Saved as a Painting

Saved as a Painting

Tali Geva

Translated from Hebrew by
Daniella Givon

Impleo

To my daughters, Noga and Zohar
To my sisters, Vered and Tsofnat
In memory of our parents Ahuva and
Dov Ketzev

Part one

Seven Minutes

Black Coffee

Robert Steins sits at the edge of the bed and smokes. He is naked and his thin body has shrunk in the cold air. His round bald head is surrounded by grey, thin and long hair, braided at his nape into a lace. His neck is wrinkled, his chest hair snarled and his shoulders slack.

The room is dim. Heavy smells of old sweat and new sweat, a brimming ashtray, and soggy clothes float in the compressed air. Two small candles flicker in round aluminum cups on the night table, and next to them rest two additional tealight candle cups, empty of wax. My clothes are draped over the chair in the corner.

Robert stretches his scrawny arms, drops ash into one of the empty wax cups, and looks at the quivering flames.

I say to him, "It's awfully cold, get under the cover." He turns his black-grey eyes to me and from his wrinkled face he smiles as one who gave up a long time ago, "Yes, cold..." His body trembles and he gives himself to the chill as though it is his intimate enemy. I cover myself with the blanket up to my neck. "Are you cold?" he asks, his voice thick and low. I answer, "no, I am covered."

He turns his face and looks at the large oil painting fastened to the wood-paneled wall with thumbtacks. The candlelight makes the shadows dance on it and for a moment I think that the painting is moving. Robert inhales the smoke and closes his eyes, opens them and gazes at the perfect rings he blows out. "Enough!" I say, "this city is totally frozen. Get under the cover." Slowly he stubs the cigarette in the ashtray and gets up. "This is winter in New York, Noa, this is not Tel Aviv... you want coffee?"

Sounds of clinking dishes come from the kitchen and in its doorway a slippery light-dark shadow moves. A few minutes later, the smell of coffee wafts from there and Robert, naked and shuddering in the chilly air, comes with two cups full of black liquid. He places one of them on the night table, sits on the edge of the bed and drinks in small sips. I sit next to him, wrapped in the blanket, drink the hot coffee and for a minute forget the cold air. "The candles will be done soon," I say. Robert looks around him, "I had more candles somewhere here, I don't know where they are." I lie down again and wrap myself in the blanket. "It doesn't matter, come to bed and get under the cover." His black-grey eyes are veiled in a purple hue and he examines my face with a soft smile.

"Why did you come here?"

"I had to. I couldn't go on without you talking to me."

"What do you want me to talk about?"

"About the letter you sent to Jessica."

"It's futile..."

"No, it's not futile. Come, lie down next to me and warm up."

***

"Noa, why do you begin the story with this scene of all scenes?"

"Because it jumps at me all the time and pulls the other scenes behind it. I have no choice."

"But this is not its place in the plot. Really! Start the story at the beginning, not at the end!"

"I don't know, Rafi, everything is a mess..."

"Begin again."

"But this story has tons of beginnings. Enough, I am tired of all this!"

"Go make yourself some coffee and start working."

{ 2 }

Shouting crows

In the summer of 2009, I was a newcomer in Tel Aviv, a city I did not know at all. When I naively mentioned this to a friendly taxi driver, he looked at me in the mirror with half a smile, "Just a minute, you were born in this country, yes? So how come a woman your age doesn't know Tel Aviv? Hey, where were you all your life?" He was right on. Indeed, I was a fifty-seven-year-old Sabra, and in Tel Aviv I felt like a tourist in a foreign city.

Despite that, I wanted to live there and become part of it. I found an apartment for rent on the internet, on the third floor of a walk-up on Jabotinsky Street, not far from Basel Square. The landlord who opened the door for me was relaxed and smiley and I took that apartment immediately. I put my desk with my computer in the living room, settled ceremoniously in my upholstered swivel office chair, and I was sure that here, finally, I would be able to write my story.

But my writing did not flow, and the city pulled me to it. And so, despite the heat and humidity, I went every day for long walks, looking at the apartment buildings standing calmly next to each other like local denizens, with their entrances and balconies and shutters and flat roofs, and I noticed that each building had its own features and expression, none wanting to look like the other. People in summer clothes walked in both directions around me, talked on their phones, chatted or were silent, and everyone's footsteps knew their path. Cyclists rode toward me or rang behind me, and at the beginning I did not understand why they rode on the sidewalk, but I learned to turn aside and let them pass. Sometimes a moist sea breeze touched me and continued on to the ornamental trees in the small yards and to the dusty bushes along the fences. The cars drove down the street, stopped - honked, continued, the city rustling around me vigorously, propelled by invisible forces.

In the evenings, I preferred to walk on Dizengoff Street, when the city turned on its night lights reflected confusedly in the large display windows. I passed clothing and jewelry shops, purses and shoe stores, groceries and bookstores, pharmacies, real estate agencies and pubs... The bridal mannequins stood in the windows in dramatic white and peered at me with dim eyes; people went back and forth or sat in cafés and restaurants which spilled onto the sidewalk in small tables and chairs crowded together, and above them towered apartments, a floor on top of a floor, and observed the street with balconies and dark or lit windows, a slip of a curtain suddenly blowing from one of them.

Thus, I walked every day in the Old North's streets, and all that time the urban clamour whirled in me, but it was not mine as I did not belong to it. My Tel Aviv friends encouraged me, "You will get used to the city and love it!" But it was alien, and when I did begin to identify some familiar rhythm in the racket, it always escaped when a shouting crow distracted me.

Six months accrued, and Tel Aviv replaced summer colours with winter's colours. I walked the streets under a canopy of dense ficus treetops. I already knew the spots where the rain which pooled in their leaves, would drip on me and my immediate surroundings were already familiar and home-like, but I still was not used to the city, and worse, I could not get ahead with my book; it got stuck in the keyboard.

And then that day of January 2010 arrived. The media announced again and again that a great storm was brewing, recommended to fasten down the water tanks on the rooftops, warned of falling trees and torn electricity cables. I was happy -- I love storms -- and I waited. Toward evening I opened the large window to the balcony and pleasant cold air entered, perfumed by the rainy city. The storm had not arrived yet but the trees along the street were already trembling frantically.

I called Avry, and he answered, "Yes, Noa."

"When are you coming? The storm is getting closer."

"Later. I'll call."

I put on my coat, put my phone in my pocket, and went out. I walked south on Dizengoff Street; heavy clouds travelled over the buildings, dyed by the last light. Wild wind began to shake the trees, as though it was checking if it could come in, and strong gusts of air sprayed small droplets on everything that was in their way. The cafés' customers looked out curiously, the street's rhythm quickened, and people rushed, opened umbrellas which immediately turned inside-out, frowned and raised their voices. Drivers honked fretfully, and torn papers scattered and stuck to the bicycles' wheels which weaved together with their riders among the pedestrians. "What's happening?" a large young man wearing a summery t-shirt yelled into his phone. He walked toward me in big steps, and as he passed me, I heard him say, "so close the shutters, I am on my way."

The wind increased, the buildings dimmed and the streetlights blinked. A sharp light sliced the air and, after it, a great thunder rolled and broke above the city. I turned to go back and rushed in the wet air and the excited gusts. At the turn to my street I stopped for a moment and checked my phone. No incoming calls. I walked fast, the rain tickled my face, and I arrived at my building exactly when a torrent of water landed on the ground, followed by a wave of blowing wind. When I entered the elevator, the phone in my pocket rang, and an hour later, when the storm outside was already revelling, I opened the door for Avry.

The water tank screeched on the roof all night and the large palm tree thumped on the shutters, slapped the shut plastic rungs with its huge palms, slammed them with its desert fingers, hit and rubbed. The sky rained with force, the wind whirled rowdily with the city and Avry and I loved.

In the morning I woke up slowly. Avry had left already and the wind outside had subsided. Daylight snuck into the room and lazy silence came from the street, as though the city had had a wild night and now it wanted to sleep a while longer. I got up, stood in front of the mirror and something in me was different, I did not know what. I looked the same in my middle height, my thick body and my brown hair wrapping around my neck. My image smiled at me as though Avry's eyes were still looking at me. His image had not dissipated yet and I was still infused with his smell.

I prepared my coffee, sat in my swivel chair by the desk and turned on my computer to catch up on the world. It has been my morning ritual for years. I surfed the internet for news sites, both Israeli and foreign, and like every morning, I was drawn to the articles about wars and natural disasters, accidents, violence and poverty. I read all the hard news items I could find, with all the photos and videos, and as always, I was pulled to a world groaning and vacillating amid big volatile powers, unknown and unclear to me.

Then I brought up my stalled story. I wanted to start writing, but I could not concentrate. My thoughts traveled to Avry, who was with me at night, and to other people whom I loved and had died, people who had nothing to do with the story I wanted to write.

I tried to chase away these thoughts, but they were stubborn and buzzed in me like wasps in a closed room. I could not get rid of them and went out to the balcony, leaned on the railing and looked down. Broken branches rested in small puddles on the sidewalk, pedestrians walked around them, cars drove down the street.

On a cypress branch near my balcony sat two crows. Their heads, wings and tails were black, and a gray hoodie seemed to lie along their backs from their nape. They had short black necks and the rest of their round bodies were covered with well-groomed black down. They looked very elegant in those suits and full of self-importance.

I looked at them, they looked at me, and one of them started to shriek in his rough voice from the bottom of his dark throat, and cawed and cawed, as though he had no choice. Again and again he repeated the sentence which had three syllables, each of a different length, turned his round head from side to side and looked at me severely, once with one button-like eye, and once with the other button-like eye. The other crow spread his wings for a minute, and maybe it was a female. She approached the male and their thick beaks faced each other. He bobbed his head to her, and it was clear something strong and intimate was between them. Suddenly the female flew away and landed on the rooftop across the street. The shrieking crow looked at her, cawed his sentence again and she answered him from the roof. But she probably meant to say something to me.

Fine, fine, I hear you, but I do not understand any of it.

{ 3 }

Guests in my Living Room

I left the house and walked to the Yarkon River. I tried to shake away the thoughts about those people I loved and had died, but they did not desist. I accelerated my pace, I breathed in and blew out, and in the end, I grew tired and slowed down. The Yarkon water moved in a dark and angry urgency. The sky was heavy with clouds, the eucalyptus leaves shook, and I walked flaccidly and dragged out the time like filling paper bags with wet sea-sand, only not to return to the keyboard.

In the evening I returned to it after all, but then the ruckus began. The city penetrated my living room through the closed shutters and via the fastened balcony windows, entered with the voices of people on the sidewalk below, the screeches of the large airplanes gliding toward the airport, the roars of the scooters and the honks of cars – Tel Aviv drivers have a strange habit - they honk a tad before they resume driving. I could not concentrate.

When I lived in Northampton, USA, I could easily concentrate. I lived in that peaceful town in northeastern United States for ten years and wrote with no interruptions in the constant silence of the corn fields surrounding it. I used to walk in the unhurried streets and gaze at the grey wooden houses with their roofs of black asphalt shingles, and with their white framed windows, pass by the evergreen lawns to the small town centre, which was always frequented by countless students in colourful clothes, hats, scarves and sweaters, sit in the corner café facing the church which was built of heavy grey stone, and then visit the chockfull bookstore, which always smelled of mint tea. From there I would enter the indoor mall with its many little shops and booths, check them out and sometimes even buy myself a shirt or a pair of pants, and on the way home walk by a flower shop, and inhale the fragrance of daffodils that always wafted from it. I loved the poplar and maple trees of Northampton, with their thin trunks, which towered in every corner, their leaves rustling in the wind, and the music that played there...

But now Tel Aviv blares at me, boisterous and impatient, self-important, running around, rushing from day into night and from night into day in a rhythm that is foreign to me and wrecking my concentration. What am I doing in this city? And why did I think of my Deceased Loves? What is happening to me?

"Too-bad, you-move-away-from-your-story!" I heard Moosh's voice, my dead childhood love, with his rapid speech that strings the words together.

And immediately I heard another voice, "No-a, stop with this hogwash and drivel. Start writing!" That was Rafi, my dead editor. Maybe he meant to scold me, but there was a soft kink in his voice that gave him away. He is always like that, hiding his fondness under heaps of coarseness.

I knew that any minute I would hear my other three Deceased too, and I said aloud, as though I was talking to myself, "OK, OK, come!"

And in my mind's eye, they indeed came into the living room, all five of them together.

Childhood-Love-Moosh, who died at age fifty-three, settled on the carpet cross-legged.

Highschool-Sweetheart-Itamar, dressed in army fatigues, sat on the carpet as well, and gathered his knees with his arms. He died at thirty.

Editor-Rafi, sixty when he died, sank into the couch with all his portly rolls.

Old-Prince-Shaul who died at eighty-six, sat on the couch next to Rafi, crossed one knee over the other, and his slight body leaned back.

And Husband-Yossi, solid and muscular, waited politely for a minute next to the armchair, sat down and put his arms on the armrests. He died when he was forty-five.

The five of them indeed died and disappeared from the world in which I live, but they remained as they were during their life. I could see them breathing, moving, and batting their eye lashes, smiling, and becoming serious, I could hear the tenor of their voices and sense their smells. They were confusingly tangible, almost like the living Avry, who was with me last night.

A strange smell spread around, a light smell of something moldy. It must have come from them, I thought, I cannot do anything about it. I did not know why they came, but their presence made me patient. "Listen," I said to them, "it's good that you came, and it's important for me to hear what you have to say, but don't start having lengthy discussions now, I need to write in peace and quiet."

Childhood-love-Moosh sent me an understanding smile from his oval face. Highschool-Sweetheart-Itamar, raised his fawn eyes to me, and agreed with one blink. Husband-Yossi, serious and focused, nodded twice decisively. Old-Prince-Shaul looked at me as though I sang a song, and Editor-Rafi wore an expression of impatience.

They are here.

MOOSH

Childhood-Love-Moosh looks exactly as he did in life, heavyset and smiley. His eyes are brown and gold, his face is lit in a smile of a man in love with himself, and his hair, thick and grey, falls on his forehead like oily straw stalks. He stretches his arms to the sides, and as when alive a sour smell of a man who forgot to shower rises from him.

"Noa, why-did-you-move-to-this-city? Tel-Aviv-is-not-exactly-your-type!" he says in his rapid speech.

"Yes, Moosh, I've been living here for six months already and I haven't gotten used to it."

He gets up, shoves his hands into the depths of his pockets and, as in his life, unthinkingly pushes low the blue cotton pants that slowly glide halfway down his flat buttocks. He paces back and forth in the living room, stops and gallops his sentences to me, "Anyone-who-grew-up-like-we-did with-the-music-of-the-pine-trees   has-a-hard-time-learning-urban-music-in-adult-hood..." The melody of his strung words makes me nostalgic for our childhood and I sigh. "Right, our roots are in the woods on Mount Carmel, but I'm far away from there now."

He was a talented and successful author, and everyone knew him by his nickname Moosh, which stuck to him at age five and stayed with him until his death. "Moosh" even appeared next to his first name on the obituary notices.

The last time we met was in Haifa when I came home for a visit. We sat in a café in the Carmel Centre, not far from our childhood neighbourhood. We talked about our long-standing friendship with its latent eroticism that never materialized, not even in a kiss. Moosh became contemplative, "it-is-very-strange, no?" and immediately became excited and described to me in poetic words his intimate relationship with his current lover. He was already sick but looked happy. Suddenly he became solemn, "tell-me-Noa, what's-the-use-of-all-these-loves   when-there-are-wars-and-violence-everywhere-all-the-time!?"

We always loved each other, although in our adult lives we rarely met. He died when I lived in Northampton. Now I imagined him here in my living room in Tel Aviv, pacing back and forth with these pants which slide to mid buttocks, and I knew that he hears everything, even what I do not say, because that is the advantage of my Dead, they hear all my thoughts.

I extended my arms for a hug, but he shook his head and looked at me like a child explaining the rules of the game, "no-touching-Noa."

"I know, I just tried, I thought it might work."

"It's-good-that-you-started-writing, your-story's-just-about-complete."

"Are you kidding? The story has been stuck for six months by now and I can't manage to write it!"

I opened the balcony's window and cool air entered the room. My two crows in their elegant suits arrived in graceful flight and sat on a palm frond. The male shouted something to me resolutely and when he finished, his friend nodded her head like a preschool teacher and cawed her caw at me. What do they want from me?

ITAMAR

I sat in my chair and turned to the computer, uploaded my book to the screen again and put my hands on the keyboard, but all of a sudden, an undulating siren infiltrated the room. I froze, that's it, here it is. The war siren grew louder, the air was filled with it, and I froze even more, is this really it? A prolonged fear paralyzed me. I could not think. Then I realized that it was the noise of a motorcycle accelerating as it sped away. It got farther and sounded like a real siren fading. I thawed slowly and took a deep breath, OK, it was only a motorcycle again.

I prepared my coffee and when I returned to the living room I found my five guests sitting and waiting for me. They looked so completely real that, had I not known they were dead, I would have thought they were alive. "I know I am alone in the living room," I heard myself, "and I know you are only imagined, so what? To me you are real."

On the carpet, next to Moosh, sat Itamar in his army fatigues. He raised his dark eyes to me, always reminding me of the earth in the Jezreel Valley after rain and said in his whistling voice which sounded like asthmatic breathing, "it's good that you are getting back to your writing, Noa."

Itamar was my boyfriend in high school, fairly tall and fairly large, with large fawn eyes far apart, a sharp nose and a shy smile. His light hair was short, his shoulders somewhat droopy, and he had the stillness of forested high mountains. After his death one of his army subordinates told me, "in the war he was our father." And they were the same age.

Itamar never spoke of his feelings for me, but he had a way of making me know how he felt, I do not know how. I loved his embraces and his kisses, but I never slept with him. One night it almost happened, but I flinched, because I thought, albeit mistakenly, that I did not love him.

A number of years passed in which we did not meet, then one day, when I was already married and a mother, as I walked in my neighbourhood on the Carmel, suddenly, up on the sidewalk, a reservist in fatigues walked toward me. Itamar! The world dimmed around me and there we were, only he and I and green and yellow leaves in the background. His shy smile ran to me and my heart ran to him, as happens to two people who belong to each other in the simplest and most wholesome way existing.

We sat on a bench. I told him about myself, he told me that he researched something in psychology and was writing a PhD dissertation, and we were silent together too, maybe we had similar thoughts. It was the last time I saw him. He was killed in one of the wars.

Itamar was thirty when he died, and that is how he looks here in the living room, a reservist sitting down on the ground. "You always loved writing," he says, "don't stop now."

HUSBAND-YOSSI

Yes, my story is done, the only thing left is to type it. My fingers are on the keys again, but suddenly Avry jumps into my thoughts. The previous night's storm, Avry standing at my door extending his arms to me, and I am swallowed in his embrace. There is no connection between the two stories. Why did I remember him now? My concentration is gone, the writing does not flow.

"Try to concentrate. Stop thinking of other people!" Husband-Yossi's baritone reaches me. I turn to him. He sits straight in his buttoned-down cotton shirt, his hands on the armchair's armrests and his round shoulders tensed. Never, during all the years of our marriage, did these shoulders slacken, or surrender. His brown eyes focus on me, and his brown curls are shoved aside. His parted lips reveal his straight teeth, the top row attached to the bottom one like lines of fortification against anger attacks. He says, "Write only about Kata! That is your story, no?" I remember that my Deceased hear everything that I think, and it is clear to me that he is bothered by my thoughts about Avry. Husband-Yossi was always careful to distance me from any man in my vicinity, it was an obsession.

Maybe he should not be here when I write? He will not understand. We connected on other planes, creativity and imagination not being part of them, although I always shared my ideas with him and I always let him read what I wrote. I think it was a mistake. One time, while writing, I fell in love with my protagonist. When I finished I let Husband-Yossi read the manuscript. He read it in heavy silence and when he finished, he looked at me as though he was betrayed, "I don't like this book." I heard in his voice his restrained anger which did not explode even once in all the years we lived together.

But he belongs in this group... he may stay here. Now I try not to remember the furies he hoarded until they clouded his vision while driving, and I also try not to remember the terrible blow that hit my heart when I was informed about it.

Enough, it was many years ago and I have already forgotten that pain.

OLD-PRINCE-SHAUL

"My precious", I hear Old-Prince-Shaul's raspy voice, "resume writing your story!" He sits on the couch, one knee over the other, and a smile of acceptance rests on his dry lips, which were glorious in his youth, according to an old photo he showed me. His yellow cheeks are droopy, his high forehead is dotted with old age spots and his brows rebel, but it is still possible to see in his face the graceful lines of his youth, the beautiful head like a renaissance painting. Leonardo would have loved it.

I met him on one of my visits home to Israel and we fell in love. He was already old, very wealthy, living with his wife in a swanky apartment in Ramat Gan. After we met he visited me in Northampton eight times. There he was happy and free, but on my visits home, in our clandestine meetings, he was anxious and worried. Our relationship lasted almost two years when he ended it for fear of being discovered.

He was born in Israel to a farming family in one of the Judean Lowlands' communities, and made his money in some defense export, something connected to submarines, although it is better not to talk about it, and anyway, I did not want to know. But I was happy to hear that for years he donated to a not-for-profit which supported underprivileged youth. I said to him, "this is wonderful, Shaul, you're some modern Tzadik!" He raised his hand dismissively, in an attempt to be modest, but his smile revealed conceit. All the same, I ordained him "prince" because of his imperial kisses. There was such a gap in our ages that I could have been his daughter, but I loved him the way a woman loves a man, with great desire.

"Writing is good for you. Write, write, my beauty," he says with a smile, and Editor-Rafi, who sits next to him, hyperventilates impatiently and explodes, "No-a, start writing already! What's with you?!"

EDITOR-RAFI

As in the past, the feeble sound of a heart broken from birth echoes in his voice. His big body squeezed onto the sofa, his arms rest at his sides seemingly calmly, and his gut slopes down under the large brown and green checkered buttoned-down shirt, as it lays in untidy folds over his pants. His thick hair is cut short in one uniform dark layer of untrimmed stubble, his frameless glasses sit on his nose, and his fat cheeks are unwrinkled, as though his sixty years filled with lustful eating did not affect him.

We met twice.

The first encounter occurred when I was in my mid-thirties. I was seated at a large round table at some wedding. To my left sat Husband-Yossi who chatted for a long time with a man seated on his other side. To my right sat a big and fat man of about forty, his short hair was black and thick, and he wore glasses. I peeked at him and he straightened and leaned back on his chair. I straightened and leaned forward some and folded my arms. I felt his presence behind me, and at the corner of my eye I noticed that he did not move. I turned to him without unfolding my arms, looked at him, and he looked at me. His dark small eyes shone through his glasses. His upper lip was plump, as though bitten by a bee, his lower lip was narrow, and they were parted, as though at the beginning of speech.

He frowned slightly, and I thought that the loud music was bothering him. I said to him, "the clamour is rejoicing here," and immediately I was angry at myself, why do you have to try to impress with such language? I wanted to correct myself: it is very noisy here, but the line was already released into the air. Instead of giving me a predictable reply, he flashed me a charming smile that immediately extinguished, "this noise is a curtain you can hide behind."

An uncontrolled smile appeared on my face, and maybe my eyes became bright, and I said to him, "So let's hide behind the noise!" He put his left arm on the back of my chair and kept looking at me. I unfolded my arms and put them on the table. "Green eyes," he said, as though choosing a name of his own for me, and immediately began between us a conversation, shifting and moving back and forth, made of short blazing sentences, once he, once I, without a subject, only scenes, what he sees, what I see, what he does, what I do. I leaned on my elbow and turned my head to him as though we were engaged in some random chat. He embraced me without moving his left hand, which was leaning on the back of my chair, mussed my hair and felt my body without moving his right hand, the one far away from me, and I embraced him, clung to him and stroked his body without moving. When everyone stood to line up for the food we stayed seated, and without getting any closer to each other, we kissed in imaginary words, long and lustful kisses.

He did not tell me his name and I did not tell him mine. Husband-Yossi's eyes drifted to us, and oddly he was indifferent to the fact that I was talking to a stranger. Maybe a curtain really hid us. I did not drink a drop of wine, but I was a little tipsy.

We met the second time two years later at a publishing house that accepted my first book. When I signed my contract, the publisher said to me, "your editor will come in in a minute." I stayed alone in the room and looked at the wall with its many book covers next to each other.

"it's you!"

He stood at the door, tall, massive and black-haired. For a minute I did not know where I was, but then I composed myself and smiled at him, "yes, and that's you!" He came closer and extended his hand, "Rafi." And when he looked at me through his glasses, he radiated youthfulness.

Since then he was my editor and guide as I was writing my books, always with me, behind the curtain of noise. Sometimes I wanted to turn it into a tangible experience, and maybe he wanted as well, but it never happened. And we never discussed it.

Saved as a Painting

Our meetings took place in Tel Aviv. I used to take the train from Haifa, and from the train station a taxi to the publishing house – an apartment on Yehudit Boulevard in the dusty Montefiore neighbourhood. I would enter the apartment on the first floor of the old building, closet myself with Rafi and together dive into my texts. After a few hours I was back in the taxi to the train station and from there to Haifa. I never stayed in Tel Aviv, neither for shopping nor for entertainment, it was a foreign city to me. When I described a scene taking place there in one of my early manuscripts, Editor-Rafi erased it contemptuously, "you don't know this city!"

Now he gets up, his upper lip, the bitten one, separated from the thin bottom lip in one of his on-off smiles. He stands next to me and gazes at the computer screen. "Remember, Noa," he states, "authors must write only what they know!"

Okay, what do I know? I know something about love, and I have some understanding of beauty, although beauty and love, on my part, are like two tails on one cat. I know a little about death, and I know, of course, Kata's story, the story I want to write.

***

I heard Kata's story in 2008 from my good friend, Agi, when I lived in Northampton, and when I came home for a visit I rushed to tell it to Rafi, my editor. I recited it excitedly, with waving arms and in flowery language, and he listened as he devoured a sandwich with salami and mustard in big mouthfuls. When he finished eating, he wiped his mouth with his checkered sleeve, "this is excellent material, Noa, and I want you to start writing it, you hear?" and showered me with instructions on what to look for in a literary research and how to document it. I was excited, "Rafi, my friend Agi scanned a few photos of Kata for me, I can show you, they are here, in my computer." But he preferred to postpone it because he was tired. We decided to meet again before I went back to the United States, but all of a sudden he became ill, his health deteriorated quickly and in two months – he was dead.

I did not get to ask him if I must mention in the story which of the scenes I write about are real and which are the fruits of my imagination; and so it happened that on that winter day of January 2010, after the stormy night in Tel Aviv, when I was imbued in Avry's smell and my five Deceased Loves were seated in my living room, I started to write a string of scenes, real and made up, that for me were all true.

{ 4 }

Vera

Budapest. The prestigious Dohány Street was suffused with elegant ambiance. The large apartment buildings stood next to each other in a sophisticated European style, white and quiet, their elongated windows facing the street in strict symmetry and their entrances decorated with long columns and ornamented cornices. The owners – rich Jews and non-Jews alike – were full of pride when they walked from the city centre to their Dohány Street and passed by the building site of the Neolog synagogue. Anyone following the construction understood that the Temple compound was going to be one of the most magnificent sites of the city and, accordingly, that street's residents would only leave their homes when dressed appropriately and meticulously from top to bottom.

Vera's grandparents had a flair for investing, and they acquired a family home on Dohány Street, not far from the building site. The house was big and white. At the entrance stood two tall round columns supporting a gable decorated with a relief of leafy branches held together by a curly string. From the sidewalk across the street the relief looked as if it were a copy of the emperor's wife's throne. Vera was born in the family home twelve years after the festive opening of the big synagogue, which was, as expected, breath-taking in its splendor.

"Well," remarked my friend Agi, as she told me the story, "this synagogue is the largest and the most beautiful in all Europe. But there are beautiful cathedrals and beautiful mosques too. That doesn't make a better world, does it?"

Vera's grandfather, who purchased the house, used to stand by the window in his old age, look at Dohány Street and marvel, "there is no city like Budapest! It is the best city in Europe!" And the rest of the happy citizenry believed that too, because when the city was united after years of war, it began to grow and afford them a life of safety and pleasure.

In 1889, Vera was eighteen years old, a pretty and educated girl who knew not only her mother tongue, Hungarian, but also Russian, German and French. She sat in the living room of the big family home on Dohány Street and played piano. Her forehead was broad, her nose large and prominent, and her pale brown eyes followed her fingers on the keys. She raised her eyes to the notes, returned to the keys, and every so often forced herself to play again a passage that did not go smoothly, saying to herself, even if I am not the most talented musician in the city, I must practice, because music is important for broadening the mind and enriching the soul.

From the next room she heard her mother calling the family to get ready to go to the opera, and Vera stopped her playing, lowered the piano fallboard, and went to her room. Half an hour later she stood erect at the door, wearing a long, pleated cotton dress in cream colour with a shiny white sash belt. On her shoulders stood out layers of large fabric leaves, starched and ironed like huge rose petals, and two thin muslin sleeves went down from them to her hands. Her aubergine coloured hair was gathered at her nape, rolled upward and fastened with a golden pin, and on her neck she wore a thin gold chain with a round pearl.

Her parents were well-to-do wine merchants, who raised her and her brother with only faint affinity to tradition. "They even considered converting to Christianity," my friend Agi told me, "but in the end they decided it was not necessary and did not bother." Like many of their acquaintances, they belonged to the Neolog synagogue, and like them used to go to that stately temple for holidays and special events. But not all their friends were Jewish. In fact, their social circle was mixed and included non-Jews as well.

I do not know why I even mentioned the fact that they were Jews. Why is it important? Religious affiliation never interested Vera. Politics interested her, social and philosophical new ideas attracted her, as well as literature and art, and those had no religious affiliation... Although maybe there was some connection after all, because somehow there were many Jews among the educated and professionals she knew, and somehow, in the various municipal offices and organizations everyone knew who was Jewish and who was not. Maybe secret lists were kept in locked drawers. Indeed, sometimes some people whispered and looked at her askance, and sometimes they excluded her from a conversation, but she considered them rude and preferred to ignore them, because in the end, what all rich people wanted was to go to the Opera, the theatre and ballrooms dressed in their finest, rub shoulders, see and be seen.

To see and be seen was important in their circles, and Vera would go out with her parents or her friends, beaming in the exclusive chic of Budapest's ladies, wearing dresses sewn for her for that purpose, rich with pleats and gatherings, lace, ribbons and muslin, decked out in expensive jewellery and wide brim hats decorated with big clusters of colourful silk flowers.

She attached great importance to appropriate attire and used to tell everyone that people should be careful how they dress, "because that is what holds a person upright!" They would hear her in amazement and shift uncomfortably. They intended to have small talk about fashion and pepper it with some gossip, and this one comes out with overbearing statements. Vera would scrutinise their faces seriously, "anyone who neglects their appearance would end up in life's dark corners."

Her parents did not make it a secret that their daughter had a sizable dowry, but young men avoided her, and one of them, articling in law and of a very respectable family, whom everyone thought would make a good match, told his friends, "it is better to marry less money and more woman."

Already when in high school, Vera read classical and modern literature in four languages, read the papers and kept herself informed on current events. In the circles of the rich and privileged in which she moved, she was considered opinionated, one who used affected language and a critical tone – the kind of sharp speech that was emanating with precise inflection, soaring from under her large nose accompanied by a piercing look at her companions who usually tried to avoid her.

Nevertheless, she had five or six friends from high school, smiley girls who accepted her into their fold even though she was, in their view, "serious and strange". On weekends they used to sit together in the most prestigious cafés in the city such as Café Gerbeaud with its Viennese style, where everything was polished and shiny as though any minute Emperor Franz Josef, his Sissi and their entourage were about to enter. The girls used to look at the many café goers, enjoy the heavenly pastry served there and chat, although Vera did not participate in the conversations, only to add her opinion when the discussion turned to world affairs.

But mostly the girls preferred to sit in the bohemian Fészek Art Club, also known as Fészek café, which was designed with mixed styles of art nouveau and oriental ornamentation, and on its walls the local artists displayed their paintings. The girls tried to sit at a table near the painters, authors and musicians, who talked loudly, smiled at the girls, winked at them and sometimes even said something to them. And they would giggle – except for Vera, who was indifferent, and men's gazes did not interest her. She heard what they said, examined them curiously, and noticed those who were careful dressers, but they did not arouse admiration on her part. "She is as cold as a marble statue," whispered one of her friends when Vera went to the restroom, and the girls around the table nodded their heads in agreement.

A FULL LADLE

One day Vera and her friends arrived at the opening of an art show of young artists at a new art gallery. Painters, authors, poets and musicians gathered there and mixed in with the crowd that came to rub shoulders with them: dolled-up gentlemen and ladies - proud Budapest residents who love themselves and their city. People stood or moved about in the melee full of bows and smiles and smells of eau-de-cologne and cigarettes smoke, and in the throng there stood Gabor Pahl, a red-haired young man named, who had just returned from Paris, where he studied art.

He was a twenty-three-year old Hungarian, thin as a twig with bright brown eyes like the eyes of a wolf. In spite of his young age, his cheeks and chin were covered with an orange beard, thick and curly, that united with a reddish moustache, its sharp ends standing out, which gave him the look of a refined savage who painted his own image.

Gabor Pahl wandered among the guests in the gallery, examined the ladies in the room with hot eyes, and breathed heavily in admiration at every dress rustling next to him and every whiff of perfume wafting to him. Women fascinated him in their walk and their stance, in their sitting and their lying. He noticed every detail about them, the way their head moved and their hair swayed, their expressions and their words. Their sensual secrets drove his imagination wild, and he thought life converged in the female body like light beams gathering in a diamond.

His gaze scanned the crowd around him and when his wolf eyes caught Vera, they seized her light-brown eyes. She halted not far from him and looked at him, and he bounced the end of his reddish mustache in an intimate smile, as though he had discovered her secret. She felt a kind of a sting in her eyes, and a pleasant heat spread through her body; she was immobile for a moment, and then turned and scurried out.

Outside the gallery Vera began to run, and for the first time in her life she ran for a long time, with hair flowing, hurried breaths and burning cheeks. Finally, she stopped, calmed her breathing and fixed her hair, and when she looked about her she realized that she had reached the market. Smells, colours and voices descended on her and raised in her a strange gaiety. She started to walk among the booths, and for no reason stood next to a booth of housewares, whose owner was a good looking young man. "Right away she knew he was Jewish," my friend Agi said to me, "people knew these things."

The man straightened up on the other side of the counter laden with pots, skillets and eating utensils, looked at her in puzzlement and called, "Madam!" spread one arm like an operetta singer and with the other he handed Vera a large metal ladle, "Madam! This is for Madam full of love, and there is much more in the pot that is inside here," and laid his operetta-hand on his chest.

Vera looked at him surprised, and he bowed so low, that his forehead almost hit the counter, "I am Ferenc, at your service." His voice sounded like a storm in the forest and he had the scorching gaze of a gypsy lover. Vera felt the pleasant heat that passed through her earlier in the gallery returning and flowing in her body, getting stronger and pooling in her eyes. Then, all of a sudden, a smile surged from inside her to this Ferenc, and she spun like a bird in a wild whirlwind of falling in love.

Two months later, when she informed her parents of her love, they were stunned.

Her father rose, exhaling in anger, and exited the room, and she was left sitting motionless at the dining table. Her mother walked back and forth in front of her, shot her angry looks and breathed fast "how? how?" She stopped and stretched her arms wide, "what are you doing to your life!?" and raised her voice, "he is nothing, a poor nobody with no social standing!" Vera looked out the window and was silent. Her mother returned to pace the room and her quick panting got stronger, "how do you let yourself do such a thing to us?!" She put her hands on her waist and went to Vera with exploding anger, as though she was going to slap her, "what do you think you are doing?!"

Vera did not flinch back and did not lower her eyes.

The door opened at once and her father walked in in quick steps. He stopped in front of Vera stiffly erect with his hands behind his back and looked at her as if she were a business partner caught in embezzlement. "Listen," he said in a stony voice, "we have nothing more to discuss. If you do not stop this thing right away, you are not our daughter!"

Vera got up, looked at her father, looked at her mother, and said in a steady voice, "then not." She went to her room, packed her summer clothes and her winter clothes, several books and her jewellery in two suitcases, slung over her shoulder a cloth bag with two hats in it, and when she left the house, she closed the door behind her quietly. Ferenc came from the corner, kissed her cheek and took the suitcases off her hands. They got married, and her parents penalized her with silent estrangement, deprived her of any assets, and abandoned her to life of poverty.

***

"Rafi, look how stupid people can be! Look how they destroy things! It was true love but, despite that, Vera's parents disowned her. Can you understand such a thing?"

Editor-Rafi stares at me through his glasses with his little dark eyes, looks at me as if I am beyond help. "Damn it, Noa, why do you even think about it? It's obvious why Vera's parents disowned her!"

Why does he get so hot and bothered...? Ugh, he heard my thought.

"You get out of rhythm; you always do that! You start great, let the scenes flow, and all of a sudden some gnat gets into you and stops you!"

He talks to me as though I have started to give a Speech From The Throne in bed... But anyway, why is it so obvious that love is regarded as less than money, social status or pedigree? "Shaul, what do you think? Why did Vera's parents disown her?" Old-Prince-Shaul puts on a fatherly smile, his old head with its thinning hair leans a little to one side, and a light grin appears on his yellowish face, "to our chagrin, most of humanity is like that, people do not understand how important true love is," and suddenly his old face creases. Maybe he remembers that he decided to leave me exactly when we were at the apex of our love.

I look at Childhood-Love-Moosh, "what do you say?" he must have a better answer, he is a writer, is he not? Moosh raises heavy eyelids to me as if I pulled him out of a nap, and removes the oily straw strands off his forehead, "isn't-it-clear?"

"What's clear?"

"Noa, most-of-the-rich-and-privileged see-love-as-something-silly-or-a-disease. They-run-the-world-without-compassion and-they-wage-wars. Enough, continue-writing."

***

Vera and Ferenc traveled for two hours in a horse drawn public wagon, and arrived at Pesterzsébet, a poor suburb on the outskirts of Budapest. The suburb was not built according to a city plan but simply assembled, when multitudes of poor farmers streamed to the city carried on the sweeping waves of the industrial revolution. The farmers became labourers and worked in the large factories growing outside the city next to the railroads. These were large yellow buildings with tall and thick walls and small barred windows. Inside these buildings stood new industrial machines, and masses of labourers worked there from the first light of dawn to the darkness of night.

Not far from the factories, the labourers erected huts or little stone houses with thatched roofs and settled their families there. A hut touched a hut, a house touched a house, and a crooked street was formed, from which another crooked street branched and another crooked street and another one. Later little grocery stores opened between houses, booths for used cloths and old shoes, and fourth-hand furniture and patched blankets, like a burgeoning flea market looking for suitable corners in the alleys.

A much trampled-on unpaved road crossed the length of the emerging suburb and became the main street, where horse drawn wagons traversed it back and forth, paused, loaded and unloaded goods. A church was built at the end of the street with a spire, a bell and a priest, and devout labourers in clean shirts gathered in it on Sundays.

In the adjacent quarter, among huts with sinking roofs, a little synagogue was built, and next to it a mikvah. On the Sabbath the synagogue gathered to it the pious Jews, who also donned their clean shirts.

Fifty years later the crooked streets were paved with small cobble stones, and low-rise slums with tiled roofs were built along them. The huts with the sinking roofs which were abandoned were rented out for living quarters or were used for storage. Two or three elementary schools were opened in one storey buildings built in patch work, and small rooms without doors were used as classrooms for the workers' children. The flea market also became a slum, and now meat, vegetables and fruits were sold there. The district was destitute and crumpled in its wretchedness, but it drew increasingly more people who came to live there, practically all of them poor.

Vera and Ferenc rented a wooden hut with one room and a kitchen in one corner, a little storeroom outside with a separate entrance, and a minuscule wooden cubicle for a toilet. "All right," said Vera and looked around her "now we will create a home here." Ferenc was excited. He hugged her and said, "Anything you say!" They bought an armoire in the flea market, a bed with a straw mattress, a table and two chairs. "First thing Vera cleaned the armoire, and immediately hung her dresses in it," my friend Agi told me.

They lived in the wooden hut and opened a small grocery store in the adjacent storeroom. Vera managed the store and Ferenc continued his small trade of housewares he bought and sold on long winter journeys to faraway towns and villages. "In winter people are stuck at home, and that's how I get them to buy," he explained to Vera.

"Not exactly," my friend Agi remarked mockingly, "the housewares business was only a front. Nobody checked what he hid in his crates, you see? He had all kinds of shady businesses, but he couldn't turn them into money."

***

1891. Vera stands in the snow in a grey woolen coat, and her head is wrapped in a green woolen scarf covering her mouth. Her large nose peeks above it and her broad forehead is bare. An alley in Pesterzsébet can be seen in the background. There are no paved roads there, and no sidewalks, only a white winter blanket spread among the low houses.

Vera is pregnant, the coat doesn't close over her belly anymore. Her hands are in a fur muff and her fingers are intertwined. Ferenc leaves the house, walks to her in big steps and stretches his arms to her. She pulls one hand out of the muff, extracts the other hand, and moves heavily from the little depression in the snow into Ferenc's embrace. He lays his hand on her belly and feels it like a Gypsy lover. Vera looks around and shoves him away with a whisper, "enough, not in the street..." and he laughs with his loud voice rough from smoking, "so what, you are my wife, no?" She looks into his big eyes, which are black-grey and veiled in purple, "there is so much snow, maybe you shouldn't go away today?" he kisses her on the mouth, "I must leave." He hitches himself to his two crates and tows them in the snow to the trolley station. At the end of winter, when the snow melts, Ferenc returns and finds in their tiny home a baby called Katalin, Kata.

***

I saw many images of the couple in Pesterzsébet, like the snapshot of Ferenc, the handsome talker, where he puts on his heavy coat to leave on his winter trip and suddenly takes it off, pulls Vera to him and crushes her breast, "come, one more time before Kata wakes up..." But I became very tired, my eyes burned, and my hands grew heavy on the keyboard. Shall I call Avry? He will come and charge me with energy... No... it has been less than two weeks since he was here last, better not call him. I turned to my five Deceased. Old-Prince-Shaul sat in old people's peace of mind, his long body slack and his lower lip droopy. "I have no energy," I said to him and he straightened and gathered his lip.

"You do look tired, love of my heart," he said, and his quiet voice sounded as if it emerged from a very dry mouth. His Israeli pathos of the forties of the twentieth century never seemed preposterous to me, though at this moment it sounded pathetic. It doesn't matter, I was tired of writing and needed him to give me a boost. Old-Prince-Shaul smiled generously and quoted his usual declaration he made when he was alive, with eyes closed and an enthused sigh, "I love you so much!"

And it worked immediately. I read the last lines in my text and a sharp pleasure ran through me, as though I was Vera lying with Ferenc on their bed before he went on the road. Ferenc moved his lips from her face to her throat, slowly-slowly lower-lower. "Continue like this," I hummed, "simply continue like this."

White Orchid

Faint daylight trickles into the small grocery store through the doorway. Vera stands on the far side of the wooden counter, which is old and worn but clean, and it is obvious that the stains on it are from times before it arrived at her store. On the counter there is a scale with weights next to it, and on the wall behind Vera there are two shelves. On one of them stand a few jam jars, arranged by height, and on the other wooden boxes and cloth bags containing coffee, lentils, rice and other grains. A cabinet with spices and medicine is attached to the wall next to the door, and under it, on the floor, rest three large bags with flour, sugar and salt. The store is dark and unaired, but Vera stands there like a white orchid, dressed in one of the dresses she brought from her parents' home. Her face is clean, and her aubergine hair is combed and gathered with a golden pin.

***

Kata was the oldest, and a year later Ilona was born. Two years after Ilona, Ernő, a boy, was born, and after his birth

Vera avoided any more pregnancies. Nevertheless, in the coming years she yearned to give birth again, but she restrained herself, preferring not to provoke her poverty.

On snowy winter days, when Ferenc went with his crates from village to village and from town to town, she sat with their children in their little home in Pesterzsébet, occasionally wearing coats and scarfs to save on coal, and wrapping themselves with blankets as they sat huddled together on one of the two beds. Vera would tell them many things, from folk tales to historical events, from scientific inventions and important discoveries to current philosophical ideas. The children listened carefully, even if they understood little of all that, and when they grew older she explained to them current affairs and showed them photos of Emperor Franz Joseph sitting on his throne, as they appeared in the newspapers. She also showed them the picture of the Empress's throne, which the Empress did not occupy much. Sometimes Vera sang to her children deliberately and in a strong voice but off key, which made the street dogs howl to high heaven. And when she spoke of Ferenc her eyes shone. "You'll see, when the snow begins to melt, you will know that papa is on his way home!" When Ferenc returned he found the small hut decorated with greenery, full of baking smells, and four pairs of eyes shining happily at him.

"What are you telling me here, Noa?" Editor-Rafi bursts at me, "what's this liquid sugar you pour that will bust your keyboard any minute?! A man leaves a young woman and three children for the whole winter, they hardly have any coal for heating, not a fucking penny to their name, and you expect me to believe that she received him with flowers and a cake in the oven?"

"It's a bit strange, but that is exactly what happened. I think that Vera enjoyed being independent, and clearly preferred to be alone with the children some of the time, without her husband's pestering. This arrangement of parting for the winter suited her. Ferenc chatted endlessly and was not very smart. Rafi, she was a different person, and if you think that there were no such women at the end of the nineteenth century, you are wrong."

During the spring and summer, the children had a father at home, with a strong smell of cigarettes and a strong and hoarse voice. A cuddling father, warm-hearted and talkative, who loved to sing at the top of his lungs, drumming with two metal spoons on a big pot to accompany himself and tell them – in an inarticulate language his wife forgave him for – about far-away cities, about other landscapes and people who spoke foreign languages. "And these people buy your goods?" asked him seven-year-old Kata, in a twelve-year-old's practicality. "Sometimes they buy and sometimes they don't," he replied and raised guilty eyes to Vera.

Ferenc did not speak explicitly about his shady businesses, but Vera understood their nature. During the first years of their marriage she begged him to get rid of them, raised her voice and accused him of irresponsibility. Next to the welcoming receptions which waited for him upon his return, there were also hard rebukes with a firm demand to stay away from what Vera called "the band of criminals." She conducted these conversations far away from the children's ears, and tormented Ferenc with harsh reproaches. He promised again that everything would be fine, but in the end she saw it was in vain and left him alone.

At night they would enter their little kitchen, Vera would cover the entrance with a curtain, and they would stretch on the straw mattress, which each night would be rolled out and each morning rolled back to lean against the wall. "Remember, the children should not sleep with us in the same room," she whispered to him. Ferenc smiled, and his eyes turned purple, "anything you say," and clutched her in his loving desire which did not wane over the years. To him Vera was a princess, daughter of kings, and he did not understand how he had won her.

Once or twice every summer she left him with the children and went to the centre of Budapest to visit the new art shows and buy a few books and magazines to check the latest fashion. "When the children grow, I will take them with me," she said to him, "now it is too early for them."

A JEW WITHOUT A SYNAGOGUE

On Friday nights Vera lit two candles, without a blessing and without saying "Good Shabbos". She only lit and gazed. A light smile hovered on her lips and drew two thin lines under her eyes, which emphasized her large nose. "I am a Jew without a synagogue," she used to say to the nosy women who came into her tiny grocery store, and they said nothing. "The Modern" they called her.

Vera considered herself secular, and when she read in the newspapers about Theodore Herzl, she thought he was like her, and she like him, both secular Jews, citizens of the world, whose roots were nourished by the same culture. They both grew up on Dohány street, and she remembered hearing her parents talk of his family, which later left the area. When she was a young woman, Herzl was already famous. She read about him with much interest and considered him one of the people she held in high esteem - educated, articulate, and with original ideas. She also secretly expected that Herzl would blaze a trail as a cosmopolitan intellectual, free of symbols of any religion and nationality. "But then he invented Zionism!" she protested to Ferenc, who stared at her with questioning eyes. "Tivadar Herzl concerns himself with nationalism! He is wrong, but that's what he wants. For me it doesn't work!"

"These days it's not necessary to establish new countries," she said to eight-year-old Kata and six-and-a-half-year-old Ilona. Little Ernő played quietly in the corner, and the girls stood next to her in the kitchen while she peeled potatoes, rinsing them in a bowl of water. She lectured with shiny eyes, and they, without understanding her words, felt their categorical importance and were attentive. "Instead of establishing countries, the economic system must be changed!" Vera said. Ilona asked, "what is an economic system?" And Vera answered, "it's the way in which people organize work and money distribution according to what is important to them." Kata said, "my system is to work hard and save lots of money." Vera asked her, "Why do you want to have lots of money?" and Kata answered, "to buy a house for us and food and clothes." "This is really important," answered Vera, "but remember, girls, what's most important is to live by your own truth, and it doesn't matter what others say." Kata and Ilona did not know yet what their truth was, but they nodded dutifully.

The children did not know their grandparents on either side, but Vera worked hard and took pains to teach them that the Sabbath and Holy Days were important for Jews, especially Passover, Rosh Hashana and Yom Kippur. "It doesn't obligate us, but it's good for you to know," she said to them, "the same way you know about Christmas and Easter. We have to be familiar with the world in which we live." Every Yom Kippur they went to the synagogue and stood outside with all the people who went once a year to hear the Shofar being blown, and Vera explained what the Shofar was and why Jews blew it on Yom Kippur. On Passover they ate matzo next to bread, and Vera explained to them the reason for eating matzo. "Are we religious?" asked Ilona, and Vera replied "no, but it doesn't matter." Kata had no interest in the conversation and was astonished that Ilona kept asking, "how do people decide who is religious?" "Those who are religious are, and those who are not are not," explained Vera. "Faith and the observance of mitzvah are a private matter for each person. There are those who believe in God, and those who don't." The girls heard about God at school, and the conversation ended there. Vera did not say explicitly that she did not believe, but neither did she say she did.

Husband-Yossi gets up and walks about the room. "Noa, it's not right!" he says crossly to me, as though I portrayed Vera as a non-believer just to annoy him. He is a secular man who wholly believes in God and always yearns for religion. It is not surprising that he interferes precisely at this point. Another minute and he will lecture me that even if I am a non-believer, there is no need for everyone to know it, because it is a shameful weakness. "What's not right, Yossi?" I ask, but he sits down again, and it seems to me that he changed his mind. Ugh, what does he know?

"Noa," sighs Editor-Rafi and shakes his head in expressed helplessness, "why do you get into this subject of religion and faith? Must you?"

***

Once, when I lived in Northampton, I sat at a dinner party next to a pleasant older woman who wore a small hat, round and light blue. I knew her slightly and knew that she was a devout Christian.

"Are you the Jewish lady from Israel?" she asked, and something unpleasant went down my spine. We exchanged pleasantries with corresponding smiles, while I forked a bite of roast on my fork, added a spoonful of cream sauce to it, and put it into my mouth. I chewed with pleasure, and suddenly I noticed that the woman with the light blue hat examined me with wide open eyes. I smiled at her, "this is tasty!" and she replied with a lopsided smile. I sensed that she, as a devout Christian, saw it her duty to ensure that I behave like a proper Jew, and I imagined her scolding me, what's this? Meat and dairy together? With a look of concern, she asked, "do you believe in God?"

I was silent for a long moment. Maybe I was too surprised to think that she was insolent, and maybe I am simply a slow person who reacts like a tired turtle. I did not want to hurt her feelings and answered, "no, not so much... I don't believe..." The lopsided smile returned to her face and I regretted my answer.

I had learned that Northampton prided itself on the conviction that religious faith is something wholly private, but it was obvious that the lady with the small hat did not think so. She looked at me as though I displayed such a bad flaw, that she could practically smell it. Her smile turned into a look of revulsion as if saying, I liked you earlier, but you went and spoiled everything. Then she was silent for a long while and in the end a smile of pity spread over her face, "I will pray for you to believe in God."

Later, when I walked home, I told myself, let's say that that woman had a gun, and let's say that someone would have told her that she had to wipe me out in the name of her God to purify the world from people like me with the smelly flaw of nonbelieving. And let's say that she would have hesitated to shoot me with her gun, and then she would have been told that it was not personal but an important religious mission – would I have continued to walk in the safe streets of Northampton, or would a bullet have struck me? But this is nonsense, no sane person here would shoot me for God's honour.

***

Old-Prince-Shaul was a secular man, whose Judaism did not concern him. In his youth he fought to create a state for the Jews, won his war, and until his last day he was involved with his security activities. "My beauty," he says to me from the couch, with the self importance of old people who know everything already, "it's better that you don't get into this God business. Better leave it be." Why leave it? And why doesn't he take a clear stand? He should say something, he is a man of convictions, he considers himself an enlightened liberal. It is important for me to hear his opinion when I write.

"Go on writing, go on writing," his voice is hoarse, "as long as you are happy." Why is he harassing me? This 'go-on-writing, go-on-writing' sound like go-on-dancing or go-on-giggling or go-on-masturbating. Old-Prince-Shaul smiles as though I complimented him. It is true that he is a charming man and a pleasing lover, but really, under this engaging Sabra mannerism a little chauvinist is hiding. How did I not notice it in his life? It turns out that my prince is simply a macho in a "tembel" hat, just like Husband-Yossi, who actually prefers tweed caps.

{ 6 }

A Silent Crow

In Pesterzsébet Vera was considered a strong and brave woman, because any woman who had a husband who traveled every winter and was not afraid to stay alone with her children must have uncommon strength. Women admired her, men respected her, and when she walked down the crooked streets in her well-cared-for dresses, no child pestered her, and no dog barked at her.

People would follow her with their eyes and would tell once and again the story everybody knew about a grocery store owner who left a palace full of riches for a life of poverty with her man, and since then she has been protected by a halo of love. Jews made bets when she would return to the palace she had left, and the others chose to forget she was Jewish. Everyone was proud that such a woman lived among them, but for the same reason they kept a distance of respect and rarely entered her grocery store.

Vera treated everyone politely, women, men and children alike. She ridiculed prejudices, and antisemitism was, in her eyes, a marginal matter that need not be concerned with. When Kata and Ilona left every morning to go to the workers' school, she sent them washed, their hair brushed, and their uniforms ironed. She taught them that clothes and the ways of speaking and walking made the person. "And of course, cleanliness," she said, "because people will treat you the way you treat yourselves."

"Always remember," she carried on, "clothes do not have to be expensive. What's important is how you wear them and how you treat them." Kata nodded and added, "and they don't have to be new," even though she dreamt of new dresses she never had. Her mother looked at her with full approval, "yes, and never have any stains on your clothes, mend any tear or unstitched seam right away, iron and fold nicely, and don't wear wrinkled clothes." She stood erect and tied her apron around her waist, pulled the ties tightly and smoothed the front "like this. Always stand straight and walk straight and then even an apron will look like a bridal gown, remember that."

Their house may have been the bastion of a close-knit family, but food and heating were scarce because the grocery store barely provided for them. Kata asked her sister in a worried voice, "what do you think, Ilonka, why don't we have many customers?" and the latter answered, "really, why? I don't know."

***

At the beginning of the twentieth century, Kata was nine, Ilona was seven-and-a-half, and Ernő was five-and-a-half. The transition from one century to the next meant nothing to their daily lives, but despite that, on the snowy night of the thirty-first of December, I heard Vera saying to the children in her strong and authoritative voice, "When Papa returns home it will be the new century. May it be a good century." Ilona asked, "what is a good century?" and Vera answered, "a good life and no wars."

Vera charged her daughters with strength and self-confidence, but Ernő grew up frightened and frail. "I am not worried about him," she told Ferenc, "when he grows up he will become stronger." Ferenc looked at his son and wondered, where is that confidence coming from?

Kata was strong and quick. At age nine her energy, determination and efficiency were already apparent. A serious girl, who was not deterred by hard work. She lugged charcoal bags and water pails, carried laundry basket and cleaned the house. Ilona did help, "but you are still little," Kata said to her and did not let her do "adult jobs".

One summer day, when Kata was thirteen, she heard her mother tell her father, "Tivadar Herzl died." Kata thought it was one of the money lenders who lent them money to save the grocery store from bankruptcy, and asked her sister, "Ilonka, who is the man who died?"

"He's the one who wanted to create a Jewish state in Palestine."

"How do you know such things?"

"I read it in the newspaper Mama gave me."

"But who cares? And where is even Palestine?"

"It is after the Mediterranean Sea. There are Turks there."

***

A year later, when the sky was blue and the air warm, Vera informed Ferenc, "tomorrow I'm taking the girls into town, it's time they get to know Budapest!" Ferenc was excited, "sure, go ahead! I'll stay here with Ernő." And next morning he stood at the door of the grocery store with an apron tied at his waist, waived his hand and called after them, "don't forget to return to me, my pretty girls."

Kata was fourteen and a half, and Ilona thirteen. They donned straw hats decorated with cloth flowers made by Vera, and wore dresses sewn from old material on a squeaking sewing machine that Ferenc brought from his travels. The white dresses were floor length, belted with ribbons tied at the back, and looked as though they were made of new material. "Vera loved designing clothes," Agi remarked appreciatively, "she was always drawn to it." Vera herself wore an old long pink dress she had brought from her parents' house which still looked like new, and over the high lace collar which was buttoned to her chin glinted the thin gold necklace with one round pearl.

They marched along the Danube on a paved path, mixing in with the many ramblers there, and stood to gaze at the view. The girls held their breath, clasped hands and looked at each other, enchanted by the big river flowing in front of them in a powerful serenity. Afar, on the hills of the other shore, rose Buda's picturesque palaces. Between the riverbanks the great bridges spanned like regal jewels on the river's neck, and steamers cruised its blue water. Kata inhaled a lungful of air and Ilona pressed herself to her in an excited sigh.

Then they walked to the city centre, passed the large steps of the Opera House and went past the other extravagant buildings which looked to the girls like huge white temples, with their tall columns and ornamental tops, and with the cornices decorated with reliefs and statues. The richness of the magnificent architecture moved them, and they did not know where to look first. Ilona held Vera's arm, "it's so beautiful here!" And Kata said with a full heart, "Budapest is a fine city." On the street with the exclusive shops, made up and perfumed ladies passed them wearing stylish clothes and modern hairdos, attached to small purses, clicking with their heels in a stately walk, as though declaring their exclusivity on the city. Kata examined them and wanted to be like them when she grew up.

Vera led her daughters to Dohány street, and when they reached the big synagogue they stopped. The twin towers at its façade with the black apple turrets decorated in gold gave the temple a charm of an eastern palace and Vera said, "this is the largest synagogue in Europe!"

Kata said, "It was built by rich Jews for sure."

Dohány street was wide and clean, and all three marched quickly until Vera halted, and the girls stopped next to her. "I grew up here," she said dryly and pointed at her parents' home across the street, "I told you already the whole story." They stared silently at the big house with its two columns at the entrance supporting a decorated gable which looked to the girls' eyes as though it was copied from the Empress's throne. Suddenly Kata crossed the street in vigorous steps, approached the door and knocked on it. No one opened. She knocked again, but the door remained shut.

On the way home, they sat on the tram which screeched on its tracks and rocked them from side to side, and Ilona said to

Vera, "I am sure that the kitchen in your parents' house is bigger than ours." And Kata added, "too bad we don't live there." She has no idea how rich people lived but she did know the poorest quarter of Pesterzsébet. Once, when she walked through it with Ilona, men and women with bad teeth and dirty children, all wearing rags, gathered around them. They stretched their hands for alms and they smelled offensively, quarreled, yelled and bellowed in coarse voices. Kata did not want to look at them, but her eyes were drawn to look, and she saw something shattered apparent in their expressions, their speech and their movements, a repulsive and ugly despair. She was terrified, "come quick, Ilonka, I can't stay here," and since then she never again entered that quarter.

The image of the big house of the grandparents she did not know did not leave her thoughts, and when she went to sleep cuddled to Ilona, she whispered, "listen, Ilonka, the most important thing in life is to not become poor." Sleepy Ilona answered, "yes..." and Kata raised her voice some, "it will never happen to us! I won't let it!" Ilona mumbled, "enough, go to sleep." But Kata was agitated, "you know what the worst thing about poverty is? Not that there's no money to buy things, but that there's no way out, you see. Those who are touched by poverty are lost and gone, it's worse than death."

Ilona fell asleep and Kata thought admiringly about their mother, who watched over her family day and night not to become poor even though poverty was so near. "I don't understand," she said to her slumbering sister, "Why did Mama prefer to leave the good life she had in a rich home? Just for love?"

Saved as a Painting

***

1907, a summer excursion to the centre of Budapest. Kata is a sixteen-year-old girl-woman, dressed in a long light blue bell skirt with a stylish matching jacket which Vera designed from another dress modeled after one she had seen in a window shop. Kata feels that people on the street look at her and a sense of obligation to appear at her best fills her for her mother's sake and for Ilona's, and for all the things she herself dreams to attain.

Indeed, she draws gazes at her erect and calm walk which she learned from her mother, at her long and heavy auburn hair, and at her sturdy build. She inherited from her father his black-grey eyes, veiled by a purple hue, his straight nose and sensual mouth, although she presses her lips together, while her father smiles copiously.

Ilona is fifteen years old and still maturing. Her nose is as big as her mother's, her mouth as sensual as her father's and her hair dark brown, curling over her forehead. She does not look like her sister, but the sisterly resemblance is unmistakable.

Going into town still excites the girls and they are delighted. Vera lectures them like a teacher doing her hallowed work, "today we're going to the new hall at the National Salon, to see a show by an artist named Gábor Pahl. I read about him in the newspaper. He is showing more than a hundred and fifty oil paintings, most of them portraits, as I understand it, and there are a few paintings of historical themes. It will be quite interesting to see his art!" The girls become serious and nod their heads.

When they arrive at the gallery, Kata enters, stops and looks around, Ilona enters after her, and Vera puts her arms through the girls' arms, one on each side. "Let's take a look. They say he is a very talented artist." Kata remarks practically, "I see that his prices are high."

In the corner of the gallery they see a throng gathered around a man with orange-red hair and beard with silver strands entwined in them, and his eyes sparkle like a wolf's eyes. A colourful kerchief is tied around his neck and his brown coat reaches the floor. His body is wide and full, and he stands in an ostentatious erectness explaining something excitedly, waving his hands and raising his voice. "He must be the artist," Vera says to the girls. She does not remember that sting his eyes had sent to her eyes eighteen years earlier, but he sees her and he remembers her. Gábor Pahl never forgets any woman's face his eyes capture, not even after many years. His monologue breaks for a moment then continues, but even before he finishes orating and his audience disperses, his gaze already follows the woman and the girls whose arms she holds, one on each side.

These girls, he thinks, resemble each other and do not resemble each other, identical and opposite. The cute brunette, I could devour her, and the auburn one, I could drink her whole in one gulp like Pálinka. Kata lifts her eyes and they meet his. Yes, the story repeats itself and it is likely to repeat, because, during all the years of painting, the artist has drawn tens, maybe hundreds, of eyes to him.

He smiles, and his short thick beard moves with his head as he nods in greeting. Kata nods her head in a polite response and her heart beats quickly. She sees his smile widening and feels something in her eyes, as though tears pool in them, but they are not tears. She looks at Gábor and blinks, and he catches her gaze and does not let go, she blushes, heat rises in her. Her mother presses her arm, "I heard that this artist is brazen. Kata, don't look at him."

Kata diverts her gaze, but Gábor Pahl quickly grasps what is in her eyes and thinks, wow, she has little purple imps in her eyes, and the one who wins her love will be a happy man... And I say to him, you had a self-fulfilling prophesy just now, Mr. Pahl. You don't know what's going to happen in thirty years, but I know. That's the problem, that I know, and I am both happy and scared. Mostly scared, damn it.

The artist continues to look at Kata as she advances from painting to painting with her mother and sister and waits for her to turn her head to him. He sees that the paintings are of no interest to her, notices her examine the prices and almost bursts in a loud laughter. Mother and daughters pause, whisper to each other, and Kata turns her head and directs her eyes straight at him. They look at each other, he is forty, she is sixteen-and-a-half, he knows a woman's soul, and she, at that moment, is agitated and does not know her own soul. He wonders where that Gypsy purple in her eyes comes from and says to himself, the mother gave this beauty the alabaster skin, and the father, he may have bestowed upon her the purple imps in her eyes.

"Beware the portrait painter Gábor Pahl!" declared a newspaper headline in Budapest which has published an interview with the artist, "you sit in front of him, and in one look he discovers all your innermost secrets!" Indeed, even without sitting in front of him, Kata feels naked before him, and piercing waves traverse through her, like the waves which traverse through me when I am with Avry.

Someone approaches Gábor Pahl to speak to him. He abandons Kata's eyes, and she returns to the paintings on the wall. She does not know that a few minutes later his eyes revert to her and capture her head movements, her hips movements, the tilt of her neck. She does not know, but I know that he says to himself, I must paint her naked.

What does he see in her? What is it that arouses him so? Maybe he is reacting to the same things I react to one hundred years later.

My friends, to whom I showed Kata's photographs said to me, "she wasn't all that pretty, why are you getting excited?" How can I explain? There was a primal beauty in Kata, a kind of unique consequence of the lavish smile Eros smiled when he saw Ferenc hand Vera a ladle full of his love.

***

1908, end of winter. Ilona stands and cooks, Kata sits at the table and darns socks, and Ernő sits opposite her and reads a book. Vera's voice drifts from the other side of the wall as she talks to a customer in the grocery store. Ernő asks quietly, "when are we eating?" He gets up, opens the door and looks out. A black and silent crow alights on the ground in front of him which that morning still had remnants of muddy snow and now turned into a puddle. The crow waits for Ernő to throw a piece of bread to him. They know each other. Ilona looks out through the entrance and says to Kata, "Mama didn't eat anything today."

Saved as a Painting

The customer leaves, and Vera gets ready to lock the store and enter the house. She looks about her as she does every evening and verifies that everything is in its place. It has been nineteen years since she got married, and her daily war with poverty exhausts her and paints an expression of constant irritation on her face. Her mood too has lost its optimistic sparkle, and now her large nose looks like an angry protruding centre of continuous worries.

She is thirty-eight, and these days she would have been considered very young, but old weariness has leapt into her eyes and every so often she sighs as though something hurts her physically. She need to feed her family, debts continue to mount, and Ferenc, who was supposed to return from his journey and bring home some money, is late to come back. Kata and Ilona work, sewing and mending clothes for rich women from the centre of Budapest, cooking and cleaning the house, washing, ironing, and helping in the store. Vera would have liked them to have a proper education, play piano, and move about in respectable society. And the boy, he needs to learn a profession. But there is no money. The snow has melted, and the road's cobblestones peek out again... Vera inhales deeply. A quivering wave rises from the bottom of her stomach, moves to her lungs, to her throat and from there to her lips in the same manner that was formed in her over the years: when winter is over her body wakes up in an expectation of her Ferenc's homecoming. She wants him already with her, her Gypsy lover, in the little corner of the kitchen.

Ernő's silent crow lands on the doorstep before her. He lifts his little head with its thick beak to her, turns it this way and that and Vera smiles at him, "in a moment we'll eat, and you will get your share." Suddenly he flies away with his wings spread wide, and two policemen stand in front of her. They state her first and then last name, as though verifying that they came to the right place and fall silent. Vera confirms and looks at them, and maybe they are a little surprised to see a noble-looking woman in such a derelict store. She asks them politely what they want, and one of them clears his throat and informs her that her husband was killed.

The City's Roar

I managed to see that Vera paled and leaned on the door jamb, I felt the dreadful blow to her heart, and I paused. She froze on the screen in front of me with her hands over her face, and I could not continue writing. Suddenly I was seized by a pain resembling hunger, a sharp contraction in my gut and a pinching emptiness in my lungs. Where is Avry? Why doesn't he call? It has been almost a month since we last met.

I got up, exhausted, and opened the shutters wide. Wintry afternoon light flooded my living room, and with it the city entered too, as if it waited for me in its whirling clamour, with its sparrows and their urban tweets, its crows who knew everything, the people who chatted on its sidewalks, the airplanes screeching in its skies... All right, all right, I am going out.

I walked and walked. Rain dripped, and evening fell, car lights and streetlamps glittered in the damp roads and the buildings along the sidewalks bounded a route for me. Ferenc loved Vera so much, what will become of her without him? And why is Avry not calling? If I think to him with all my might, maybe I can draw him to me with telepathy, maybe he will come by inadvertently. And what if Ferenc is only injured and the policemen made a mistake? No, it is not possible to change the story. He did die.

I returned home and my legs hurt. Vera waited for me, still hiding her face, but I did not have enough energy to write her. I did not call Avry, I waited for him to remember me and call.

✱✱✱

Avry and I were born in the same winter month of the same year, when the country was four years old. He was born on a kibbutz on the shores of Lake Kineret, and I on a small moshav on the periphery of the Galilee region. He was seven years old when his family left the kibbutz and moved to Tel Aviv, and I, at age six, moved with my family to Haifa, to a house on Mount Carmel. We grew up in similar families, who read the same books and voted for the same workers party with romantic leanings toward the labour movements and the communities they established. We were raised on the Israeli mythology of Elik Who Was Born from The Sea. Had we been raised on a different mythology maybe our lives would have been different but that is how it is, constant wars. When we met, we were fifty-seven, parents to grown children with their own families, I alone and Avry alone, in some sort of nomadism of life's refugees.

Avry is of medium height and full body. His stride is measured, but there is always some urgency to it. His honey eyes are framed by long straight lashes like a fence of cypress trees along an old cemetery, and above them spans his forehead with dark gray bangs, thin and long, a vestige of a 50s and 60s fashionable top curl shoved aside. At the back, his hair reaches his nape, although never beyond his collar, "the barber always catches it in time." His neck is quite thick, his ears are large and flat on his scalp, and his cheeks are daubed with a dark veil of stubble that no amount of shaving can hide; as soon as the blade glides over it, it grows out twice as hard. His round chin gives the impression of softness and lines descend along his nose. His lips are neither wide nor thin, his teeth straight and grey and his breath is reminiscent of peeled apples.

I see an image from our last meeting on the night of the storm. Avry lies on his stomach naked, his face on the pillow is turned away from me, and his arms are stretched to the sides. I sit next to him at the edge of the bed and glide my hand over his shoulders, from this one to that and back. He takes deep breaths. I write with my finger on his back, "I love you," and smile creases form on his exposed cheek. He turns and lies on his back with his eyes shut, feels around for my hand and grips it. With my free hand I smooth the hair on his chest and write on it with my finger. Avry smiles, his eyes are still shut. My pencil finger continues to move on his chest and stops left of centre, next to three longitudinal lines, doughy lumps of skin, one long and two short, where the hair is reluctant to grow. These are the marks with which the war stamped Avry.

"It was a small hell there," he told me on our first night together, and he sounded as though he was talking of a stranger. There was shooting all around him, something entered his chest and he almost died. But the surgeons operated on him and saved him. I asked if it hurt, and he replied that he did not remember.

Since then he refused to talk about it again. "It is unnecessary," he said. My pencil finger skims over his three scars in a foolish attempt to bypass Avry and talk to them directly. His breath is irritated, and he opens his eyes. I whisper to him, "fine, fine, sorry." He shuts his eyes again, pulls me to him and hugs me... Where is he now, why doesn't he call?

INTOXICATING WORDS

I walked out again to wander the streets which looked like empty wind tunnels. The city hushed her sounds for me, leaving me to be sucked into myself without her running around me determined to distract me. I walked against the cold wind and made it to the beach. The water was green-blue and full of foam, moving with force and producing roars of whirlpools and abysses. Waves came and went, indifferent to me and full of themselves, the sky was heavy, and a forlorn silence rested on the empty beach.

When I returned home I stole a glance at the computer screen. Vera was still standing at the entrance to her grocery store, but I could not go near her.

Next morning, I told my five Deceased, "I'm going out, wait for me," but on Dizengoff Street, on my way to the bus number 5 stop, I discovered that four of them were walking with me. Highschool-Sweetheart-Itamar was not among them, for some reason he stayed home. What are you doing here? Why did you come?

Editor-Rafi walked on my right in his large checkered shirt gasping with each step. Moosh the writer, my childhood love, walked next to him, dragging his legs and pulling up his slipping pants. To my left marched Husband-Yossi, his jeans fit him as if he were born in them, and his folded sleeves exposed his arms' muscles. Next to him Old-Prince-Shaul strode like a camel, his neck pulled forward and his knees bent somewhat. All four matched their steps to mine and their faces bore a ridiculous determination of soldiers. Just don't pester me to return to Vera! It won't help, I say to them in my mind.

They climbed on the bus with me, although suddenly they disappeared from my sight, and when I got off at Habima Square they were next to me again. There is a different atmosphere here, I thought to them, do you feel it? At the beginning of Ahad Ha'am Street we stopped. Look, this street is one hundred years old, one of the oldest in Tel Aviv, and I am so new in it... Avry came back into my thoughts and a pain of emptiness tugged in me.

Come, I said to my companions and we walked slowly down Ahad Ha'am Street. Old three-storied apartment buildings crowded together on both sides of the narrow street, dolled up in seeming simplicity, each building with it unique angles, with its staircases, its windows and shutters, porticos and balustrades. The renovated ones looked like architectural models of their Bauhaus youth, full of their self importance, and among them stood their neighbours waiting for renovations with sooty walls and peeling plaster, faded entrances and crooked banisters. But even from them a haughty whiff of old-timers hummed to me, some Tel Avivian breath of air I have already learned to recognize. A green palm tree stood erect like a poem next to a white wall, and in the small gardens the entangled greenery grew high, with full-grown trees and thick bushes, supported by shaded and sunny walls. All of them looked time-honoured and filled with proud urban history. Look, this sign says that the poet Shaul Tchernichovsky had lived near by. I see him with his big mustache and his bushy hair, sitting and reading a book in old Greek, smiling to himself. Amos Oz wrote about him that he had a brown smell. How beautiful.

Cheerfulness is knocking at my soul, but I refuse it and Childhood-Love-Moosh scolds me, "enough, get-over-it!"

As luck would have it, we reached Ahad Ha'am Street just before garbage collection, when the overflowing containers stood on the narrow sidewalk and blocked our way in an arrogance which said why-are-you-making-such-a-big-deal-go-around. We stepped down to the road and treaded on pages with writing which were scattered there, got back on the sidewalk side-stepping dog's excrement which was smeared on it with its foul stench. I saw old clothes flung on the stone fences, a strange local custom of those who have leaving them there for those who have not. A Mediterranean complacency of an endless siesta imbued everything, a yawning tranquility of beauties who are late to get up and have not yet washed their faces.

A winter sun emerged briefly from among the clouds and touched me with a placating private warmth. I pulled the telephone out of my pocket and sent a text message to Avry's telephone: "call me!" and he immediately called. My voice trembled, "Avry, it's been three weeks..." and he replied, "I thought I told you I was travelling. Didn't I tell you?" I whispered, "you didn't tell me, but it's not important, come over." He asked, "tonight?" and after a short pause he added in the same drunken tone he had at the beginning of our relationship, "I miss you already too." What words do to me, how they intoxicate me! All at once winter rejoiced again. A large cloud covered the sun, the wind cooled the air, and it began raining in long clear drops.

Avry arrived at my apartment in the late afternoon and, as we loved to do, we sat together in the living room, sipped wine and talked. He told me that he had gone with his daughters and their families for a week of ski in Switzerland. He is very close to his daughters. I told him about my writing and about what happened to Vera. Then we got into my bedroom, and after Avry left I fell asleep wrapped in my down blanket.

Next morning, I found my five Deceased Loves sitting each in his place in my living room. I stretched. "Mmm, what a night I had! But actually, you saw, you see everything. Well, come, we are going back to Pesterzsébet."

{ 8 }

Moving to Budapest

The policemen who informed Vera of Ferenc's death told her that he was found on the road, that it seemed he was knifed and bled to death but that it was not known who stabbed him. In replying her they said that no boxes were found next to him, only his satchel. "We don't know what happened there," they said and left.

The Jewish community of Pesterzsébet provided burial to all Jews, and Vera said, "we are Jews, so let him be buried with Jews, it's fine with me." Her three children surrounded her silently, looked at her and did not know what to do. Suddenly her face became despondent, and she stretched her arms crying, "who will love us now?"

I had never seen Vera cry. She had a strange cry, like bellows that erupted from her chest. Ernő thrust himself into her arms weeping, Kata and Ilona cried and hugged both of them, one on each side, and their bewilderment was crushed between them – I know.

After the funeral Vera emptied Ferenc's satchel, searched his clothes fretfully and strew them around her. Her hair became wild and her face contorted. Her children had never seen her like that before. "Where is it," she mumbled angrily, "I know it has to be here!" A single sock fell out of one of the shirts. Kata picked it up and shoved her hand into it, showed Ilona the rolled bills which were in it, and said to Vera, "here, I found it! Enough, Mama, calm down!"

That night Vera could not fall asleep. She rose and went to the kitchen and sat in the darkness next to the rolled mattress which leaned against the wall. Kata rose, brought a chair from her room and sat next to her. Vera hid her head in her shoulder and emitted a deep moan. Kata hugged her, put her chin on her mother's head and was silent.

Few people came to the wooden hut to offer condolences, most of them creditors who had lent Vera money. They sat before her with a sigh, spread their fingers on their chests and closed their eyes with a promise not to abandon the stricken family, but on their way out entered the small grocery store and looted anything they could lay their hands on.

Kata and Ilona went in there in the evening.

Flour was sprinkled on the floor dotted with footprints, and little mounds of sugar were piled everywhere. The large sacks disappeared. On the wooden counter lentils and grains of buckwheat swam in puddles of vinegar and olive oil. The scale with its weights disappeared. The large metal spoons, the pots, the ladles and other housewares disappeared as well. The shelves were empty of jars, the wooden boxes and the cloth bags, some of which were scattered on the floor. The spice and medicine chest was uprooted from the wall and thrown outside.

Kata looked at the destruction and her face reddened in fury. Ilona hugged her waist, "such mean people!" Kata inhaled a lungful of air like a swimmer before the crucial competition of her life, "that's how poverty begins! Now I have to put our life in order. Mama is not up for that. We are moving to Budapest!"

WOLVES HOWL IN THE WOODS

Two weeks after the funeral Vera, Kata, Ilona and Ernő sat mutely around the table. Three big bundles of tied blankets sat in the middle of the room, inside them were clothes and bedding, housewares and small items. Two nails protruded from the wall opposite the entrance, where framed photos of a long-ago love used to hang, and on the stove set afire with the remains of the charcoal, the soup bubbled in a pot. Ilona got up, "Let's eat." She wrapped a rag on the edge of the pot and put it on the table, "we have a potato soup." She ladled a little into a bowl and handed it to Vera, "eat, Mama." Vera looked at the bowl and did not touch the spoon.

Ilona filled Kata's, Ernő's and her own bowl with soup, sat down and the three of them ate in silence. Kata finished her food, leaned back and quickly gathered her disheveled hair, waves of shiny auburn mop, which locked in them feminine secrets that she herself did not yet know. The brown woolen shawl fell off her shoulders, she bent to pick it up and when she straightened her eyes met her mother's eyes. Kata said, "Mama, please eat!" Vera picked up her spoon, dipped it in the soup and began eating.

The oil-lamp's light lit Kata's white forehead. She wrapped herself in the shawl, folded her arms under her breasts which filled already in an accelerated maturing, and said in her metallic voice, "tomorrow we'll get up early!" Ilona smiled at her fondly, "everything's ready to go," and her alto voice spread in the room like the soup's aroma.

I sat there with them, and Ilona's pleasant voice relaxed me. To me it was more pleasant than Kata's voice, which was full of metal shards, and I found it easier to love Ilona than her sister, but I cannot help it, the story is about Kata.

When morning rose, four forms laden with bundles like war refugees left the hut. Vera was wrapped in her grey coat and her green woolen shawl, her large nose protruded from her face which became gaunt in two weeks, and her eyes darted. Kata and Ilona were bundled in long blue coats, and Ernő, whose face was dotted with pimples, wore a coat a few sizes too big. His mute crow followed them to the tram. They boarded the car, laid the bundles next to them and departed to Budapest, Ernő's crow flying behind them.

"After about a year the piano arrived at the apartment they rented in Budapest" said my friend Agi. "They had a piano?" I was excited about the new item that was added to their lives, and Agi said, "one of Vera's parents died, I don't know if it was her mother or her father, and she inherited the piano they had bought for her when she was a girl. But only the piano. Not a penny did she see from them."

I did not have a photo of their apartment in Budapest, but I clearly saw the piano and Vera trying to teach her children to play. The girls were busy, and did not have time to practice;

moreover, Kata was not interested, and Ilona, who loved music, showed no talent for playing. But Ernő spent long hours on the piano. He was a gentle youth who grew up quietly, diffident and self contained. His pimples stayed on his face for a long time, and when they finally disappeared, they left dark marks on his cheeks. He went out every morning to feed his silent crow and then went to school. It was strange that this crow did not find a mate. I read that crows find life-long partners.

***

Ilona sat by the table after dinner and read the newspaper. She was seventeen and radiated energetic loveliness. Her light-brown eyes went rapidly over the lines and her eyebrows were somewhat furrowed. Her big nose gave her a look of determination, the same as her mother's when she was young, and her full lips, like her father Ferenc's lips, were parted some, as though constantly waiting for a kiss that was about to come. She used to gather her hair at the back with a strong bind, but if a curl freed itself and fell on her forehead she did not bother to put it back in place and her face became whimsically sensual, the one the artist Gabor Pahl noticed and said to himself, the brunette, I could devour her. She was lively and intuitive, with a spicy sense of humour, with generous measures of cynicism and a leaning to playfulness. Sometimes she teased her sister, but Kata did not understand jokes.

"What are you reading there in the newspaper for a whole hour?" complained Kata, and Ilona replied pensively, "politics in Europe is only getting more complicated. Problems, all the time problems."

Saved as a Painting

Every morning they dressed for work and stood next to each other in front of the mirror, both of them of medium height, with a small waist and large hips. Ilona's posture was a little slack, not maintaining the tense erectness of a king's daughter, and it gave the impression that her breasts were smaller than those of her sister's. But no, Ilona's breasts were just as full as Kata's, but less mischievous. The sisters combed their hair and chatted like two pigeons who always had something to burble about to each other.

Every morning Vera asked the girls, "maybe I should look for a job anyhow?" And like in a refrain they would stand in front of her and look straight into her eyes. Ilona would kiss her forehead, "it is enough that you cook for the whole family!" And Kata would put her hands on her waist and shake her head like a senior executive, "Mama, you are not going out to work!"

Maybe they were wrong. Maybe it would have been better for Vera to go out and shake herself out of her mourning. On the other hand, had she wanted to go out, nobody would have stopped her, but Ferenc's death extinguished her.

***

The girls left the house, Ilona accelerated her pace and Kata held her elbow, "walk nicely!" They talked about Ernő, whose school they paid for, and about his two new friends who came over every day and cloistered themselves with him in the small room. "What do they talk about?" wondered Kata, and Ilona answered, "about girls."

"It would be better if he studied for his exams and played the piano, why does he need these friends?"

"He studies and plays, Kata, what do you want from him?"

Then they talked about their mother, who, in spite of her lingering despondency, went back to reading in four languages and played extensively on the piano.

"I'll be rich, Ilonka, and Mama will become again the respected lady she used to be."

"If you say so, it will happen! Even your God will not change what you resolve to do."

"What?"

"Yes, Kata, the one that sometimes you call 'the good God', I know you have a relationship with him. Keep it up, maybe we'll need it some day."

Ilona worked as a clerk in a metal casting plant, and every morning she sprinkled her "good morning" on everyone, which was like a promise of good weather that day. That is where she met Aladar, a Jewish engineer, whose Jewishness was not very important to him, a tall and thin young man, with an Adam's apple that moved as he spoke. His nose was thin and big and his eyes, which were close together were blue and clear.

They talked about politics and current affairs and sparred with witticisms. Aladar made Ilona laugh with his jokes, and she made him laugh with her quips. They fell in love and stayed together forever. There are people who are fortunate to be planted into each other with long-lasting love, and cruise through life together until they die at an old age. I never experienced such love, sometimes I think it is a literary creation, but there you have it, it exists.

Kata worked at a tobacconist shop. She herself never smoked and even forbade smoking at home, although Ernő smoked secretly with his friends. The shop was one in a line of prestigious stores in the centre of town, its many customers visiting the shop regularly, and profits were high. Kata observed the running of the business, quickly perceived the addictive nature of smoking, and understood that it was a gold mine. When she had some ideas about increasing sales, she shared them with the owner who listened to her appreciatively and immediately made her his personal assistant. "Katalin has a good sense for business," he told anyone willing to listen, "she is a gift from heaven to us."

"She made good money," said my friend Agi in satisfaction, "and her employer gave her nice bonuses not to lose her. And he treated her like one of the family and used the familiar form of speech when he talked to her."

"Wait a minute, Noa!" Husband-Yossi called to me. He looked a little less tense than usual and had an expression of a fascinated child on his face, "look, something doesn't work here. It's not logical that the people in the story speak Hungarian while you don't understand one word in this language."

"What's the problem? In the story I understand them and can talk to them."

"But how is it possible that someone who doesn't even have any family connection to Hungarians all of a sudden understands Hungarian?"

"It's a story, Yossi! It is like in a dream where everything is possible."

"So, what, in your story you are an Israeli who understand Hungarian, like, from the air?"

"And how do you think I'm talking to you now? You are dead."

***

Kata saved some of her salary, the rest she added to Ilona's portion of her salary and created a tight budget. Overseeing expenses and saving were foremost on her mind. She planned to purchase an apartment for them, furnish it, buy new clothes, enter a respected social circle, and buy a subscription for the theatre and the opera, to see and be seen. She wanted to get the best and the most beautiful of everything and even contemplated studying something.

No, that is not true. Kata did not consider spending time on schoolbooks, I invented thoughts she did not have. But why, Kata? Why didn't you want to study?

Editor-Rafi gets up and his face changes expressions, wavering from deep affection with a flash of a soft smile to angry impatience. I see that the anger is winning. His wide shirt shakes, and he approaches me like a big checkered animal. His little eyes shoot daggers at me through his glasses. His upper lip, the thick one, is fastened to the thin one and his bald head is inclined toward me like a dark watermelon, "what do you want from Kata? She doesn't feel like studying. It's not her thing! Let her be what she is and don't push her around with your blowhard ego. Keep your stuck-up ego to yourself."

"You have to be so coarse? You can say the same thing differently."

"What does it matter how I talk to you? What matters is what I say to you!"

"But you're insulting!"

"If you are so dainty, write for housemaids! Authors have to be fighters without Kleenex in their pockets!"

Old-Prince-Shaul nods his head in agreement. Why doesn't he support my point of view? What's with him?

Husband-Yossi announces in his baritone, "Kata is not the type for schoolwork!"

Great, now he too.

And Itamar in his fatigues doesn't get up. From the moment they sat down here he has not gotten up from the carpet.

"Itamar, I can't leave Kata with elementary school education!"

"But she didn't study, that's what the story tells you," he answers me simply.

Moosh the author straightens his legs, stretches his arms to the sides and spreads his sour smell in the room. His face looks like an egg with a face drawn on it, and his eyes shine at me, "Noa, when-we-write, we-need-to-give-the-characters-space. Move-away-a-little!"

He talks so fast that sometimes it annoys me, but he is right. OK, all five are right, so what? I can't stand Kata's materialism! She dismisses anything that enriches the soul. She does not appreciate any literature, any art or any music, she buys an opera subscription only to see and be seen! "Moosh, did it ever happen to you that you wrote about a protagonist who irritated you?"

***

"Kata was like a bulldozer," said my friend Agi to me, "nobody could stop her." Yes... I see Kata marching down the street in Budapest. Her body erect as though it is held in a corset, her little purse is hanging on her forearm. Her heels tap on the sidewalk in a moderate but determined pace. She never runs and never becomes winded or sweaty, but these manners of aristocracy do not stop her from going from store to store and comparing the prices of food and clothing, housewares and furniture. Tirelessly she patrols the rich neighbourhoods, checks where buildings are being built and where renovated, writes down the contractors' names, gets to know the municipal offices and knows whom to turn to for any question or any subject.

She is eighteen and a half and the first decade of the twentieth century is coming to a close. She does not know that in five years a great war will break that will last five years, and that millions of people will die as a result, and then there will be a deluding lull of twenty years, and again a great war will break and another tens of millions will die. She doesn't know but I know. She is full of optimism and I am full of fear. Wolves howl in the woods of Europe. The authors and the poets, the painters and the musicians, all the artists and the intellectuals sense some tremor in the earth or the air. They themselves do not know what they sense. Something begins to crumble, but the sun shines every morning on Budapest which ingratiates herself on it, and I – I calculate the times again and again, like an obsessive search for a mistake that may have occurred in my calculations, that if I find it I can repair the timeline and rescind the moment of Kata's death. How silly, it is impossible to change the timeline. I am here and now with Kata in Budapest in 1909 and also here and now in Tel Aviv in 2010.

{ **9** }

László

Kata ambles down the street in her moderate pace. Early spring's morning light illuminates her face and dances in the chestnut hues of her hair which can be observed through the brim of her green hat. The air is still cool, but Kata is already dressed in a green spring suit – a long skirt tight at her waist, widening from her hips to her ankles and a jacket whose wings are short at the back and a little elongated in front in an elegant angle. The sleeves are folded once on her forearm, revealing the dainty cuffs of her pink shirt's sleeves, linked by two small cloth buttons. A black leather purse is slung over her arm and in her hand she holds a bouquet of violets.

Every Friday, two boys bring to the flower shop a basket full of perfumed violets whose short and delicate stems were carefully lopped. The shop owner gathers them into bouquets, attaches around them a few of their heart-shaped leaves, and binds them with a purple ribbon. "Put them in water and they will last several days," she tells her customers, and by noon all the bouquets she prepared are snatched. Every Friday Kata buys a bouquet of violets and brings it to the tobacconist shop.

The shops on the street are still shut and will be open in fifteen minutes, but Kata always comes a little early. She passes by the large fabric store whose owner stands outside holding a long wooden pole. He attaches the pole to the end of the door's shutter to push it up, but when Kata passes him he props it on the wall and takes his hat off before her, "good morning, Miss Katalin." She nods her head to him without changing her expression, "good morning", and notices the quiver of excitement between his nose and eyes. He leans on his pole in her direction, "Miss Katalin!" Kata stops, and he tells her, "You have a guest in the shop!" She does not respond. Ilona would have broken into a large smile and ask, really? Before the shops are open? Who could it be at this hour? And maybe that is the question the man with the pole wants Kata to ask, but she does not ask, and continues walking. Her fastened lips stretch lightly. A day earlier her employer told her that someone who would like to meet her would come to the shop.

The glass door is still shut, but Kata can see through it the shop owner's shadow with his back to her talking to another shadow. Ilona would have put both hands on the glass and fixed her forehead to it to see better what is inside. Kata stands and waits, and the shop owner opens the door, "good morning, Kata."

A tallish and thin man stands in the middle of the room, his eyes are green-brown, and his big balding head is encircled by yellowish-grey hair. His face is pale and his lips are paler. He wears a long spring dark grey coat, made of fine material, his white shirt's collar is high and tied with a grey tie. His black pants are carefully ironed and his black shoes shiny. Kata sees his black hat set on the table. She guesses that the man is rich and realizes that he is a Jew. I do not know how she realizes that; I would not have. She also sees a sign of gentleness in his face, which he may be trying to hide.

The shop owner introduces Kata to him, "Sir, this is Miss Katalin, our senior sales clerk," and turns to her, "This is Mr. László Steins, he's a fabrics merchant." Kata extends her hand to him. Her fingers are long and thin, and her nails are white and well kempt. The merchant László Steins leans to her and takes hold of them, hovers with his lips over them and says, "how do you do, Miss Katalin." His voice is thinner than expected, and there is something in its melody that inspires trust. He unbends, Kata looks straight at him and a blush tints his pale face.

He lifts his hand to his gleaming bald head and smooths it back with splayed fingers from forehead to crown, moves it in slow motion, once then once again, then puts his hand in his pocket. He is twenty years Kata's senior, but he is like a boy before her. As far as he is concerned, she is ageless, only a presence stronger than any other presence he has known. She is beautiful, he tells himself, and beyond that he has no words to think with about her beauty.

Kata's pressed lips stretch to the sides and separate into two fleshy leaves. "I heard about you, Mr. Steins, how do you do." She turns in a deliberate movement, walks to the back of the counter while removing her hat. László looks after her as she walks with her skirt swaying lightly and the jacket accentuating the outline of her body. The shop owner looks at them from the side, as though overseeing an event that takes care of itself without his help. No need to mix in, Kata knows what to do. He joins her, takes a cigarette box made of thin yellow metal out of the drawer, opens it and offers one to the guest, who refuses politely, "I don't smoke." Kata is pleased.

She stands next to the counter without leaning on it and puts the bouquet of violets which she brought with her in a small vase. László Steins observes her fingers and then her neck, face and lips, and Kata feels that he tries unsuccessfully to detach his gaze from her. She knows he knows it is not polite to stare and she smiles to herself.

Now she raises her eyes and smiles at him with her pressed lips, a friendly smile of a fellow expert-merchant and also a smile of a woman who knows her strength, who has built a thick wall around the wild imps inside her who whisper and fan the secret yearnings of her body. She never responds to them only locks them in her in firm determination so that they do not pester her. At this moment they are completely asleep, László Steins's presence does not wake them.

Kata sets the vase with the violets in the centre of the counter and says, "please, sit down, Mr. Steins, we'll have coffee." A whiff of her perfume reaches him, mixed with the scent of the violets, and he fills with desire.

***

"No! No!" I turn to my Deceased Loves quintet, "the story is going sideways! This László Steins doesn't suit Kata!"

Childhood-Love-Moosh, the writer, raises his face to me and looks at me with rancour, but I ignore him and raise my voice, "how can a beauty like Kata's find a place in the soul of a man for whom commerce is his essence? Look at László, he doesn't understand what he sees! It is a wrong match. This beauty needs to be ravished with love." You have to know how to ravish such beauty with love.

If I could, I would have altered the plot now, removed László Steins, at least temporarily, and put the artist Gábor Pahl in his stead, to love Kata the way she needs to be loved.

Moosh gets up and stands beside me, and I raise my head to him. He looks at me as though I am one of his students in the creative writing workshop for beginners. "So-what-if-László-Steins-is-a-rich-merchant? He-can-be-a-butcher-or-an-opera-singer-or-a-tailor! What-difference-does-it-make?"

"But he doesn't suit her, Moosh! You yourself always told me how you make love with words! You even crowned yourself the champion of lovers with words. And it is important to me too to be loved with words, at least as much as with kisses and caresses. How can I abandon Kata in the hands of a mute merchant?"

Suddenly I notice that my breath has quickened.

Editor-Rafi rises like a gun ready to shoot. Here he is the authority, all the others are just hitchhikers, maybe except for Moosh, because he is a writer. "Noa," Rafi sounds full of self satisfaction, "if you can climax just from talking, it does not mean all other women are like you."

"You don't get it! Kata cannot be happy with a man like him!"

"You are just picking on László," states Rafi, "consider what Vera's granddaughter told you when you visited her in the Seniors' Home." He is right. I remember my visit with Edit, Ilona and Aladar's daughter. I came to the Seniors' Home in Tel Aviv and recorded her additions to the story. When I asked her about László's character, she smiled, "Laci had a strong intuition, he was a good man, not anxious."

It is obvious that Editor-Rafi is trying to restrain himself, but he raises his voice all at once, "you see? You wrote every word she said to you. Where is your notebook? Why is it shut? Open it. What else do you have written there? 'László Steins loved children and knew how to communicate with them... and anyone who loves children etc. etc.', so?" Yes, this is the portrayal I got from Old Edit. She was five years old when László Steins, her aunt Kata's husband, took her by train from Budapest to Novi Sad, but she didn't want to go and cried. László hugged her and wiped her tears, "come, come, Edit'ka, don't cry... You know what? Your two cousins are waiting for you at the station with lots and lots of flowers. Each one is holding such a huge bouquet that you can't see their faces, don't cry."

"You see? That's László Steins! What do you want from him?!"

"I don't know, Rafi, he simply doesn't suit Kata!"

Rafi raises his voice again, "even if you write one hundred times that László isn't the right man for Kata, and even if you add every time ten exclamation marks, it will not make a difference. The story itself will show if they are suited for each other or not! What's with you? I see I have to teach you everything from the beginning!" He is agitated. He cannot work differently; his feelings lead him and some inner aesthetics press on him from inside. He looks at me in protest and moves to the balcony.

Itamar, who has not gotten up yet, sits with his arms leaning on his knees. His uniform sleeves are too short and pull upward, the open cuffs look to me like alluring entrances to secret caves. He lifts his fair head, looks at me with his brown fawn eyes, and I remember that in our youth he never talked about his feeling for me, but he had a way about him to make me know, I have no idea how.

Suddenly I hear Husband-Yossi's voice, ", tell me, what do you have against László Steins?"

Really, what do I have against him?

I have nothing against him, on the contrary, I like him. The problem is that I am not attracted to him... Kata is not attracted to him. I know what wild fervour she possesses, and that is exactly what makes her so beautiful. She must have a relationship of passion! But it is not going to happen, and it is not László's fault, it is Kata's fault. Why did she choose him?

A PURPLE HUE

László Steins courted Kata the way gentlemen traditionally courted in those days, when the old and orderly world of the Austro-Hungarian Empire was a source of security and pleasure for them. That was the world that the artist Gábor Pahl so often described in his oil paintings, in which he presented Budapest's society women wearing their house robes and street clothes, fully naked and partially naked, in the pampering settings in which they lived, in the elegant cafés, in the well-cared-for gardens and in the high-ceilinged and well-lit rooms furnished in urban splendor. That was what their world looked like, adorned and decorated, full of self marvel and blind to bad omens.

It was then that Gábor Pahl left with his family to the United States on an artist's tour planned to last one year but lasted ten, and László Steins remained in Budapest persistently courting Kata.

The flowers he sent her every week, the restaurants and cafés he invited her to, the theatre, the opera and the balls they frequented, all these made him happy, and he believed that he was paving the way to the young woman's heart. She thanked him for his gestures in graceful politeness and pretended that his wealth did not impress her.

László did not comprehend. He always trusted his ability to understand women and men, and when he first met Kata he immediately felt they were a good match. Was he wrong in his supposition? True, she was different from the women he courted in the past; those women were so eager to catch him for a husband because of his wealth that they exasperated him. But she did not reveal her wishes, although it was clear that she was attracted to the good life. He wondered why Kata, who was the only one he wanted, on whom he bestowed of his riches, that if she only asked he would bring her the moon, did not hurry to fall into his arms. She did show affection to him and chatted with him in a captivating openness. They already use the familiar form of speech, and when they danced she brushed against him every so often in a way that made his ears burn, but what did she really want?

Kata was for László a magic secret that he wished to cup in his hands, not necessarily to crack, but to be only his. He did not imagine that already after their second meeting she told Ilona, "I can't love him... but he has a good heart and he is rich. I will marry him." Ilona, who already talked marriage with her Aladar, hugged her sister, "are you sure, Kata? Without love? And he is too old for you, he is Mama's age. Twenty years is a lot, no?" Kata thought for a minute and said, "maybe love is important, but there are other important things. We need to be settled. Life without money is poverty, and poverty is worse than death." And at night, when they went to sleep bed next to bed, Kata whispered, "listen, Ilonka, he is a nice man and he deserves to feel good. So he will make a great effort and work hard, and in the end, he will get me. That way he will always feel that he made the deal of his life."

During the wedding ceremony Vera stood with her hand covering her mouth and examined her daughter's face through her veil for a long time. Ilona pressed herself to her mother and whispered, "she'll be alright, Mama, don't worry, Kata is life's commander-in-chief." Vera removed her hand, "instead of loving, Kata does business."

***

I never played catch or hide-and-seek with the men I loved. When I loved them and wanted them, I announced it in clear words and body language which did not leave room for misunderstandings, and I always believed they wanted me just as much. That is how it is now with Avry.

Kata would have seen in my behaviour a sure sign for unforgiven stupidity, but from the start I knew we were different, almost opposites. If we were to sit together, I would have said to her, "Kata, you and I belong to different periods and different backgrounds," and she would have dismissed my words with a movement of her white hand, "No! There is something different here." Suddenly I realize that I hear her metallic voice close by and smell the scent of her perfume. I quiver, she is here in my living room! I must bring her a chair; she can't sit on the carpet.

I bring her a chair from the kitchen, but she prefers to stand. Her auburn hair is gathered at the back and lifted, and a blue velvet robe rests on her like a royal cloak over an off-white silk negligee trimmed with lace at the front. It is obvious that Kata is not comfortable with my familiarity. She is not used to it, but surprisingly enough, she adjusts herself to me. "It has nothing to do with background or the times," she says in the determination of an empress, "the question is what kind of a woman you are. A woman who chases a man is foolish, excuse me."

"No," I answer her, "the question is what the woman wants. What did you want from László, Kata? You wanted the financial security he could give you and your family and which he gave whole-heartedly. Maybe it is necessary to play catch or hide-and-seek for such financial security." I restrain myself and do not say that László would have given her all his fortune to win her love, and I forget that she, like my other Deceased, can hear all my thoughts.

She raises her brows and says, "what does a woman want from a man except for financial security, especially if she is not yet nineteen and has to care for her mother, sister and brother? In order to live in a comfortable house, eat well and dress properly, learn a profession and enjoy what Budapest has to give you need money, no?"

"Yes, true, Kata, you really understand life. You put your hand out and held it, life, tight, commanded it, managed it, and got everything you wanted: a large house, good food, dresses and coats and shoes, hats, purses and jewellery, an indulgent social life and entertainment. But sometimes," I raise my voice, "sometimes a woman doesn't seek financial security from her man. You see, Kata, what I want from Avry and what he gives me, is something completely different!"

She probably senses where my thoughts pull her, but she does not give in. It is not her way to open her heart and reveal the hunger that was eating at her soul all her life with László Steins. You do not tell things like that. Ugh, again I forget that she hears my thoughts. She looks at me stiffly. I gaze at her through Gábor Pahl's eyes, and suddenly the imps in her eyes go wild and spray both of us with purple hues. I whisper to her, "Poor Kata, you had only six love encounters in your life."

"This is killing me, Noa," Editor-Rafi's voice explodes at me and robs me of this moment with Kata. She disappears from the living room and he scolds me, "Again you force Kata to be what you are! Let her be herself!"

"Why, what are you talking about?"

"Poor Kata..." he quakes his voice disparagingly and his compulsive tones increase, "Kata lives the way she lives. Don't interfere with her story!"

"What do you mean not interfere with her story? Her passion never found a release and was never acted upon, and it hurts me!"

"So what if it hurts you?" Rafi's face distorts with frustration, "your pathetic pity on her does not convince me. If she lacks anything, show it to me!" He almost weeps, and I avoid looking at him not to see what ensues in his loins. Once in a while it happens to him when he gets overly excited. "Write only what you see in pictures! You have enough pictures for ten books, but you insist on writing the non-pictures. That's not how to write!"

"Maybe when there is no passion there is no picture, but that's how Kata lives!"

"If there is no picture, then there is no picture. Move on!"

He wants to banish me from the story, that's what he wants.

Old-Prince-Shaul straightens like a Supreme Court judge, "my beauty, I think it is fine and natural that you describe your feelings toward Kata, there is no reason not to." Mmmm... I hum to him just to demonstrate I am paying attention.

Itamar lifts his arm like a student who wants to say something, and his fair head is raised to me, "Maybe what is important to you was less important to Kata?" I do not comprehend him and do not even try. My patience is short, "Itamar, she lives without her passion, isn't it clear?"

Rafi does not give in, "She and her husband fucked regularly, what did she lack?"

I overcome the repulsion I feel for his bluntness, "Passion is much more than a sexual relationship!" And suddenly a sticky frustration spread through me. Even though Rafi is always with me behind the noise curtain, in the same fantasy, he does not understand what passion is to me. He feels my pictures differently, and I fail to clarify what is inside me.

Moosh the writer gets up resolutely and stands next to me. He stretches his arm, almost-almost touches my shoulder, and glances at me with the same air of closeness we had in our childhood in the wadi on Mount Carmel, "look-Noa, your-editor-deals-in-styles, your-high-school-boyfriend-deals-in-contents and-your-prince, with-all-due-respect, is-not-interested-in-your-writing-only-with, let's-say, what-his-old-penis-dreams-about-you. Allow-me-not-to-comment-on-your-husband..." He pauses for a long moment, "and-I-tell-you, what's-most-important-is what-happens-to-you before-the-words-appear-on-the-screen. That-is-your-purple-hue, Noa."

He bends toward me and looks into my eyes as before kissing.

Point of Intersection

I heard Kata's story, as I had mentioned, from my good friend Agi when I lived in Northampton. She told me the whole of it except for the last chapter, which we completed later on, and the story moved me so much that I forced all my friends to hear it. I told it excitedly again and again, in English and in Hebrew. My friends listened to me patiently and somewhat perplexed, because I probably seemed a little peculiar in their eyes – an Israeli woman, a widow who has been living alone in the United States for ten years, when her children, grandchildren and the rest of her family lived in Israel. But possibly there were other things that puzzled my friends. Once, one of the women in our group asked me, "Noa, apart from this story, you never feel like talking about fashion or the weather?" And I thought she was complimenting me.

I got hooked on Kata's story, and when I finally relaxed and began to think about writing it, a great need to go back and live in Israel rose in me. "I have to go back now, and stay," I told my friend Agi and felt it necessary to apologize. "I know this is sudden but that's how I am... we will fill in the missing last chapter some other time." That was in November 2008. I packed my belongings and returned to live in my house in Haifa.

I found it hard to be a returning resident. I could not extricate myself from my Northampton self, and I missed it as though I was on a visit to Israel that lasted too long. I walked every day from my house to the Carmel Centre and I did not recognize my image reflecting in the shops' windows. The city I grew up in was strange and uninviting, and in addition, when I tried to write Kata's story it did not flow.

It was quite dispiriting, but two months after my return Agi called me from Northampton to inform me that there were new developments. "That's it, now we can finish the story," she said in an uncharacteristic solemnity, "and for that we need to go to New York. Are you coming? We'll take my car."

"Of course I am coming!"

I felt as though I was going home. I bought a plane ticket, took the train to the airport, and there on the train I met Avry.

Editor-Rafi coughs artificially from the couch. What does he want? He sends me a sharp look through his glasses, "you deviate from the main plot and it disrupts the sequence of your story. Enough! Go back to Kata."

"Listen, I have to explain a little about Avry and me."

"But why here of all places?"

"Because I reached the point where the stories intersect."

"OK... But make it short! You drag it out too much."

At the beginning of January 2009, I took the train to the airport. I sat with my face forward, next to the aisle, and all the way from Haifa to Tel Aviv I watched the scenery running to me and away. It was a regular grey day that flattened all my thoughts.

The soldier who sat on the bench facing me by the window, leaned his head on the wall and his body was slack. His eyes closed and opened intermittently, and from his headphones echoed the monotonous bass of a rhythmic music. Every so often he pulled his phone from his shirt pocket, pulled out one of the earbuds and his expression did not alter as he talked or listened. His gun rested next to him, and in my mind's eye I saw him crawling on the ground in some battle shooting with this gun, shooting and shooting, the earbuds stuck in his ears and he is deaf to the moaning and screaming around him, even his own.

At the 'Tel Aviv Centre' station, a man in sunglasses entered the car, carrying a bag over his shoulder. He stopped and laid his bag by the aisle, sat facing me next to the soldier and removed his sunglasses. I pulled my legs in to make room for his and looked at him. Although I have trouble recreating those first moments in which Avry was still a stranger, I remember clearly that there was something crude and snubbing about him, rebuffing and attracting, and that his presence filled the space around me.

I strained not to stare at him but was not successful. He had fairly big honey eyes, surrounded by dark lashes and wrinkles which crisscrossed around them. Thin dark-grey hair hung on his forehead, like bangs that used to be a fifties-style pompadour, and his nose looked bulbous. Dark stubble shaded his pale cheeks, and his lips were moist. He leaned back, looked around and suddenly turned his eyes to me. Our eyes locked and I was overcome by an excited bashfulness. He gave me a pondering smile·as though I spoke to him, and his smile confused me. My eyes bolted to the window and I felt that his eyes stayed on me for a few moments of sweet eternity. I spread my fingers on my knees, which touched and did not touch his, to parade the only ring I wore, a non-descript silver ring with a red stone, and for a moment I was ridiculous in my own eyes.

I looked at him again and he pulled a paper bag out of his jacket pocket, opened it and handed it to me, "You want?" There were peeled chestnuts in the bag and I asked, "Chestnuts? Where did you find them?" He leaned into me, "What?" I raised my voice a little, "Where did you find chestnuts?" He smiled apologetically, "Just a minute, I can't hear." I understood that he had a problem hearing, so I leaned forward and said, "Come, sit next to me." He raised his eyes to me and smiled appreciatively. Heat flooded my face and I moved to the window. He sat next to me and left some space between us, in a touch-no-touch of a shoulder to shoulder, an elbow to elbow, a thigh to thigh. I felt his heat seek me and I did not move. We leaned our heads back, only pillows were missing, and eyed each other.

He pulled a chestnut out of the bag and handed it to me, pulled another one and put it in his mouth. We ate his chestnuts together and he tugged at his left earlobe, the one close to me, and said, "this one hears, the other not so well. Now we can talk." His thick voice sounded to me as if it came out of some darkness. I smiled at him, "So I am on your right side?" and dim echoes came back to me as if we were alone in a space shuttle cell.

"Flying today?" he asked in a soft voice. "Yes, flying," I responded to his whisper.

"For how long?"

"For a month... And you?"

"For a week. Where are you going?"

"To the United States."

"Ugh... that's far."

"Where are you flying to?"

"London... I am Avry," he lowered his voice further, as if trying to keep our privacy in the little space we had. I answered in a whisper, "Noa." He looked to the sides and smiled for a second, "Noa, let's think we shook hands." His quick blink, his stretching and contracting smile and his sideway tilt of the head out of shyness or excitement, were like echoes to enchantment that pulsated in me with a heart's rhythm. From the corner of my eye I saw the dark shadow of the stubble on his cheek and rounding chin, and when he turned his honey eyes to me, we were already speaking, and did not use any words yet.

He asked, "Do you live in Tel Aviv?" I swallowed the little saliva I had in my mouth and said, "In Haifa, but I may move to Tel Aviv." "That's good," he said, "there is no place like Tel Aviv." I asked him if he had ever been in Budapest, and he looked at me in surprise, "Budapest?" I did not know why I asked and I felt confused. He asked if I was taking time off work. I replied, "I used to work, now I don't. Do you work?" He pulled his shoulder, "Yes, at Tel Aviv City Hall." I asked, "Were you ever in Northampton?" He peered into my eyes, "No, where is it?" I told him and said, "I lived there for ten years. It is a beautiful town with an addictive loveliness."

Saved as a Painting

We talked in a crammed, dense conversation, and later I hardly remembered what we talked about. When the train stopped at the airport, Avry helped me drag my big suitcase, and in the departure lounge we stood and looked at each other as though the exchange of words still continued. Avry took a blue business card out of his wallet. "Take it. Write to me from your Northampton." And I said, "I will write, and you will answer me." He hugged my shoulder, "of course I will answer," and I did not want to leave his embrace.

Next to Avry's name on the business card, it said "Observer" and under it several phone numbers, a fax number and an e-mail address. What kind of a profession is Observer? I never heard that there was such a job at City Hall, only in war areas when the UN sends observers there. What does he observe exactly? And how does he do it, with binoculars? What kind of training do you need for this? But these questions dissolved and only his face with his honey eyes surrounded by sad lashes and the expression of wonderment was left.

***

I got to Northampton, settled myself in Agi's house and counted seven days before sending Avry an e-mail, "I hope you enjoyed London." I described the wintery cold in the town and the snow falling on it, and at the end I asked, "Observer is a type of a critic?"

He answered quickly, "No, it has to do with screening of actions and processes. I will tell you about it when I see you." Then he described the rainy street he sees from his apartment window in the Bavli neighbourhood of Tel Aviv, as if he is also overseas.

The last sentence, in a separate line, was "I am a widower. And you?"

He is a widower too? In all the years since Husband-Yossi died, I met divorced and married people, separated and single, but I never met widowers, and in fact, I forgot that I was a widow myself. I was widowed from my loves five times. I was widowed from Husband-Yossi, my children's father, whom I married in accordance with the law of the State. I was widowed from Childhood-Love-Moosh, from Highschool-sweetheart-Itamar, and from Old-Prince-Shaul, to whom I was married in accordance with the law of the heart, and was widowed from Rafi my editor, who was woven into my life for the purpose of writing. I was widowed from them, and each one of them was widowed from me when he passed onto the other side. And now suddenly I had a living widower.

I replied, "I am a widow too," and then described Northampton, "which is covered with a white blanket," a banal description... So what, I tried to be light, but in the last sentence my keyboard took over and discharged, "I am craving more e-mails from you." Avry replied, "I waited for your e-mail. Our meeting was wonderful. I keep talking to you all the time."

In ten days our correspondence turned into a flood of yearnings in daily texts full of the excitement of discovery. Avry wrote at length about himself in animated words as he marvelled about my writing, which was no less lengthy and no less animated. We saw ourselves as soul mates, and after three weeks our e-mails attested to our being spectacularly in love. But when Avry explicitly wrote, "this is love, Noa, I love you," I was startled: already that explicit word? So fast? And in the next moment I gave myself to him in a soaring e-mail, "my love, I fly back in two days."

I did not write about the trip Agi and I made to New York in a downpour the likes of which I had never ever seen before. It was an important trip, where we completed the last chapter in Kata's story. I planned to tell Avry about it at a festive occasion, as the crowning glory of our sweeping falling in love, and I was sure that after telling him, I would start writing, and my writing would flow.

The day I returned to my home in Haifa I called him and said in a quivering voice, "it's me, Noa." Avry replied, "I want to see you," and a fierce quiver was in his voice too. Next day we met in Tel Aviv. He waited for me at the train station, and when he saw me approach he removed his sunglasses and spread his arms to the sides. I sank into his embrace and embraced him, closed my eyes, and suddenly, apropos nothing, Kata appeared to me sitting in her blue velvet robe and her black-grey eyes looking directly at me.

***

Avry's apartment was neat and pleasant and had the good smell of cleanliness. We were excited like children, even though we were rather mature and rather jaded. He looked into my eyes and asked, "it will be good to be together, right?" I hugged him, "clearly, we are twins, aren't we?!" In my eyes Avry was attractive and wise and wonderful –

"Commercial! You are writing a commercial here. Noa, you went too far!" Editor-Rafi's voice pulls me out of the screen.

"'Attractive and wise and wonderful'" he mocks, "don't try hard to sell him! It's not possible to believe you, you are biased!"

"Great! But I am biased about Kata and about Ilona too, I am biased about all the characters here, you as well."

"But you didn't write such a stupid sentence about any of them. You are simply a gas artist."

Ugh, he is so crude! It is absolutely insufferable! Of course, he hears me, I don't have an ounce of privacy with these Deceased. I can do nothing, let him hear me, let him react, or not, it's his business. What did he actually say to me? That I write poorly? That he is jealous? Maybe both.

"You write poorly. You blather."

"Noa," Moosh calls to me and his brown-gold eyes shine, "when-we-are-too-close-to-the-character-in-the-story we-cannot-write-it. Step back!"

I prepared a cheese and olives sandwich and ate it at the small table in the kitchen. Moose came after me, sat in the chair opposite me and looked at me with our old childhood fondness. I said to him, "too bad you are dead, too bad you cannot eat with me, "and he said, "I-am-dying-to-eat-with-you."

THE MONTH OF HONEY

During a month of honey Avry and I met almost every day, most of the time in my house in Haifa. We held wild lust parties, we ate and slept, walked and returned, and most of all we told and got excited. Avry lectured to me and I lectured to him, about our lives and about the world, about the country and about current affairs, about literature and about art... I trusted our words, especially the beautiful ones, and I believed that they would lead me into Avry's soul and him into mine.

And the words did pave the way for us, but only to the place where they always stopped and dissipated, and suddenly a bewildering silence fell between us. I searched urgently for topics to talk about, determined to save us from the hush that overcame us, but I did not manage to bring back the flowing exchange that we had at the beginning. Avry became completely quiet, and I managed to dribble a few more sentences and, in the end, I fell silent too.

We peeked at each other, for a moment his eyes dove into my eyes and mine into his, and suddenly, as though binoculars from Mount Nebo, I saw into his deep layers and I noticed the pain hidden there in the darkness, a reflection of my pain, the things never spoken about with anyone. I did not say a word and I did not even bat my eyelids to indicate that I saw. And Avry too, if he saw my deep layers and my pain buried there, he did not indicate that he saw and did not say anything. These are unconnected stories that I may write one day. We sat silent on the carpet, touching shoulder to shoulder. And then, out of the silence, without speech, gentle feelings appeared between us, displayed in Avry's expressions, and probably were visible on my face too. When words ended a closeness arose between us. But it startled me, and maybe Avry was startled as well. I did not know what to do with such closeness. How to exist in it? How to speak it?

I was confused. Every word I said to Avry made me feel unnatural and forced, and maybe Avry felt the same way as he spoke to me. I avoided his eyes and he avoided mine, and together we escaped to the bed with the wide mattress covered with a smooth sheet. There, in the skill of the seasoned and the experienced we submitted to sex dances, and easily hid in ourselves, he from me and I from him.

At the end of the month of honey we separated. We did promise each other that we still loved, but parting was inevitable. "Something did not work out," I summarized impatiently, and I was a little ashamed of my efforts to flatten the sadness between us. His fingers toyed with the car keys, "right..." he said, "we can't manage to talk, and we can't manage to be silent. It is strange because there is love here."

His words pained me so much that I immediately erased them, as if they were never uttered, but suddenly Kata came into my thought and I changed my tone against my will. I heard myself talking to Avry in a pleading voice as if fighting for my life, "listen... Let's not sever it completely. Let's meet once every two weeks. No obligations!" I did not understand why I talked that way and why I suggested such an arrangement. Avry looked at me in surprise and shook his head, "It won't work." His dark hued cheeks paled, and he said, "Such a together-arrangement will only hurt you, Noa." He got up to leave, hugged me and looked at me in a questioning expression. "I am fine," I said, "everything is fine."

He left and I felt a relief. I missed the story and I wanted to start writing it without interruptions. But when I sat at the computer, I discovered to my great bewilderment, that the story became mute. I tried to revive in my mind Vera and Ferenc, Kata and Ilona, but no picture came up, the screen stayed dark.

Saved as a Painting

I closeted myself in my house on the Carmel and sank into despair. I did not have Avry with me, and I did not have Kata's story, and on top of it all I was a returning resident who failed to fit in.

***

But soon I recovered and decided to make a radical change in my life, as if the return from Northampton was not radical enough. And so, in the hot summer of 2009 I moved to Tel Aviv, a city I did not know. I found a three-story building on noisy Jabotinsky Street, and I rented my pleasant apartment on the third floor, with a tall palm tree reaching its balcony, and next to it a soaring wild, dark-blue cypress. On my first week, while I was still settling into my new abode in Tel Aviv, Avry called me unexpectedly, as though the city crows announced my arrival. We hadn't seen each other for five months, hadn't talked and hadn't exchanged emails, five months in which I tried not to think about him or Kata's story which became mute in me. But when his name appeared on the telephone display I cried with happiness, "Avry!" We talked, we became giddy, and he immediately came. He came around noon, went away toward evening, and left me melted.

And this is what happened: the minute Avry entered my apartment, Kata's story commenced beating fiercely in me.

That night I could not fall asleep, the story churned in me and I believed that finally I would be able to write it, but my writing did not even trickle. Days passed, and the story remained stuck. I went out for long walks, I got together with friends who lived in Tel Aviv, excellent people who did not belong to the story, and every three-four weeks Avry and I met. In reality, his apartment was a short drive from mine, but he would arrive as though he came from far away.

Sometimes we walked to the beach and back, sometimes we sat in a café, a pub or went to the cinema, but mostly we preferred to sit and chat in my living room. And each time we ended our dates in my bedroom. Then Avry would get up and leave.

My yearning for him would strike me after about two weeks, pinching and distressing me so much, that more than once I said to myself that this arrangement was too cruel to bear, and that I would not wait for Avry any longer. But I continued to wait for his call until I no longer could, and I would explode and call him, asking him to come. And he came excited and full of longing, as if missing me revitalized his feelings. Thus, he came and left, came and left, without making future plans and without knowing when I would see him again. I could not understand why I had instigated such a tortuous relationship, which had no constancy and no exclusivity, and why I became accustomed to it. My logic and my emotions cried in me to stop it, but I could not give Avry up and I did not know why.

In the meantime, I continued my futile attempts to write Kata's story. Once I managed to fill a few pages, my writing began to flow and I got into a rhythm, but I stopped again, the same way it happened more than once in bed with Avry, when the climax was so close and suddenly it stopped three breaths away.

And then, in January of 2010, when that night storm raged in Tel Aviv, there was something in the moment in which Kata,

Saved as a Painting

Avry and the wind's roars of joy converged in me. Next morning my five-Deceased sat down in my living room, I began to write, and this time it poured.

{ 11 }

The Novi Sad –
Budapest Line

The Danube river flows east through Europe, from Germany to the Black Sea. On the way it runs through Budapest under the bejewelled royal bridges, and further on it glides by Novi Sad under its big and picturesque bridges. It cruises by other beautiful cities and other impressive bridges, but only Budapest and Novi Sad belong to my story and I see only them now.

Serbs established Novi Sad on the shore of the Danube at the end of the seventeenth century, and over the years its inhabitants built wide streets, churches with Gothic towers, magnificent public buildings and elegant apartment blocks. It was so central and picturesque, that it received the name "Serb Athens". But the city was not lucky. One hundred and fifty years after its birth the Hungarian army besieged it and bombarded it, conquered it, destroyed and killed and slaughtered, and murdered half of its residents. Why destroyed? Why murdered? Because. War is about slaughtering and destroying. And like any war, this one broke out of destructive motives, devoid of humane compassion.

Serb Novi Sad stayed under Hungarian rule, and like after any war, it restored itself. Eighteen years later, the Austro-Hungarian Empire was established, and the emperor decided to develop the city. Many Hungarians moved there, opened businesses, established cultural life, and it became a city of mixed population of Serbs and Hungarians. However, the mix was not successful. Novi Sad's residents spoke different languages and used different alphabet. They stayed aloof from each other, and deep hatred ensued, covert and overt. The Serbs did not forget the killing and destruction of the war twenty years back, and the Hungarians – they had their own accounts to settle. "The city was a keg of explosives", remarked my friend Agi knowingly.

László Steins' Hungarian parents moved from Budapest to Novi Sad and paid no heed to the tension and the hatred there, maybe because they were concerned only with their livelihood. They opened a fabrics store, bequeathed it to László, and he, who spoke Hungarian, Serbian and German, expanded the business, sold fabrics in Budapest and other cities in Central Europe and made his fortune. At the end of the first decade of the twentieth century, when he was thirty-nine, he met nineteen-year-old Kata at the Tobacconist shop. They got married and he brought her to Novi Sad where she joined him in running the family business.

In keeping with their financial standing, Kata and László purchased a large home on Dunavska street, a one-story house with white front overlooking the street through five long windows and with a large entrance boasting a brown door of carved wood. Above the arch of the entrance there were reliefs of flowers and curly branches, and above them, all along the front, stretched a cornice decorated with squares and embossed in the baroque style, the same decoration as the other rich houses of the city. The house had high ceilings, a fully equipped kitchen and a well-lit dining room, six bedrooms, a vast living room, a room for small gatherings, and three Serbs who were responsible for the upkeep and domestic chores.

Kata and László moved into their new house, and shortly after that Vera and Ernő arrived from Budapest and moved in as well. Sixteen-year-old Ernő registered in the local high school to complete his education and become a clerk, and when László brought Vera's childhood piano it was placed in the living room and Ernő played old and new pieces on it every evening. Ilona and Aladar got married and stayed in Budapest.

Agi told me, "today it takes about 3 hours to travel between Novi Sad and Budapest in a car. But in those days, it took six or seven hours on the train, but it didn't bother them, and they visited often."

***

Novi Sad, 1912. Kata is twenty-one, devotes her time to the family's fabrics business together with László, and their cooperation goes smoothly and efficiently. They have a circle of rich friends, Hungarian speaking like them, with whom they spend considerable time. After each social event Kata and László exchange impressions, which are always similar, at times even identical. Her opinions suit his opinions, and his taste suits hers.

Saved as a Painting

Ernő, who has finished school, works as a clerk for a shipping company which ships merchandise on the Danube. He is thin, his face is fair, and his cheeks are pockmarked by acne scars. He says little, and when he is spoken to, he smiles shyly, lowers his eyes and answers in brief sentences.

Vera is in charge of the food and the cooking. "It is good for her and good for us," says Kata to László, and he nods. Vera is only forty-one, but something in her is dark like premature aging, maybe her eyes, maybe her gait, maybe the longing body that is too thin. Her considerable nose protrudes even more, her sunken cheeks are pale, and her aubergine hair is dull. She strides erect from stall to stall in the market dressed in her long blue dress, like an exiled queen. Two of the Serbs walk behind her, stop when she stops, and wait for her purchases to carry them home. Vera instructs them in fluent Serbian which she learned in one year since her arrival in Novi Sad. She has no complaints. Her life is comfortable, she cooks when she feels like it, she plays the piano when she feels like it. She reads books and newspapers, goes to the theatre, and her elegant dresses are made by the best seamstresses of Novi Sad, but the despondency of mourning has lingered, heavier than before.

Kata is not troubled by her mother's despondency. "It will pass!" she says confidently to László, and in the summer, when Ilona and Aladar come for a visit, Kata hugs her sister and whispers to her, "you see, Ilonka, mother is again the lady she was at the beginning!"

A SOUVENIR PHOTOGRAPH

Summer days in Novi Sad are clear and the gardens bloom. Kata and László, Vera and Ernő, Ilona and Aladar, clad in light cotton clothes and summer hats, walk together by the Danube, and I walk with them. They chat in hushed voices, and the waters of the large river, wide like a lake, flow next to us silently. Aladar, whose Adam's apple moves and his blue eyes clear, stops for a moment and all of us stand around him. He tells a joke, everyone laughs in a familial intimacy, and they carry on.

We reach the beach. At the entrance there is a wooden gate, with the sign "Strand" above it in Serbian and Hungarian. Under it a few young men and women stand in bathing suits, about to be photographed. Large straps, tight shorts, horizontal lines and vertical lines. They laugh, freeze for the photographer, and run back to the beach.

Now we are going to be photographed under the sign too. "We should have a souvenir from the Strand," says Kata in her metallic voice, and everyone gathers around her for a family photo. I stand with them, even if I am not in the photo. Later on, the photographer will send them three copies with his name and the date stamped on the back.

The beach is padded with soft and dry yellowish-grey sand and on it wooden recreational facilities are scattered, swings and ladders painted in white, and white benches and beach chairs. A garden is planted to the side with a café and straw sun umbrellas. Large white swans glide on the river, their necks twist, long and reedy. In the fall they will fly away, but now they are here, on the Strand, where everything is tended and clean, everything is quiet and full of promise.

The family walks slowly on the sand, and they have no way of knowing what will happen thirty years later on the Strand. That's the problem, that I know, and they do not. I walk with them, adjust my steps to theirs, and a mortal fear freezes me. An undulating alarm reaches me from the street below. I tell myself it is only an accelerating motorcycle, but the taste of dread stays in me long after it speeds away.

My imagination hits me: what if in some future time someone will write about Tel Aviv's Old North where I live and write now? Someone will tell about this neighbourhood flooded with hedonistic atmosphere and will describe the people who are dressed to kill and maybe will focus on my daughter and me, sitting in our usual sushi restaurant in a corner of Basel square. Or on Avry and me, sitting at a small table in a charming wine bar intermingling with each other in smug mid-weekdays, when suddenly a real alarm begins to wail, and a shower of missiles rains on us.

But now we are in 1912, walking along with ease on the banks of the Danube in light clothes, white socks and light summer shoes punched with small holes for ventilation, and Vera says, "it's lovely and beautiful here."

***

Two years later World War One broke out, during which Kata gave birth to two sons, Sandor and Miklos, whom everyone called Miki. Both boys were born at the margins of the war, the first at the opening margin, and the second at the closing.

Sandor, who was born to the guns' rumble, was a shrieking baby who became a sullen and exceedingly thin boy, whom no amount of food could satiate. "Grandma Vera was worried about him, and said that they should look into it," my friend Agi told me, "but Kata didn't get excited and claimed it was his character, that there are people who are never happy. He's a bitter boy, she said" Over the years a sense of deprivation was added to his bitterness, which grew with time, and in the family he was known as a scowling and grumpy youth.

Whereas his brother, Miki, who was born to the sound of bells ringing the end of the war, was a content and satisfied baby, grew to be a round and smiling boy and became a handsome youth. "Good fortune stuck to him," Agi smiled the way you smile when you hear of someone who has won the lottery, "he always had lots of money."

I imagine that due to its wealth the family went through the First World War unharmed, and the business did not fail. Had anything extraordinary happened to them during "The Great War", Agi would have no doubt told me about it.

At the end of the war political agreements were signed and borders were rearranged, and Kata and her family residing in the house on Dunavska Street received Yugoslav passports. Austro-Hungary was undone, and Novi Sad became part of the newly formed Yugoslavia.

A GRIM ROSE

Europe licked its wounds and insisted on healing fast, filling the trenches with earth and erasing the ugliness of the war scars. Everyone wanted to forget the great bad war.

The artist Gábor Pahl returned from the United States with his family successful, rich and famous. He was fifty-six upon his return, and apart from his improved English, he was essentially unchanged: he had a full head of hair, his short thick beard still curled in a sensual untidiness of red and silver, and his wolf eyes shone. The erotic fire burned in his bones as in the past, and his creative passion was as strong as ever.

Budapest, however, changed and did not appear to look like the city he had left before the war. The roaring creative atmosphere turned melancholy and the arts were hard to recover, but he kept painting with excitement and worked vigorously to inspire the artists with a spirit of renewal. On winter days they crowded by the fireplace in his favourite Fészek Artists' Club, sipping Schnapps and Palinka, and solved the problems of the world in long discussions and arguments. During summer days they preferred to be seated in the café's inner garden and exchange glances with the ladies who sat there too.

***

And Kata - the long journey by train from Novi Sad to Budapest did not deter her, and she traveled often to see Ilona, who was her only close friend. During their reunions they talked in the doves' cooing sounds of their childhood, and when Ilona asked cautiously, 'Kata, what is going on at home with Laci?" she responded in a smile of everything-is-fine accompanied by a light sigh that only close sisters could hear.

When I sat in the Seniors' Home in Tel Aviv with eighty-six-year-Old Edit, daughter of Ilona and Aladar, I asked in a direct way which may have embarrassed her, if she thought her aunt Kata's marriage was a happy one. Old Edit looked pensive, as if there were subjects which were not talked about at home and nobody knew about them decisively. "My aunt... she was twenty years younger than my uncle," she said, "so... maybe there was something, but I never saw... They were quiet people and got along well."

***

Kata sits in the First-Class compartment on the Novi Sad – Budapest line. She is dressed in an olive travel suit, her stylish hat is resting next to her, and on the table in front of her lies her documents case with business accounts. She peruses them with deep concentration, looks through once and again, marks certain lines with a pencil, and mumbles to herself. This is a good time for her to work, quietly without interruptions. The rushing scenery outside the window does not attract her attention, and if I were to ask her, she would have probably responded that she has traveled this route so many times that she knows every tree on the way.

In my opinion she does not know any tree on the way. She does not look at the corn fields which stretch to the horizon nor at the small structures at the corners of the fields, like elevated small train cars, in which the farmers dry the corn ears. When the train goes through villages, Kata does not pay attention to the vegetable gardens full of pale cabbage heads and the farmers' wives sitting among them with knives and collecting them into sizable baskets. Later, the train passes through the plain, which does not interest Kata either, and she doesn't see that the view becomes arid and the rich earth turns into dry and wind-blown land.

Saved as a Painting

The train rumbles on and Kata dozes or is busy thinking about her family and the business she runs, but when she returns home two days later, she tells her sons, Sandor and Miki, that the road was splendid. Because that is what should be told to children, so that they learn that train riding is comfortable and efficient, and one should not stay confined to one city, but visit other places, get to know them, and that way find more clients and expand the business.

***

Vera sits at the family dining nook and sips her morning coffee. Her cheeks are still gaunt and sunken, but they are rosy, and her expression is alert, as if she has been herself again for a while. Several books and magazines rest on the table in front of her, some in German and some in Hungarian, among them an article by the Hungarian Karl Polanyi. Vera has been following his articles for a few years, because his social and economic positions suit her own socialist beliefs. She reads his article, marks some lines and puts question marks next to them. She will take the article with her next week when she goes to visit her friend, a spirited Serb woman, a devout communist, whom Vera met at the theatre during intermission. The two women became close friends and would meet once a week in a café in the spacious square in front of City Hall for long discussions about society and state. A year later the woman moved to Belgrade. Since then they exchange letters and meet every few months, once in Belgrade and once in Novi Sad. Two friends, one socialist the other communist, delight in each other and listen to each other patiently and fondly. "When she speaks of Tito, their rising star," said Vera to Ilona, "it is like hearing the muse speak."

***

Steins's fabric store in Novi Sad moved to a larger building, and a wing was added for sewing clothes. Kata allocated a special corner in her office for Vera, who sat there once or twice a week designing coat samples. "It is good for her and good for us," said Kata to László and he nodded. They bought sewing machines and hired tailors who sewed coats according to Vera's samples and according to samples that arrived from Paris. Girls were hired to work on the finishing alongside the tailors. "Those girls, they came from all sorts of villages," Old Edit told me at the Seniors' Home in Tel Aviv, "they were expert in lace and looked for work in the city, maybe they looked for a husband too..." Edit remembered nostalgically the long summer vacations of her childhood and youth, when she came to visit her aunt in Novi Sad. "In the summer," she said to me, 'instead of the lace girls going home, my aunt kept them and paid them to sew beddings for my dowry. My aunt Kata, I was like her daughter... and if you asked, then yes, I was a bit afraid of her, but really, she had a good heart, she only wanted to give."

The volume of business increased and the sales agents traveled and sold coats all over Yugoslavia and Hungary. I am not surprised that Kata and László's business thrived. People always bought coats and will always buy them because everyone needs to stay warm, especially in the European winter, and it is clear to me that Kata relied on it, but here is the difference between us: I think of the existential need to protect me from the cold, and Kata calculated how much she can raise the price before shoppers shy away. I am busy with beauty, and she with fashion, I with love and she with business. What is there in Kata that attracts me so?

***

Budapest, spring of 1923. The rain which fell all night washed the city and now it is clean and fresh. The sun peeks behind the clouds, the scent blooming flowers fills the air, and people leave their homes to look at window shops and sit in cafés. Kata and Ilona too stroll down the street, arm in arm.

Kata is thirty-two. Her body has become rounder and her hips larger, but her waist stayed narrow – her belt buckle is fastened in the second hole to the right as it has been in her youth. The rise of her little belly can be observed through her chiffon skirt, and her breasts are prominent. Her shoulders are pulled back in her eternal erectness, and when she sees her image in the shop window she runs her fingers across her forehead to ascertain that a strand of hair has not fallen across it.

Ilona is almost thirty-one, and she does not have children yet. She had one failed pregnancy after another over the last ten years, but in the end, she succeeded, and now she is in her ninth month. She does not know, but I know, that soon she will have a baby girl whom she will name Edit. Ilona's lips are swollen, her eyes beaming, and her enormous belly bulges in the maternity dress Kata bought for her. They had a day of indulgence going from one shop to another. Kata chose, bought and paid, and Ilona accompanied her patiently, restraining herself from telling her that it is not necessary to buy so many clothes. Now, laden with bags, they go to sit in the Fészek Café, which tries hard to reconstruct the Bohemian atmosphere of the good days of old, before the Great War.

At the entrance they take off their spring coats and hand them to the coat check attendant, peek into the empty inner garden, wet from the night rain, and climb the wide staircase to the second floor. Daylight streams through the stained-glass windows and scatters around them in shades of red and blue, yellow and grey. The patter of their shoes is absorbed by the thick crimson carpet which covers the stairs. Ilona stops. She leans on the stone parapet, pants and supports her abdomen with her hands. Kata stands next to her and looks at her with softness reserved only for her sister, "it is heavy, Ilonka. Just a little longer, a matter of days!" They continue to climb slowly and pause at the crowded café's doorway. The host leads them to a side table covered with white tablecloth, and the other guests' eyes follow them.

The artist Gábor Pahl sits with his friends in the centre of the room and immediately identifies the sisters. They matured, he says to himself, and the years made them even prettier. Ilona looks to him like a peach in mid-season. The hand resting on her abdomen lightly digs under her left breast, which rests in a round calmness, and Gábor Pahl's eyes fill with fireworks. Wow, this brunette! She pulls up a chair and sinks into it, her back to the artist and her face to the window. Kata sits opposite her and looks around. "Look," she says, "the artist Gábor Pahl is here." Ilona waits a moment and turns to look at him. He plows his beard with his fingers, raises his eyebrows and smiles at her. She smiles back and nods her head in greeting. "Why are you smiling at him?" Kata scolds her, and Ilona shrugs.

Now Gábor Pahl eyes Kata. Her pink lips are pressed together, her white cheeks are powdered in blush and she seems to him like a grim rose. He traps her eyes and they move from his eyes to his beard and back to his eyes. He smiles at her but she does not smile at him. He insists and smiles, and she insists and does not smile. Suddenly, to her chagrin, she blushes and shifts her gaze to Ilona.

The waiter serves them coffee and places small plates with cake before them. Kata gazes with yearning at the Stefani cake and inhales with pleasure. Gábor Pahl observes her and imagines the moisture spreading in her mouth. She tilts her head a little, and her auburn hair, which is held by combs, smolders in the light. Her straight nose looks like a line in the centre of her face – blush on one side and blush on the other, and under it the rose lips which are pressed together with force.

She holds the fork and in a gentle movement cuts a piece of cake. Her expression is concentrated, she brings the fork with the piece of cake to her lips and spreads them apart, conceals it between them and immediately pulls it out. Her lips press together again and move a little with her chin and jaws. Her eyes flit over to Ilona and she mumbles, "Mmm..." She swallows and closes her eyes for a second, and when she opens them they are caught by Gábor Pahl's wolf eyes, and he smiles like a man with whom women are always true. Kata escapes his gaze and returns to it, escapes and returns, and in the end she capitulates in a soft smile and her black-grey eyes are veiled in purple hue.

{ 12 }

Needing a Boost

I prepared a big meal of salmon, rice and broccoli, as I used to when writing in Northampton. I wanted to eat in front of the television, and when I prepared to sit on the couch between Old-Prince-Shaul and Editor-Rafi they got up and stood by the library. I turned on the television and said to all five, "you can stay here or go away, I don't care. I need to eat." They, of course, did not go anywhere. I ate with pleasure and tried not to think of Kata, but she did not leave my thoughts. The news was on the second channel, but I did not absorb anything. I did not manage to watch a movie, and later I did not hear the music of the disc I played, and when I washed the dishes I did not notice I was by the sink. I surrendered and returned to the computer, but in spite of my dinner I had no energy to write.

I swiveled in my chair and saw that Old-Prince-Shaul was still standing by the library, long, reedy and bent. I approached, stood close to him and felt the moldy smell of his breath. His lips parted, his head tilted toward me, and in spite of remembering how foolish he acted in my living room, I was still attracted to his marvel of me. As in his life, he seemed to desire me regardless of his old body's ability. If I could, I would have hugged him, and he would have pulled me to him and charged me with the energy of his regal kisses, "but it is impossible," I said to him. He smiled as though I invited him to bed.

From the corner of my eye I noticed that Husband-Yossi tightened his hold on the chair's arms. He doesn't have it easy, I thought, but the rules of the game enable him to hear my thoughts and my yearnings. I cannot consider his feelings. If I were to be occupied with him and the four others, I would have written a different story.

I went back to the computer and told Editor-Rafi, "come help me, I can't continue on my own."

"What's the problem?"

"I don't know how to skip fourteen years in Kata's life. There is so much material that I must exclude to move forward, that I'll have to abandon many pictures..."

"If you have to abandon, abandon."

"Which pictures should I abandon? All of them? Here, look, Kata runs a business, she is a talented merchant, a housewife, a mother, a wife and a respected lady..."

"So?"

"It is not that her life was so interesting that a book is needed to be written about her, on the contrary. And she is not the first nor the last woman in history who married out of financial consideration and then was sad all her married life. I don't know what attracts me to her. She is not a prominent protagonist of a period story, she is not a character who left some personal mark, and in addition she is so materialistic that it bothers me, but I am compelled to write about her and I don't understand why."

"So you don't understand! You don't have to understand everything you write. Let it come out of you and leave the editing to me."

"No, I need to sort the material, Rafi."

"OK, that's enough! You don't hear anything anymore. What happened? All your energy is depleted? Call the guy you fuck."

"Why do you talk like that? What's your problem with Avry?"

"I don't have any problem with him!"

"But you are coarse and you ridicule me! You don't respect my love."

"What not respect? How not respect?"

"Must you use that horrible word?"

"What do you have against it?"

"To fuck is to take advantage of another person, to scam or victimise, to hurt someone. It's a word containing ugliness. Fucking doesn't fit with caresses and tenderness."

"Noa, to fuck is to fuck. Get used to the language, get down to earth."

***

I called Avry.

Avry picked up the phone before the first ring and answered like a neighing horse, "Noa!" This excited "Noa" was like a gust of air over embers. "When do we get together?" I neighed back to him. He was silent for a second as if I doused him with cold water, and asked in a matter-of-fact tone, "How is it going? Writing, writing?"

"Yes, writing all the time, but I am spent. Let's meet!"

He murmured something to himself.

"What did you say, Avry?"

He lowered his voice, "You call me only when you need me..." paused a moment and added, "but when there is love everything goes. Tomorrow sounds OK?" and sounded as if a double dose of tenderness sluiced his throat.

I almost got angry; he is the one who doesn't call me! But his "when there is love" and the tenderness in his voice melted my irritation. "Oh, Avry," I whispered, "let it be tomorrow already!" And the telephone almost dissolved in my hand.

WHITE SHIRT

It was dark when I heard a knock on my door and I opened. Avry stood in front of me smiling, his body leaning into me and his honey eyes seemed like pebbles drawn out of water. In one hand he held a big flowerpot with cyclamen and in the other a bottle of red wine. "Avry!..." I had my wits with me enough to lock the door behind him and immediately they dissipated into the coming and going movement of a wave, that wonderous movement that starts in the heart and spreads all over the body.

Avry inserted a disc and piano music filled the room. I recognized it but did not know what we were listening to. I lit candles and we sat on the carpet with wine glasses. Avry leaned on the couch and I sat next to him. For a while he told me in detail about his daughters, their husbands and children, about helping with driving them to their afternoon activities, about the baby who is crawling already... He spoke and his eyes were beaming. Then he talked about his work, about the books he read and the books he intended to read... so much trivia that I lost my patience, and he may have sensed it and became quiet.

I reclined and put my head on his lap, and from below I looked at his jaws and his rounding chin with a small double chin fastened to it. Immediately I burst out talking and waiving my hands in front of his face. I described to him how my writing was pulling me and how I became addicted to it. I talked about Kata and her family, I became excited, I raised my voice... And then I realized how melodramatic I sounded, and I shrank, but Avry listened to me with his fingers playing with my hair, his gaze focused on a far corner of the room and his breathing quiet, as if he heard me with his whole body. He asked, "when will you finish writing?" and I answered reluctantly, "maybe in the summer."

Suddenly my five Deceased appeared sitting around us and looking at us. I sat up, what do you want now? Leave us!

Avry looked at me. Maybe he wondered about the sudden change in my mood. Indeed, something in me cooled and faded, maybe in him as well. I said to myself, it's not so bad, try to fix it. I drank some wine and asked, "how do you spend your days?" I meant well, hoping he would return to the trivia he enjoyed so much, but I sounded to myself critical, as if demanding an account of his actions. He paused before answering, maybe looking for special wording, "you know how I live, work a little for my livelihood, and the rest of the time connect and disconnect."

His voice had a slight tone of aggression and he did not look at me, as if he walked alone in the desert.

"Tell me, this connect-disconnect of yours, does it not wear you out? Don't you need to rest sometimes?"

"Sometimes it is tiring, but that's the life I lead, I fuck therefore I live."

I recoiled, almost moved away, but got over it. "You know," I tried to soften my voice, "you never told me about your wife." He sent a quick look my way, "you never asked."

"I am asking now; what kind of woman was she?"

"She was delicate."

"You mean... physically?"

"In all ways... she was delicate. The girls are like her."

A loneliness descended upon me.

"Do you miss her?"

"Sometimes, yes. But life goes on, the dead are not with us."

"Sometimes they are with us..."

He nodded his head as if knowing.

"What do you feel when you miss her? I mean, what kind of mood does it put you in?"

Avry pulled his head back, closed and then opened his eyes, "longing is really only a mood, some kind of sadness. But it passes." I said to him, "even now, when we are together, I long for you," and he was silent. I wondered if he missed me sometimes, and suddenly I did not know why we broke up, we do love each other.

"Avry, why aren't we a normal couple, like other couples?"

He looked at me with the expression of leave-this-thing-alone, but I insisted, "Is it because of me? Something in me puts you off?" He did not answer, and I continued talking like bringing up bile, "Husband-Yossi said once that it's impossible to have simple sex with me, he called it 'quickies'. 'It is impossible to have quickies with you,' he said, 'with you it has to be a special event, for which it's necessary to get ready and after it take a day off.' Do you understand it, Avry?"

I almost cried. I felt sorry for myself for not being a woman who could enjoy talking trivia, who did not flinch from the word fuck and with whom it was possible to have quickies, but Avry's face was full of amazement and his gaze was open to me as it never was. "For me," he said, and his honey eyes widened, "when I go to meet Noa, it's like putting on a white shirt and moving from the profane to the sacred."

Great, I thought, he and Husband-Yossi sing a duet.

Avry looked moved, he pressed me to him, "I love you," and his words were as good as old and comfortable piece of clothing that washes and irons well and for a moment seem new. Avry felt me with his lips and we kissed. "I wish we could be more together, Avry! When I want to be with you and you are not with me, it hurts me physically."

"I told you once that this together-arrangement would hurt you. If you can't carry on, I'll understand."

Ah, he will understand... I was startled, he may simply get up and leave! And immediately I told myself that our arrangement indeed felt like Chinese torture to me, but so far I could stand it. I did not know why I was prepared to be tortured like that, but I could not give Avry up and accepted the knowledge that so long as he was with me, in the few hours he allocated to me, I choose not to leave him of my free will. "In the meantime, we are together," I mumbled.

We kissed again. I heard the sound of our kissing lips and I straightened, "say, what do you think is the connection between kiss and kill?" He opened his eyes, and the lashes of cypress trees around a cemetery bordered them, no one goes in or out. "It doesn't matter now," he muttered and neared his mouth to me, "come, one more..." but I moved away from the kissing scene, and insisted, "why is an action which is so pleasant and human reminiscent of a violent act? It's horrible, no?" He smiled, and I scolded myself, that if I had not talked so much, we would have moved to the stage where words go to rest and a love dance takes their place.

The candles flickered. Avry was lying on the couch shirtless and I knelt on my knees next to him and moved my fingers over the furrows of the scars on his chest. Suddenly I bent over his hearing ear and whispered, "I despise the people who used killing machines and injured you in the war." He opened his eyes, smiled forgivingly and closed them again, "it was a long time ago." His voice was steady and flat, like nothing happened, and I knew I should leave him alone. I did not want to hurt him, but some warrior in me did not cede. I did not have any pity in me, only some dull ache, and I said, "they wanted to kill you." He answered without opening his eyes "it wasn't personal".

I remembered Joseph Heller's Yossarian, who piloted a jet fighter and yelled, "they are trying to kill me!" And I thought about Highschool-Sweetheart-Itamar, who was shot at and run over by enemy soldiers in a galloping tank, and I thought about Kata, and I wanted to tell Avry that the people who shot at him in the war did not know him, but they directed their guns at him personally. He too shot and killed, and it was personal, because when you kill people, it is personal.

My lips grew cold and I was defeated. I rested my head on his chest, felt the scars' ridges on my cheek and discharged one squashed last thought, "I still don't like that kissing and killing are so similar." Finally, I fell silent, and Avry got up, and shaking himself he pulled my hand and we rushed to the bedroom, and my five Deceased stayed in the living room. I spread out like a fan and Avry spread out like a fan, and we became one fan, and there was wild vitality in us in a continuous together-time.

I fell asleep intoxicated and in the morning I found a text message that Avry had sent when he left my apartment, "I feel alive kissing you. It was a wonderful evening." But why did he not stay with me till morning?

DETACH

"OK, now get up and get back to what's important."

"What's important, Rafi? I will sit in front of my computer and again I will find no solace."

"What solace? How come solace now?"

"Listen, from the day I returned to Israel I am worried that a war would break again. You saw, even when I am with Avry I think about that. I have nowhere to run away to and no solace."

"Enough, Noa! It must be the stinky news you read every morning. It poisons your mind. Snap out of it. Go back to Kata's story."

Why does he hassle me?

"My precious," says Old-Prince-Shaul in a scorched voice, "maybe you look for solace in the wrong place?" He moves in his seat uncomfortably. What is he hinting at? Hush spreads in the room. None of the five Deceased men looks at me. "Why are you silent? Shaul, what are you trying to say?" He does not answer. The old man chickened out.

Nu, talk already!

"Children and grandchildren," says Husband-Yossi crossly, "if they are no solace for a woman, she is simply not right in the head!"

How dare he?!

Moosh, the writer, chuckles, "you-are-more-writer-than-mother, huh?"

Editor-Rafi smiles meanly and his little dark eyes shine through his glasses, "you are like Kata. She, too, was more interested in business than in her children. Noa, you lived alone in the United States for ten years, far from your children. No wonder you don't find your solace in them."

Highschool-Sweetheart-Itamar hides his face in his arms which are resting on his gathered legs. The other four Deceased stare at me with vulture's eyes and chop me into a salad of guilt feelings. A weight lands on my lungs.

***

The elevator descended too slowly. I exploded out of it and ran almost all the way to the Basel Square which welcomed me with its apartment buildings that surrounded it with the crooked awnings, the rusted banisters and the junk filled balconies. I walked fast along the white plaza which could be a beautiful piazza if it had large planters with geraniums around it like in Northampton. They are cheap, they are simple, need only a little watering, but that is how it is, Tel Aviv loves its ugly corners. I rushed from there to Dizengoff Street, where slim mannequins in colourful dresses stared at me stupidly through the shop windows, scruffy street cats burrowed through the foul-smelling trash cans, and a long-tailed rat ran on a black cable from balcony to balcony. I panted, and a bitter flow streamed through me... Right then my Deceased appeared. Itamar stayed home but the other four marched next to me, two on one side and two on the other, full of childish remorse. Had they tails, they would have wagged them. "Go away, toadies!" I said out loud.

Suddenly I heard Itamar's screechy voice speaking to me from my living room. "You should detach Noa the writer from Noa the written," and I halted. What?

"You forgot that you write about Noa who writes a story, not about the whole Noa who is real."

How come I did not think of that? The whole Noa who is real came back to Israel from Northampton and integrated into her family with her children and grandchildren, and lives a normal life, like everyone else, and only part of her is in Kata's story... Right, Itamar, right! And if so, how does Avry fit into this story? Why does he insert himself into it?

{ 13 }

Good Days

Novi Sad, 1936

"Laci, Mama wants to go to Belgrade again! Can you talk to her?"

László smooths his bald head with his hand, once and a second time and looks at Kata with a smile, "Don't worry, she just meets her friends there and sits with them for a nice chat."

"No, she needs to stop meeting them! I asked Ilona to explain it to her, but she and Aladar agree with Mama. You don't get it that this is dangerous?"

"Your mother didn't join the Communists. She only supports their ideas."

"Why does she need to support them? It's not good for the business."

"Her opinions can't hurt the business. You don't have to worry."

Kata nods her head, "Fine, if that's what you think." She reverts to perusing the orders and László enters the sewing department, as he does every day, to check that all is well.

He is sixty-five. His bald area expanded, long wrinkles line his face, and his shoulders sag a little. His general look has not changed since he met Kata in the tobacconist shop, but his soul is gentler. From the family business boss he turned into the boss's assistant and he is satisfied. In his eyes, Kata is the epitome of business acumen, and he is her most suitable helper. He is also their children's father-mother.

***

The atmosphere in Europe's cities was becoming tense. Bad and threatening sounds were rising from Germany, but in Novi Sad business was as usual and people were busy with their routines, like birds who wake up to a new morning every day, as if there was no yesterday and no tomorrow.

Sometimes, Kata and László went to Budapest with friends to take in art galleries and theatres, concerts and the opera. They would stroll around the centre of the city and see only what they wanted to see. When Szálasi's fascists walked past them screaming and raising mayhem, Kata whispered to László, "The police will disperse them any minute," and he answered, "but they will return later." She held his arm and they continued on their stroll with their friends, all of them Budapest natives in every way, although they were from Novi Sad, a Serb city.

Kata and László perceived themselves to be lovers of culture, even though sitting during concerts tired them, and more than once they fought their drooping eyelids. They did not read much good literature, but when Kata read an interesting book, she gave it to László. They read and immediately forgot. "I read on the train to help time go faster," she said to Ilona, "and I am content with simple books without all kinds of philosophies, or where the protagonists work out their problems." Poetry intimidated Kata and alienated her, but when any of their friends who was a 'somebody' suggested to go hear a famous Hungarian poet read his poems, they would join the group and go hear him. "I don't know what people find in this performance that they pay so much money for the tickets," Kata said to László as they left the reading. "Right," he answered, "there was nothing special in what he read, but he has a beautiful language, and it was nice to be with everyone." He pressed her arm to him and she smiled in pressed lips.

But Kata very much enjoyed social gatherings, parties and balls, one time in this rich house and one time in another, when they assembled dressed in their fineries, stood or sat and chatted pleasantly, ate, and at times even danced among the staged décor of expensive carpets and sheer curtains, splendid furniture and original oils of the best Hungarian artist, which hung on the walls in gilded frames.

Every so often Ernő joined his sister and brother-in-law and went to these gatherings, sat by the piano and played for the guests. People smiled at him and clapped and he thanked them in a whisper and a shy smile. At the beginning friends would ask Kata or László, "Why is he alone? He is such a pleasant young man!" But stopped when they were answered with reservation. "What do they expect?" wondered Kata to László, "Every group has it singles. That's the way of the world."

I have dozens of images of their lives in Novi Sad of those days, although there are some things that are impossible to see in these pictures, for example, the envy and scorn their Hungarian neighbours held against them, especially the richer ones, who smiled pretending good neighbourliness but secretly made lists and marked the Jewish homes.

✻ ✻ ✻

Kata and László formed a coordinated team. He knew her thought patterns, she knew his, and during all their years together they never clashed or fought, neither regarding the business nor regarding domestic issues. A peaceful agreeableness existed in the reality they created for themselves, with small indulgent habits, and with their good health, which is not a simple matter, and they delighted in all the goodness life bestowed upon them. As it was, every once in a while László would say to himself, we were lucky, it could have been different.

Sandor, their twenty-two-year old sullen son, worked in the thriving family business, but hoped to leave, be independent and reside away from his parents. He wanted to get married, but when he could not find a mate, his temper grew. "It is hard for him," Kata said to László, "he doesn't know how to be happy, and girls don't want someone like him." Whereas seventeen-year-old Miki was handsome, cheerful and surrounded by girls.

Kata turned forty-five. Her face filled and rounded, and a thin line like a streak of sadness stretched down her right cheek. In fact, it was barely noticeable, but it softened somewhat her hard expression. She was satisfied with her life, but had we had a heart to heart conversation, I would have asked her, "How can you be satisfied when you live without giving way to your desire?" She probably would have said to me, "I have other things in my life. You are making too much of this. I married very well." I would have said, "But Kata, your purple side has never been realized, it must have made you feel that something central to your being was never satisfied." She would have looked at me with reservation and would have sharply dismissed me, "Rubbish."

But Ilona, too, saw Kata's streak of sadness and said to Aladar, "What can you do, that's the life she lives." Ilona also slightly changed. Her sharp tongue, which exuded generous sense of humour, became prickly toward women. "She had no patience for silly women." my friend Agi told me. "Ilona would destroy her with words anyone who uttered nonsense or behaved vulgarly".

Ilona was more forgiving to men, because to her they were like youth in the eternal process of maturing. But women who were interested only in fashion and gossip earned her scorn. She was a clever and sunny woman, so much so that it was a pleasure being with her and talking to her, but her good comportment was reserved only to those she appreciated, and over time she showed arrogance and envy. Her arrogance probably came hand in hand with her interest in social issues and politics, it happens to opinionated people, and her envy - most women I know are envious, it is natural, and no one is perfect.

Kata did not possess even a drop of envy. Her personal relationships were built on business contacts, and the women in her social circle did not interest her and did not threaten her self-confidence, even if they were attractive, rich or famous. "Fine for them," she used to say, "I have what is mine."

Her family was always her main concern – her husband and children, her mother and sister, brother, niece and brother-in-law, eight people, whom she viewed as her full responsibility and whose welfare she tended to generously and steadfastly. She was the head of the family, everyone's financial security. Everyone came to her to consult about property and money and to receive her gifts and went to Ilona to pour out their heart including László and Sandor and Miki, and even Vera and Ernő, because it was good to talk to Ilona.

Ilona had three close friends with whom she met regularly. They told each other the details of their lives and they were jealous together to boot. Kata did not have even one close friend, and she was only thickly bound to Ilona. "It is nice to have friends to go out with and sit in a café," Kata said, "but to spill your guts and gossip, that I don't need."

Indeed, twice a week she would go to the magnificent Lipa Restaurant in the centre of Novi Sad to meet ten ladies of her circle. They would eat lunch together while casually chatting, celebrating each other's birthdays with cards and little gifts, all of which Kata enjoyed very much. All the women of this circle liked Kata because she was always warm and welcoming and her conversation clever, always dressed well, and when they told her personal stories she listened courteously. "Katalin may be a little reserved," they would say to each other, "but she is OK."

*** *

Kata is sitting at her vanity table wearing a light blue camisole and looking at the mirror. She pays no attention to her beauty and is not glad about it, she is not spoiled and not busy in self admiration, and besides, she is not the kind who is impressed very easily. At the same time, she is not one of those who find fault in everything. In her dialogue with herself she does not say, for example, gosh, another wrinkle on my face, and not, I have pretty lips, or I have a lovely neck. Instinctively she avoids the word "beauty," which she feels has something wild, uncontrolled in it that creates a turbulence behind her wall of restraint and self control.

She carefully examines her skin, her brows and teeth and wipes her forehead as if trying to erase any signs of worry, even though she has no reason for worry. Her single fear in life is poverty, a vague fear at the edge of her consciousness.

She is careful about her appearance and endeavours not to gain weight, although now, with the pestering hot flashes, she gets food cravings and has a hard time curbing them. Vera said to her, "I started early too. A year or two and it will be over."

Kata pulls her shoulders back and checks intently the very full brassiere under the camisole, then she opens the eau-de-cologne bottle and perfumes her wrists. Soft fragrance spreads in the room. She returns to her image and meets her eyes. I know that the perfume arouses her, smells have a huge effect on the spirit. Suddenly something starts to run amuck in her stomach and lungs, like a draft which enters through the window and throws havoc in the room. Kata gets up all at once and pulls in her breath.

She slips on a blue-grey silk dress, which reaches to her ankles, wears her high heeled shoes, covers her front with a gauzy make-up cape, and returns to sit in front of the mirror. She applies thick lines on her upper lids and thin lines on the lower lids with black kohl. She uses her powder puff to spread blush on her cheeks and colours her lips with the pink-purple lipstick. Now she removes the make-up cape and dons the white gold earrings László bought for her birthday. Her image stares back at her from the mirror, neat and made up, as it should be. She gets up and attaches a purple silk flower to her décolletage, lays on her shoulders a blue silk scarf intertwined with silver strands, and informs László, "I am ready."

They go to the summer ball at their friends' house down Dunavska Street. Warm air caresses them and they stride with her arm, as always, in his, and he, as always, adjusting his steps to hers. "It will be interesting to see who is invited," Kata says clicking with her heels, "they like to invite lots of people. "Yes," answers László, "they feel good when they have lots of guests," and his eyes smile at her.

BEAUTIFUL LIKE A RIVER

The invited guests had already gathered in the big house – all of them Hungarian speakers – and Kata gracefully mingled in the decadent-polite atmosphere with the bows, smiles and hand shakes, the custom-made dresses and the jackets and blazers cut in the latest style, the gold and pearl jewellery, the ties and scarves, the belts and the evening purses, the luxury leather shoes and the American silk stockings, the cigarettes in the thin long cigarette holders and the thick cigars... everything elegant and respectable.

The hosts invited the guests to gather in the salon to view a new and grand oil painting of the hostess, a smiley woman by the name of Vivi. "Gábor Pahl is in town!" she declared in a loud voice and a smile. "He is the most famous artist we have today in Hungary!" She walked back and forth in front of the portrait, encouraging her guests to compare the original to the painting, and stopped, "He is visiting Novi Sad right now, and already painted several portraits." Her smile widened and revealed a line of small teeth, "We were lucky to be at the top of the list. It is so long that we would have had to wait for weeks." Her guests murmured appreciative assents.

This was one of the dozens of portraits done by Gábor Pahl on his journey through Yugoslavia that year. He was well known and well sought after in Central Europe, and leaders and the nobility asked to sit before him, the rich and famous boasted being painted by him and gallery owners invited him to show his works with them. He loved money, loved women, and above all loved painting. He knew how to grasp and transfer the person's essence to the portrait, and even if strong public relations together with the forcefulness of celebrities were part of his fame, his rare talent and engaging personality were what paved the way.

László viewed the portrait for a long time. Background colours surrounded the hostess in orange and gold tones, and her image stared out with the smile which exposed her small teeth and her typical head tilt and her seating position which attested to her impatience. It seemed to László that any minute her ringing laughter would burst out of the painting.

Vivi stood close to him, but he did not hear her take pleasure in her guests' reactions, nor did he hear her husband who spoke loudly about the high price the artist demanded, nor did he notice the other guests buzzing around him. László heard only his own breathing and felt his heart pounding.

He never looked at a painting this way. His eyes moved slowly over each detail, caressed every line, mixed in with every hue, sank deeper and deeper into the colours and the shapes until he noticed the brush's hints and saw and heard the artist holding it and whispering to him over the lady's shoulder, I can see the laughter bubbling in her abdomen.

László's heart pounded fast, his lips paled and his hand got stuck on his bald head for a long moment. His gaze moved to Kata who was standing at the end of the room leaning over the refreshments table with a small plate in her hand. Her hair, coloured in her natural auburn, shone in the light of the sizable chandelier, the white gold earrings captured the light with a sparkle, and her blue-grey dress glided from her waist to her thighs and sashayed softly, in the clinging-separating softness of the fabric. She smiled to herself as if a wave of craving for sweets flooded her, put two marzipan pralines on her plate and straightened.

László saw her body's outline, her head tilt and her expression, and an excited movement arose in his loin, a kind of shivering rustle that climbed up his back and circled his chest, moved down to the bottom of his stomach and stirred between his testicles. His temples pounded and he said quietly to himself, "She is so beautiful, beautiful like a river, like the mountain, like the whole world."

He heard his own voice and his words were like wine in his mouth, which absorbed in his blood and inflamed his body. Suddenly his breath stopped, as if a secret which was hidden away from him for many years divulged itself, he smiled with a happiness he had never known and his face blushed.

Saved as a Painting

Kata, who began walking to him holding her small plate with the two pralines, stopped and looked at him with stupefaction. Their eyes met and for a long moment, a moment different from all the moments László knew with her, her eyes were veiled in purple hue, her lips parted, but immediately pressed together again. She lowered her gaze and all at once László understood everything.

***

They walked home wordlessly. Kata was discomfited by his silence, because she was used to exchange impressions of the evening with him. She forced herself to stay silent too until she could not restrain herself any longer, "A good portrait they got, no? The artist grasped Vivi's exact expression." László was still quiet and Kata felt even more uncomfortable, "Did something happen, Laci?"

"I want to put my name on Gábor Pahl's list, to do your portrait."

Kata fell silent.

She took off her clothes in the bedroom, put on the off-white silk negligee with the lace at the front, combed her hair, tied it loosely at the back and removed her makeup. László was in bed already, leaning on the elevated pillows and looking at her. He knew that only Gábor Pahl would be able to show his wife's beauty, and deep in his clenching gut, he felt the real price he would have to pay.

Kata lay next to him and covered herself, "What happened to you?"

"I want him to paint your portrait."

"It's unnecessary, Laci!" She sat up and looked at his face, "What do we need it for?"

He embraced her, pulled her body to him, and twenty-six years too late tried to pleasure her with his new awareness, tried with the force of his love, but she, as usual, responded coolly.

A PUDDLE OF PAIN

I could not look at this picture any longer. Two and a half weeks passed since Avry was with me, and a hunger for him fell on me at once, strong and demanding. I attacked the email, wrote him a long and eager letter, and finished with a call, "Avry! come!"

An hour later he called, and late in the afternoon – arrived.

"You wrote to me so beautifully..." he said and his pale face assumed a searching expression. "You asked me to come... and preceded me by one day." His words surprised me so much that I was not sure if I heard properly. Maybe something good is happening to him regarding me? My heart trembled, but I heard myself saying like a teacher in the classroom, "You see, Avry, we are learning to adjust ourselves with our doses!" And suddenly I had a bitter taste in my mouth.

We were in bed, Avry leaned on the pillows and I lay next to him on my side. He asked softly, "how are you?" I murmured that I was fine, careful not to discharge any more nonsense. He told me about a lunch he had with a co-worker and described their conversation and the argument that ensued. I nodded, mumbled, and was silent. Avry seized a strand of my hair, tickled my cheek with it and said, "You are beautiful." I did not know how to react. We made love wildly and I lost myself.

When he rose to leave, he was closed and remote. I wanted to ask him why he wouldn't stay with me till morning but I did not. I took comfort in the fact that he intended to call me even before I appealed to him to come.

Old-Prince-Shaul says to me, "This man did not intend to call you! He lied!" I answer him shamefacedly, "Yes, Avry can love me for only three hours a month."

"Three hours?!" Husband-Yossi's voice booms, "He doesn't love you even for fifteen minutes! He takes advantage of you! He doesn't deserve your love!"

I never heard him raise his voice like that. Maybe finally he learned to vent his rage? He continues, "When a man comes to a woman once a month for three hours it is like going to a whore!"

"A whore gets paid. Avry loves me and I love him."

"You call this love?"

"Hell, Yossi!" I raise my voice, "You'll decide for us what love is?" He looks at me in pity. I have to end this conversation, simply tell him calmly that we perceive love in different ways. But the fight sours my mood, wise words escape me, and I yell at him, "You and your stupid sense of honour and your fanatical jealousy!"

Husband-Yossi does not flinch, "How can you call this demeaning arrangement you have with him love?!"

Anger grows in me like nausea, "How were you better than him?"

"I married you! I gave you my salary, I built a house for you, and I raised a family with you. I was with you! Him, all that he is interested in is to lay with you and leave right away!"

I explode, "You still don't get it?!" All the anger and frustration I accumulated against him erupts, "My marriage to you was no less cruel together-arrangement! You were constantly irritated and you hated, you hated my writing!"

Husband-Yossi looks at me as if I am so unjust that even on the other side it is hard to bear. A blood libel. He folds his arms on his chest and lowers his head.

A grey silence falls on me. Why did I yell at him?

He insists on his truth because he believes in it. He was like that in his life and he is like that in his death. He was never mean, though. A wise and ethical man, an expert in engines who developed a small component in a big tank's engine, part of a master plan for war matters. He was self-important and proud of his expertise. "The state needs these projects," he used to say in an expression of can't-say-more-than-that, "And I am happy that I do my share." Logical, level-headed and polite, devoted and helpful. It has to be said to his credit that he passed good genes to our children and always cared for them. He will never be able to understand my protests. What do I want from him? We had a couple-togetherness. True, our compatibility was realized in the successful combination of genes in our children, so maybe this is the foundation for the right love?

I stand behind him. His nape is delicate and smooth like that of a boy and I want to put my hand on it, but it is not possible to touch. I move to stand before him and look in his eyes, "Sorry, Yossi." Not a muscle in his face moves. The other men in the room each look at a different spot and we all sit together in a puddle of pain.

FÉSZEK CAFÉ

1937. The house on Dunavska Street in Novi Sad became a little parliament. Vera and László stayed seated every night after the meal and exchanged opinions about the situation: what is happening in Yugoslavia where they live, and in Hungary to which they belong in spirit, and in Hitler's Germany, and all over Europe. They updated each other with news and with commentaries they read in the newspapers and made assessments. Vera lectured about her positions excitedly and with bright eyes, mentioning Tito every so often, and László listened to her attentively. When he disagreed with her, he explained his position, and when he agreed – he concurred. Sometimes Ernő, Sandor and Miki joined in the conversation, and Kata made an effort to sit with them despite her yawns.

She hoped that these lively discussions would push away the portrait idea, but to her surprise, László raised it again. Kata continued to refuse and he continued to remind and asked and begged in a persistence she did not know he possessed, "I want Gábor Pahl to paint your portrait!"

***

"1937?" Asked Old Edit at the Seniors' Home, "I don't remember anything special about that year." She straightened for a moment and peered out of her wrinkled face like a girl in a History exam, "the big troubles began later." I mentioned to her that I read that that year Hitler supported Hungary economically, and as a recompense Hungary implemented his Jewish policies. "Oh, sure, there was anti-Semitism," Edit replied, "but it didn't worry my parents. My mother, she was very political, but she worried about the Fascists, not anti-Semitism. My grandmother Vera, too, she came to us often from Novi Sad. She was a socialist, people thought she was a communist, but not, she told me herself that she was a socialist. She did not pay attention to anti-Semitism either."

During those pre-Anschluss days, Hungary was like a tremor before the big quake. The speeches' barks and the marches' growls in Germany spewed out of the radio in Budapest into homes, cafés and restaurants, and mixed with the sounds of the broadcasted concerts. However, the city was prosperous. Contractors built and stores sold, theatres performed and orchestras played, operettas were sung and danced, and galleries were full of art shows of ambitious artists under Gábor Pahl's spirited leadership.

The seventy-year-old artist's health began to deteriorate. Occasionally he felt dizzy and faint, but he ignored it and at the artists' gatherings at Fészek Café he attacked Fascism and the violence that was ignited in the city with youthful fervour. He liked people, especially women, and was not interested in their ethnic origin or religion, but the situation in the city worsened day by day. When he felt that it became impossible to create free art in the mounting hatred in his Budapest, he decided to leave with his family. Thus, without letting his friends know, and telling only his closest relatives, he began to plan his second trip to the United States in the fall. He packed his paintings and sent them to New York, one box at a time, "Not everything together; we don't want needless questions," he told his sons.

Saved as a Painting

One summer day, László went to Budapest on business, and upon its completion he went to Fészek Café, where Gábor Pahl and his friends used to sit every afternoon. The air was warm and some of the guests sat at the tables in the courtyard garden. László stood at the entrance considering where was best to sit. A large radio stood on the bar next to him and the light music coming out of it was cut occasionally by newsflashes and Hitler's wild speeches, but László paid no attention to them. His eyes wandered over the tables with their white tablecloth scattered among the trees in the garden, each with a red glass ashtray and next to it a blue glass vase with two roses.

As on the previous times in which he entered and sat here, an Oriental sensuality enveloped László, induced by the high Turkish arches surrounding the garden. They were painted orange and lines of dense and curly arabesques were drawn on them in black. The arches rested on tall white Greek columns, and an even taller wall rose behind them closing around the whole courtyard. László chose a small table to the side and ordered coffee.

A short time later Gábor Pahl and two of his friends stood at the entrance to the café's garden. The artist lay his elbow on the bar like someone who belonged there, and with his other hand he rubbed his short beard, a mass of dense hair sensors, which merged with his thick mustache. True, no traces of red were left either in his beard or in his thinning white hair which was coloured by light blue shades instead of dull grey. His wolf eyes shone and a brash freshness burst out of them. In his youth he had been thin as a reed, but over the years he had filled out. His abdomen was rotund and solid. His long brown coat was slung over his shoulders in a foppish carelessness and a colourful kerchief was tied at his neck – his bohemian attire for public appearances, even though twenty years earlier, in the United States, he preferred well- made three-piece suits. "When in Rome," he used to say, "dress as the Romans do."

The waiter led the three men to their customary table at the centre of the garden, and László turned his chair and looked at them from his corner. Gábor Pahl sat down, and leaned back, inhaled his cigarette and sighed with pleasure, "Hála az istennek" – this is bliss.

Hammers pounded inside László and his mouth became parched. He drank the rest of the coffee left in the white cup, rested it in the saucer and got up, approached the artist and offered his hand, "Good afternoon, Mr. Pahl."

The artist held László's hand in a firm shake and smiled like a celebrity who is used to strangers approaching him to compliment him and rub shoulders. "Who may you be?" he asked. László blushed and answered, "I am Steins." He bowed slightly, "How do you do, nice to meet you," and turned to go.

Gábor Pahl turned to his friends and lowered his voice, "who was that?" The three of them took in the elegant man leaving the café's garden and one of Pahl's friends said, 'that is László Steins, a textile merchant, a very rich man from Novi Sad." The artist raised his brows, "Aha". He was not aware of the rabbit's expression which appeared between his eyes and nose every time he spent time with rich and famous men.

***

László stayed that night with his sister-in-law and her husband and was joined on the following day when Kata, Vera and Ernő who arrived from Novi Sad. Ilona and Aladar's apartment was pleasant and the family members sat there together as they loved to do, ate, drank and chatted. Aladar always had an amused smile and always had new jokes, Ilona always had witty comments, and Kata always had stories about businesspeople, which she delivered in a profound seriousness, and which never had a point,.

László was quieter than usual and a little tense. It did not escape Kata's notice, who worried for a moment, but she relaxed when he invited the whole family to Fészek Café. "I reserved us a table," he said and Kata put her hand on his arm, "Oh, great! This is a nice café. You can meet there all kinds of artists and writers." And my friend Agi noted, "The situation in the city was already not so good, but it was not scary to walk down the street yet. Sometimes they still went out."

***

Kata and László lead the way, he in grey pants and a grey summer coat, with a white carnation in his lapel, shiny black shoes and a black hat, and she in a blue linen suit, a bell skirt which reaches below her knees and a buttoned-down jacket with shoulder pads, that fits her waist and extends to her thighs. Her hair is divided from her forehead to her nape and gathered on each side above her pearl adorned ears with silver combs. On her feet she wears low-heeled white shoes and her white purse is slung over her arm. She strides in her moderate pace, erect, her chest high, looking around and breathing calmly.

Vera walks behind them. She is sixty-six, grey and withdrawn. Two weeks earlier she was about to go to Belgrade to visit her friend but Kata asked her to abandon her plan. "We can't indulge in association with communists, Mama," she said, "you have to understand." Vera did not protest and did not say anything. She cancelled her trip, went to the hair salon and had her grey long hair cut in a modern bob, short and graceless. Now her shorn hair is combed back and makes her look like a nun who took off her wimple. She marches down the sidewalk in a long grey cotton skirt, a white shirt with a high starched collar, and a thin summer shawl covers her shoulders. Her sizable nose protrudes, her eyes stare forward and her mouth is puckered in a declaration of proud wretchedness.

Ernő walks next to her in limp steps. He is quiet and folded into himself as usual, dressed in a brown summer suit and wearing a narrow brimmed brown hat on his head.

Ilona and Aladar walk behind them. Ilona's wavy hair is gathered and her light blue cotton dress flutters as she walks, revealing her legs as if she was a dance teacher whose body is full and her limbs light. Tall Aladar strides next to her hatless, in a new sports suit which Kata chose and bought for him. First he refused to wear it, but Ilona looked at him in plea, "Sometimes you have to dress to show off, it's important to Kata!" and he agreed. Ilona holds his arm and they exchange smiles. She looks back and calls out to their daughter, "Come!" Edit is fourteen, curly-haired, blue-eyed and smiley. She rushes next to her father and looks like a blooming cherry tree in her rosy muslin dress.

Everyone, even Vera, enjoys the stroll down the street in this beautiful city, which belongs to them as they to it, dressed in her honour, as she is decorated in theirs. The citizens of Budapest love her just as the citizens of Tel Aviv love their city. Seventy-two years later Edit will tell me at the Seniors' Home, "Before going to the café we dressed right, you couldn't go out without my aunt Kata's eyes examining you from head to toe."

Gábor Pahl is already seated in his usual place in Fészek café, looking around him with pleasure. He discerns everything with his sharp senses and he remembers everything in minute details and vivid colours. I read about this phenomenon, about old artists whose senses and memory are retained in youthful vitality thanks to their endlessly abundant creativity which knows no dry season.

The family passes through the tall entry columns, presents itself at the entrance to the café and stands in a polite silence, as if in front of a photographer in his studio. The host will be there in a moment. Gábor Pahl sees them, and his eyes swoop in on Kata hungrily. That is the moment László was waiting for. He sees that Kata identifies the artist and notices her embarrassment at his devouring stare. Nevertheless she sits facing him and László lowers himself next to her with a tight throat. Let him look, he tells himself, pain and happiness comingled in him, let him see her.

The artist is impressed by their attire and exchanges appreciative looks with his friends. Vera has matured and changed, but he recognizes her immediately and remembers her light brown eyes as he had seen them for the first time forty-seven years earlier, in the young artists' new gallery. He remembers her thirty years earlier, in his show at the National Salon, walking with her two daughters, holding them by the arm, one on each side. He remembers Ilona's pear-like pregnancy fourteen years earlier, Kata's refusal to return his smile and the purple hue that finally appeared in her eyes. The images rise and move in him in a sequence, with all their details and original colours.

Now he looks at László, whom he remembers from the previous day, smiles like a rabbit, and waves to him with his hand. László responds in a friendly wave, as though they knew each other since childhood. Kata is surprised and her eyes move, astonished, between the artist and her husband. And I, my heart goes out to László, who at that moment is the most miserable man and also the happiest.

Gábor Pahl gets up and all the guests at the café look at him. He walks over and puts his hand out to László, "How do you do, Mr. Steins," and looks at the rest of them with smiling eyes as well. The host quickly brings another chair and sets it at the table, facing Kata. László shakes the artist's hand, "Please, join us, Mr. Pahl." He gestures with his hand to the empty chair and orders coffee and cake for the guest who sits down and leans back.

"What is your opinion about the situation in the city, sir?" László asks him, "And what do the artists say?" The artist shakes his hairy head from side to side. "In the United States, such wild behaviour would not be allowed. Excuse me, sir, for saying it, but you probably think the same way I do." Ilona nods vigorously and sends him a beaming smile, Vera confirms with a brief nod and Aladar leans toward him, "We're of the same mind, of course!"

They carry on with the conversation, László leading it gently, asking about the artists' activities, listening politely to the artist's answers, and then, as if in passing, he says, "I thought, I wanted you, sir, to paint a portrait of my wife."

Gábor Pahl swiftly pulls out of his pocket his notebook with a pencil attached to it and says in a dramatic voice as he writes, "Mrs. Steins, portrait!" He turns to Kata, "Would it be convenient for the lady to come to my studio next week?"

14

In Gábor Pahl's Studio

I knew that now I had to go into Gábor Pahl's studio on Izabella Street in Budapest, see how he paints Kata and be a wit-
ness to what passes between them, but I could not go there. I
was afraid of the moment his gaze would linger on her face, his
wolf eyes scan her body and begin to paint her. I was afraid
that my yearnings for Avry would descend on me at that moment and a wild craving would rise in me to have him come
and touch me with scorching strokes and roar, "I fuck therefore
I am!" And Gábor Pahl would caress Kata's white neck and put
his mouth to hers, draw into him all her purple colour and roar,
"I paint therefore I am!" And Kata will roar in his arms, finally,
for the first time in her life, "I am beautiful therefore I am!" And
all my Deceased, including Robert, will roar to me their existential roars and the air will be full of Eros's panting, and I will
pant heavily with them and type and will not see the screen.

Avry. Where is Avry? I need him to go out with me somewhere, anywhere, maybe the movies, only come to me! But I

don't dare contact him. Unplanned outings are not part of our together-arrangement. He does not like surprises.

Should I go out to one of the many bars this city offers? I have already been to a few of them with friends and had a great deal of alcohol and have seen around me people I did not know, men and women, young and old, who drank like me, and I have rejected with a smile of co-conspirators the casual courtship of men awash in longing for something they did not even remember. They were men with tired eyes, for whom the search for the nightly pastime in a strange bed became a habit, because Tel Aviv is that kind of a city, of "the occasional fuck" to quote Avry, and I overheard a complaint by a frustrated man, "yesterday I didn't have sex either," as if he looked and could not find a restaurant for dinner. I caught a fraction of a conversation between two young women, "He went down on you?" I have immersed myself in that atmosphere which tempts the soul to accept, in a Tel Avivian camaraderie, the pieces of gossip flying in the air about celebrities, meteors-for-a-night, whom you can meet on their travels from bar to bar in the latest fashion, in the latest topics of conversation, in the latest English-studded Hebrew, and I have seen people dressed in brands and with their hair made up who tried and succeeded in looking their best and I have heard Eros laughing, and I knew why.

It would have been so good to go into a bar with Avry now, sit with him at the counter arms touching, and listen to the amplified music, drink until my mind fogs, not to speak, not to listen, not to think about the story I must write. But Avry does not want to put on a white shirt every time I hunger for him. He is busy with the meaning of his existence.

I looked at my Deceased Loves, "Go out alone?"

Childhood-Love-Moosh, the writer, straightened himself and as usual rushed his words, "No-way, this-city-will-devour-you!" Husband-Yossi gritted his teeth, and Old-Prince-Shaul raised his eyes in fright and his yellowish face blanched. Itamar, in his fatigues, looked at me with understanding, and Editor-Rafi said, "You are not going anywhere, get back to your writing!"

I paced in my apartment from the kitchen to the end of my balcony and turned, back and forth, and in the end I sat in my swivel chair and said to all five, "OK, come, we are going to the studio! It's time for Gábor Pahl to paint Kata."

***

August 1937. Morning in Budapest. A scent of freshly baked goods fills the air and summer light floods every nook and cranny, as if there are no war clouds on the horizon. Tall ornamental trees planted along the sidewalk on Izabella Street bloom in pink, and white homes attach themselves to each other like a wall of dolled-up architecture, with horizontal stone slabs, elegantly designed façades and stylish windowsills. Passers-by are dressed smartly and stroll unhurriedly. Kata, Ilona and Edit march to Gábor Pahl's studio, each with her heels tapping on the sidewalk. Ilona marches lightly and Edit skips next to her. Kata walks stiffly, compressed in a brown buttoned-down jacket and a brown narrow skirt, her hair gathered with hairpins and a large bag hangs on her shoulder in addition to her purse.

"Here we are," Ilona says. She knocks on the door and Gábor Pahl opens with a wide smile, "Come in, my ladies, please, come in." They enter and the tap-tapping of their heels is immediately absorbed by the old wool carpet which pads the studio floor. Morning light flows in from the open window by the entrance and fills the small room. The three of them breathe heavily and look around, and Ilona says to her daughter in her alto voice, "You see, Edit'ka, this is what a famous artist's studio looks like." Gábor Pahl closes the door, turns and bows to her with shiny eyes.

A wooden hanger stands on the other side of the entry. Kata hangs her brown jacket and her purse on it. She holds her big bag tightly to her chest, stands and waits. The artist shows with his hand the frilly, two-panelled Parisian screen standing near the hanger a small distance from the wall. "Please, change your clothes here, madam." Kata hesitates for a moment and goes behind the screen.

Canvases stretched on wooden frames lean on each other against the wall next to the screen and above them unframed oil paintings hang close together, all of them of women. Past them, in the corner, there is a worktable with a large radio on it, from which calm concert music is heard. Small colour containers and pieces of cloth and boxes with pencils and brushes are scattered around the radio. A vase with roses would have been very befitting there, but it did not occur to Kata to bring flowers, she came here as to a meeting with the enemy.

At the centre of the room, three paces away from the screen, stands an easel with a large white canvas on it, and the artist is already standing next to it as he buttons his grey work smock, sprayed with paint. A small platform with a Baroque chair with carved arms is set on the carpet six paces away, facing the artist. To the right of the platform, facing the window – a small sofa covered with gold satin fabric, on which Ilona and Edit seat themselves. Two small unframed portraits hang on the wall behind them, and further on hangs a heavy red drape like a theatre curtain.

Gábor Pahl turns to Ilona, "Will the ladies wish to drink coffee?" She smiles, "No, thank you, sir, we just ate breakfast, and had coffee." Kata comes from behind the screen, passes the easel and climbs the little platform, sits on the Baroque chair and holds its carved arms tightly.

She is dressed in an alabaster negligee trimmed with a lace at the front and a blue velvet robe she bought for the occasion, slightly open. The air in the room is cool, and she worries that her nipples will show. She covers them with the robe and grabs hold of the chair arms again. Gábor Pahl smiles to himself.

Kata's hair is gathered at the back and lifted up, and she wears her white gold earrings, which give her regal splendor, or maybe her erect posture and her tight lips bestow on her this splendor, and maybe not these but her white skin and her restraint. What makes you so majestic, Kata? And why do I want him to paint you in the nude?

Kata leaves the chair arms and folds her hands in her lap, looks out the open window for a moment and returns her gaze to the artist in front of her. Ilona is amused, still does not get what goes on here, and Edit looks around her with curiosity. They are silent, breathing in the studio's air with its smells of oil paints and paint thinners mixed with scents of perfumes and cigarette smoke. Gábor Pahl stands erect in a theatrical pose and his hand digs into his beard. His eyes centre on Kata, he moves them to the right to Ilona, and a moment later returns and looks at Kata.

"He looked like that, one time at my aunt and then at my mother," Old Edit told me at the Seniors' Home and turned her head from side to side, "All the time his eyes moved, this way and that. Later on, when people saw the portrait, they said that he painted both sisters in the same face."

"Why did you join Kata that morning?"

"My aunt thought she would be bored and told us to come."

"And you went to the studio every time?"

"No, only that first time. Later she went by herself."

Gábor Pahl sketches on the canvas with a quick hand. A sparrow lands on the windowsill, looks in and flies away. Kata's lips part in a faint smile. Ilona whispers, "What, Kata?" And the other answers loudly, in a metallic sound which nicks silences and without batting an eyelash, "Who needs this painting? My daughters-in-law won't want to have it hanging right in front of their eyes and will shove it in the basement."

Gábor Pahl stops his sketching and bores into her as if reading her insides. "Maybe you yourself need this painting, madam," he utters in exaggerated drama, as if he acts in a Shakespearian play. Kata lowers her eyes and twists her fingers, a shiver traverses her and she hopes her sister has not noticed, but Ilona has. She leans back, puts one leg over the other, and stretches her arms on the sofa's backrest, "The maestro is right, Kata, nobody ever painted you and it's time."

***

Later Kata changed her clothes behind the Parisian screen uttering neither a sound nor a breath and came out carrying the bag with the robe and the negligee. Gábor Pahl looked at her for a long moment, smiled and said to her, "There is no need to take the bag with you, Mrs. Steins, you better leave it here," and turned to Ilona as if she were the operation's commander, "Why carry the bag every time?" Ilona smiled and her substantial nose blocked the mischief in her smile. "Yes," she said, "it's true," and imitated his theatrical tone. "The bag is very heavy. It is better to leave it here. You will take good care of it." He thought to himself, oh, I wish I could devour this brunette. She hugged Edit's shoulder and they walked out.

Gábor Pahl took Kata's jacket off the hanger and laid it over her shoulders, and while standing behind her he put his lips near her earlobe, dove into her perfume and whispered, "in two weeks, Kata. Come early, I need you in full light." His hot breath on her ear made her shiver and his familiar whisper confused her. Something cracked inside her. She turned to him with purple hued eyes, and answered in a low voice, "In two weeks, Mr. Pahl."

He decided on two weeks because he knew the duration of build-up-time and knew that it was crucial. He painted many women's portraits and was adept at the complete process from its charmed beginning to its dissipating ending. If Avry's build-up-time were dedicated only to me, he would not have forgotten me between meetings and we would have carried on countless journeys between charmed beginnings, exclusive trip of build-up and release, but he does not have steady girlfriends and his build-up-time is no-man's-land.

Kata left the studio. Ilona, who walked ahead with Edit, did not rush and did not look back, even when crossing the street, and only at the Heroes' Square she stopped at the tall column with the angel Gabriel on top, turned around and waited for Kata to join her.

***

Two weeks later, morning on Izabella Street. Kata walks in measured steps. She has arrived on the train from Novi Sad a day earlier and has spent the night at Ilona's so that she could be early at the studio when Gábor Pahl would have the right light. Her breathing is labourious and her face frozen. She arrives, stands at the entrance and her insides tighten. Her hand feels her stomach which rustles, her heart beats fast, and as she knocks on the door her face pales.

The artist opens the door and his face lights up in a smile, "Good morning!"

Kata tightens her grip on her purse, "Good morning," avoids looking at Gábor Pahl's face and walks in. He closes the door behind her and locks it. "We don't want to be disturbed," he says simply. She is uneasy and wonders when she should go behind the screen and change her clothes.

Gábor Pahl turns up the volume on the radio. Sounds of piano and strings float in the room, and he moves his head with the music's softness, "The Trout Quintet by Schubert, oh, it's beautiful!" Kata looks at him with lips pressed together and then looks around her. Everything is ready. The canvas with the sketch is on the easel, and next to it a small table with paints and brushes. The Baroque chair awaits on the little platform.

"Will you have coffee with me?" the artist asks pleasantly, and Kata answers in a fading voice, "Alright." He goes to the paints table at the corner and returns to the centre of the room with two glass cups full of coffee. "Let's sit here," he nods with his head toward the settee draped with golden satin fabric. Kata sits and presses herself to the corner of the settee. He hands her one cup and raises his as if it were a wine glass, "Good luck to us!" Kata whispers, "Yes..." without looking at him and raises her coffee cup a fraction. He settles on the settee, not too close and not too far, and his gaze flickers over her face, "When did you arrive in Budapest?" She takes a sip, and likes the taste of the coffee, "Yesterday, to my sister's," and sips again, breathing into the cup. They drink in silence, and he places his cup on the carpet by the settee. "Shall we begin, Kata?" he asks through his thick beard, "We'll catch the light? Go change."

The bag with the negligee and the robe rests behind the frilly Parisian screen. Kata changes her clothes, and when she goes out to the room she is seized by a mixture of excitement and shyness as if she were naked. She shivers and tightens the robe around her body. Gábor Pahl turns to her. His wolf eyes are shiny, his well-groomed beard and mustache expose his moist lips and his gaze follows her as she passes him and sits on the chair that is positioned on the little platform.

He stands by the easel and his eyes travel slowly from her forehead to her bare feet, as if peeling off the blue velvet robe and the alabaster negligee which is under it. Then he returns to her eyes and tries to catch them. Kata fixes her eyes to his right, moves them to the left and eventually looks straight at him and blushes.

"Purple..." he says with satisfaction and approaches her, takes her right hand and rests it on her lower abdomen, "Like that, leave your hand here," and is slow to let go of her fingers. A current traverses through her body, his hand is still on her hand resting at her lower abdomen. Finally, he removes his hand, takes her left hand and lays it opposite the right. "So that the fingers almost touch, like that, close," he says in a low voice, and he is slow to remove his hand again. It seems to her that her fingers together with his will slide lower any moment and another current traverses her, a stronger one. She nods and he moves away, looks at her and comes closer again, stands next to her and holds her shoulder softly, leans it a little back, and runs his hand along her back. "Like that, straight all the time, the way you are," he whispers and looks into her eyes in a close proximity. Kata breathes in and her mouth is dry. Usually she is against smoking, but she likes the smell of his tobacco which makes her giddy as it mixes with the taste of coffee still in her mouth.

Gábor Pahl puts his hands on her jaws, his warm pinkies underneath them, his thumbs on her cheeks and his fingers touch her earlobes under her earrings, as if he takes a rose which is open to the sun with both hands. Slowly he turns her face toward the window until the light dances on it the way he wants. "The head should be like that," he whispers and lingers, his face close to hers. Kata closes her eyes and feels his breath. Her right hand drops to the side as if fainting. The artist moves away walking backward, stops before the easel and examines her.

Suddenly the concert broadcast is cut, the newscaster's voice announces the news and the room is filled with the sound of a recording from Hitler's speech and another one from Horthy's, the Hungarian leader. Gábor Pahl turns and murmurs to himself, "What are they cooking for us." When the concert resumes he turns again to Kata and she opens her eyes and smiles to him with parted lips.

He sketches her image with the charcoal pencil, her sitting pose, her face, the robe's sleeves, the negligee's folds, the left hand at the lower abdomen, the right hand which dropped aside.

Kata moves her fingers and shifts her head. The artist wets his lips, "You can rest now, take a few minutes." She leans back and rest her hands on the chair's arms. The blue velvet robe opens and its wings slide to the side. He smiles at her and sends her waves of marvel, "Come." Kata gets up and descends the little platform, approaches him, goes around and stands behind him to look at the canvas. He turns to her.

*** *** ***

That evening, when Kata returned to her home in Novi Sad, László received her as usual with a hug and a kiss on her cheek and asked how the trip went. She said to him, "Laci, I am so tired, maybe I'll take a bath."

Five more times she went to Gábor Pahl's studio. Her portrait was his last project in Budapest. His imminent departure to the United States was prodding him, and in the fall of 1937, he sent the oil painting to the large house on Dunavska Street in Novi Sad.

At that time Vera was on a long visit with Ilona in Budapest, Ernő was not home either, and only Kata and László, Sandor and Miki stood in the living-room and looked at the messenger who removed the cloth wrapping the portrait and leaned it against the wall, "Mr. Pahl said to hang it where there's no strong sun." László saw the messenger to the door and returned to the living-room. He stood between Miki and Kata, and next to her, a little to the side stood Sandor. The painting was in front of them: a wooden frame carved with gold painted leaves, a hundred and twenty centimetres tall and eighty centimetres wide, and in it Kata's portrait painted against dense background, dark grey with some green, impenetrable like a safe's door.

Afternoon light flooded the room through the sheer curtains, and the four stood silent. Kata looked at the portrait indifferently, and László and the boys looked at it with fascination. Fifty years later, on his death bed, Miki remembered that moment, the only time in his life that he saw his father cry.

15

Hibiscus Dust

I go out to get some exercise and walk slowly south on Dizengoff Street. Spring is in the air already, or what the city believed is spring. Northampton knows other spring blooms, but they are behind me now and I am here, slowly integrating into the solid mass of "the old North." Great city, Tel Aviv. Kata would have enjoyed living here... Hey, enough with this story!

She disappears from my mind, and in her place stand my four Deceased, whom I cannot banish. Itamar has stayed home as usual, sitting on the carpet. I am tired of them and I beg them to give me some space! But they stick to me.

I try to ignore them and look around. There are always things to see, and I see them again and again, street signs for example. All the streets here are named after historical personalities. Some are better known and some less, but it does not matter, each has a sign. When I pass them and read the names, their namesakes jump and declare in my ears in a national pathos and historical excitement, "Do not forget that you walk down the streets of the first Hebrew city!"

Saved as a Painting

The elders of Tel Aviv must be trying to cultivate a sense of its own value with these nameplates of the important personalities of history, because, after all, this city is not like Jerusalem, the eternal city, or Tzipori or Beit She'arim, not even like Caesarea. Tel Aviv does not have a halo of holiness or the smell of dark burial caves. She is just recumbent on the beach, full of sun, sand and westerly winds, feather weight in the national history. But she insists on proving that she is no less important than Jerusalem.

Editor-Rafi wheezes on my right, "What do you think, that you are in some community in the Galilee, where the streets are given names of flowers and trees?" A fat peacock that he is, citizen of Tel Aviv from birth, boasting local-patriotism, "This is a city of people! It is the liveliest city in the world." And after a moment he adds with abhorrence, "An ugly and stinky Mediterranean city, full of low-life and foreign workers, crazies on bicycles, everyone smokes, you can't breathe here." Moosh the writer drags his feet next to him. "There-is-lots-of-love-here," he says enthusiastically, "you-can-smell-it-in-the-air."

Husband-Yossi walks to my left, his teeth are locked and his face is impassable. I think to him, it's too bad that you hate Tel Aviv, Yossi, your loss! But he does not react. Next to him strides Old-Prince-Shaul in his camel walk. Most of his life passed in Tel Aviv and he calls her name in a dreamy mien.

I turn east on Ben Gurion Boulevard, pass mid-day-people seated on the benches and women rocking baby strollers and talking on their phones, until I reach King Solomon Street and turn north onto it.

***

Large ficus and other trees whose names I am not familiar with are planted on the sidewalk along the street. I walk between light and shade and promise myself to learn their names. A line of parked cars stretches to my right, and they are indifferent to each other like their owners who stroll by each other in reserved disregard. People always smile to each other in Northampton and say hello, even if they are strangers. A different culture.

Why was this street named after King Solomon? It is true that he was an important politician with international connections, wisest of all men, educated and knowledgeable, a poet, and, in the eyes of the early Near Easterners, a handsome and well-groomed man. He lived with a thousand women and probably did not remember all of them by name. He was very rich and a great pleasure seeker too – actually he had all the qualities that Tel Aviv likes and always liked since the days it was called "Ahuzat Bayit" – but in spite of all this, I imagine King Solomon as lacking in fervour, a jaded intellectual bored with all the beauty and riches and wisdom. His street is more sensual than he was, with trees shading the sidewalks, dogs' excrement left on them in mounds, girls skirting them in catty charm as they talk on the phone, young men chatting back at them and humming, "what gives?", and cyclists winding between them and clanging...

What do they all have to do with King Solomon? I imagine that the elders had no choice but to dedicate a street to him, if they named another street after his wild father, King David, and dedicated a whole boulevard to David's predecessor, sad and crazy King Saul. Or maybe King Solomon got a street named after him because of his mother Bathsheba, who was, in fact, a Jerusalemite. When she bathed on the roof she knew she was being seen but she did not care, like a Tel Avivian woman on the beach... And suddenly I remember, King Solomon built the First Temple in Jerusalem, how could I forget?

I have reached the intersection, and I stand waiting for the red light to change to green. Then I cross the wide Arlozorov Street, crowded with belching buses and buzzing scooters, hooting taxis and pushy cars.

I go across directly to the supermarket entrance from which comes the sound of a man announcing something over the PA system, shouting in a Russian accented Hebrew. Every second person has a foreign accent here.

My grandfather, for example, had a Lithuanian-Yiddish accent. He came here as a pioneer during the twenties of the previous century, and went to a kibbutz in the Jezreel Valley, "to redeem our land", he used to say to me with shining eyes. But in the end he and my grandmother settled in Tel Aviv, which at the time was still a small town, proud of each new home built there. In the evening after work, my grandfather used to go out for long walks along the beach with his daughter, later my mother, walking beside him listening to him. Once they met Hayim Nahman Bialik, the national poet, on the beach, and talked to him, a formative event which was recounted in our family from generation to generation.

I leave the supermarket behind and walk on Yehoshu'a Bin Nun Street with its own large ficus trees with their thick trunks and profuse tops, reaching high out of beds surrounded by stones and scattering cool shadows about them. Apartment buildings stand on both sides of the street with their walls pimpled with air-conditioners, with cables and electric wires and pipes and cords which drop and sway and stretch on the walls. There is not one building without these cords-wires-pipes hanging from the roofs and the windows and the small openings and the balconies... and the plastic shutters...

Hibiscus bushes kiss the sidewalk in the small yard to my left, an evergreen hedge so tight and tangled that even a cat cannot go through it. I brush against their dense leaves, and they hand me their big red flowers with their wide petals which open and spread shamelessly like the flowing dresses of flamenco dancers. A long thin tongue emerges from each red flower, sticks out ready to lick, full of yellow powder of desire, and swings in a Tel Avivian indifference. Each flower and its tongue, multitude of desiring tongues, each with its own powder, scattering around gold hibiscus spray, which spreads and flows on Yehoshu'a Bin Nun Street and the streets leading away from it and those leading into it. The city saturated with hibiscus dust fills with desires, breathes in hot breaths, and is in love with herself.

The supermarket wall stretches like a fortification behind the hibiscus line, tall, windowless, and hidden by some trees and bushes grown wild. This wall, shabby and angry, dust and rain stricken and bitten by the teeth of time, precisely this wall displays two huge mosaic images. Every time I pass by I think, wonder of wonders! The images are in fact faded, missing sections and broken, but they are still real works of mosaic, like in a museum, seriously.

What do these mosaic images do in this aridity? Since when are they here? Maybe from the middle of the previous century... Once, when I was a child in Haifa, they used to decorate public walls with mosaics, but this wall on Yehoshu'a Bin Nun does not seem to me to be very public. It just connects the supermarket's main entrance with its back exit, a chaotic anus through which garbage is removed on a conveyor belt, merchandise is taken off trucks and where employees go out for a smoke. And on such a wall two works of art were installed!

The mosaics describe two military operations under the leadership of the biblical military leader Joshua son of Nun, whose street this is. One image depicts the defeat of Jericho, and underneath it the appropriate biblical verses are quoted, proof that everything is written and documented. The second image represents the war against the five kings of Canaan and their armies, when the sun and the moon stood still to the general's command, so that he could continue his operation in full daylight. Here is Joshua on horseback, galloping to combat, war-craving and merciless. He conquers Canaan. The people cheer and the dead lie on the ground. You can see the Gibeons surrender and raise their hands in supplication, trembling with fear. They will become hewers of wood and drawers of water.

It seems to me that the first Hebrew city's elders loved Joshua, because not only did they dedicate a street to him but took care to add to it a dimension of importance with these mosaics. Husband-Yossi marches next to me and does not take his eyes off them. "This is our heritage!" he says to me with that excited expression he has always worn on Independence Day, "You see, this is part of our title deed!" Husband-Yossi includes me in his "our" whether I want it or not. It seems to me that this mosaic title deed imbues him with strength and evokes in him affinity to Joshua, the brave general, who slaughters his enemies with his sword, deaf to the screams of terror and horrors of agony. He is on a mission he must accomplish. It is not personal.

I am reminded that one block away from here, on the northeastern corner of the Arlozorov and Ibn Gabirol intersection, there is a colourful mural of two jeans-clad youth sitting on a stone wall, peeking into the garden behind them, and their whole being expresses ordinary tranquillity. Not Gibeon and not Jericho, not battle cries and not title deeds, only a run-of-the-mill day in Tel Aviv on the shore of the Mediterranean. But now I am on Yehoshu'a Bin Nun and here he is the hero.

My four Deceased and I cross Amsterdam Street that immediately reminds me of Anne Frank, pass a synagogue whose façade is overlaid with green-bluish porcelain tiles like an entrance to a public washroom, and continue and cross another narrow street called Vormaiza.

All of a sudden I am seized with uncontrolled need to ascertain that there are sidewalks on Vormaiza Street, and there is no resemblance between it and a narrow Middle Ages ally amid thick wall. Hopefully no magic entry open here like in Tchernichovsky's ballad.. In it, in the eleventh century, pregnant mother of Rashi walks in an ally in the city of Vormaiza, Worms, on the banks of the river Rhine. Tall stone walls rise along the narrow street throwing shadows on the heavy woman, when suddenly a regiment of horsemen gallop toward her. There is no sidewalk there and there is nowhere for a pregnant woman to escape to. The horsemen advance, threatening to trample her. She turns to the side, presses herself to the stone wall in fear and covers her big belly. The horsemen advance, they do not slow down and do not stop, like Joshua, it is not personal, they are on a mission, and I feel her terror. Suddenly a miracle occurs, the stone wall opens and shields her. She is saved, and we have Rashi.

But how many miracles really take place? Why no miracle befell Kata, for example? And why do the residents of Tel Aviv's Old North need to be reminded every day of these horrors? Is it not enough for the city what she herself experienced from Brenner's murder to the suicide bombers? If the streets had names of flowers, trees and birds, the air would have been filled with peace and solace. But the air here is saturated with violent history and piercing stares of people from the past who emerge from the street signs in a self-righteous nationalism, wave to me with the deed titles, "A Hebrew city! A Hebrew city!" and they are more important than hibiscus flowers. No wonder there are no planters with geraniums on Basel Square, no wonder Avry's love hides in the bunker of his soul, bound and mute.

Childhood-Love-Moosh, the writer, loses his patience, "Enough, Noa!" He puts on an expression of demonstrative fatigue and disappears. Editor-Rafi informs me, "You are losing it," and disappears as well. Husband-Yossi wants to fight for Joshua's dignity but dissipates. And Old-Prince-Shaul says to me, "This is your time to stretch your legs, my beauty," and fades away too.

Finally, I am alone, strolling and giving in to the sense of freedom in anonymity, in the ever-present profane existence that swirls between the sea and the beach and the sky, and is filled with the smells of sweat and salt and powdered with the golden hibiscus dust.

{ 16 }

Bitter Cold

December 1937.

Gábor Pahl sailed to the United States with his wife, their two sons, their sons' wives and children. Even though Kata missed him, his departure relieved her and she was less concerned that she might suddenly face him in the streets of Budapest.

In the house on Dunavska Street in Novi Sad, László hung the portrait in the living room, and every morning stood long moments in front of it staring at it like a hungry man who cannot get sated. Kata was afraid that his long stares would reveal the secret hiding in the painting, but after a while she relaxed. Ever since the portrait arrived at the house, something in her softened toward László, and when she talked to him, an appeasing tone was added to her voice. Nightly attacks of sexual desire began to frequent her, and when she was flooded with longing and desire she found it hard to hide it from him. He did not ask her the meaning of the change that came over her, did not mock and did not ridicule her for becoming wild and passionate, only kissed her closed eyes and loved her as always.

***

"Let's go to Budapest, Laci," Kata said, "I want to show you an apartment building on Klauzál Street."

He smiled at her like a teacher, "How many apartments are there?"

"Eighteen. We'll take half, what do you think?"

"But maybe this is not the right time to invest? You know, the tension and street riots."

"Never mind, it will calm down. Let's go see the building."

Kata had everything planned already. She designated one apartment to Ilona and her family, and another apartment to their elder son, Sandor, who got married and his wife was well into her second trimester. "They may want to move to Budapest. We'll give him one apartment," Kata said to László, "and Miki will get an apartment too. We'll rent the rest. It's a good deal."

They wrapped themselves in their warm coats and scarves and boarded the train to Budapest. They took a taxi to District VII and stood in front of the building on Klauzál street, which was conspicuous in its white colour between two yellowish ones. The door to the building was green, made of heavy wood and carved with winding branches. Above it there was an arch decorated with reliefs of branches and fruits, and above the arch a wide overhang, made of squares of reliefs, their elegance attesting to the prestige of the building.

Kata and László entered and stood in the covered passage with its crossword puzzle of floor tiles decorated like a Persian rug. The passage led to a clean inner courtyard, open to the sky and surrounded by the four storeys of the building's apartments with their doors facing into the inner court. On each storey there was a long open corridor fenced by an ironwork balustrade overlooking the enclosure.

"What do you think?"

"It is a handsome building and well taken care of. And what do you think?"

"This is a good location."

The real estate agent arrived and joined them, took them to look at two of the apartments and gave them a file with all the details. Kata and László looked at the file and on the train back to Novi Sad perused the documents in it.

For a month they deliberated, calculated and planned, and at the beginning of January 1938, they decided to acquire half the asset. The snowy winter did not deter them, they took the morning train and traveled to Budapest. In the real estate office they were received with light refreshment and great respect. They sat and read again the sale contract, paid and signed. Then everyone shook hands and they left.

It was already dark outside. They stood on the sidewalk and Kata took a deep breath, "it's a good deal, Laci!" Cold wind blew and snowflakes danced in the air. A jumble of noises of people calling and shouting and police whistles came from one of the streets. Kata ignored it but László tensed. She tightened her fur collar and held his arm, "The snow is not so bad, let's stand for a minute and breath in the clean air. Everyone smoked in that room and it was suffocating!" But László preferred to get into a taxi as quickly as possible and go to his sister-in-law and her husband.

In Ilona and Aldar's apartment they were welcomed with warmth and smells of cooking. Kata sniffed around and call, "Ilonka! You made your stuffed cabbage!? Let's eat, I am so hungry."

I sat with them, I saw them eating and drinking with pleasure, talking and laughing, and I shivered. It was of no benefit to me knowing what the future would bring, and I did not have any message for them, I simply was terrified for their lives.

The music on the radio stopped and a man delivered the news in a restrained narration. They listened, their eyes wandering about the room, and when the music resumed László said, "It's going to be bad, this time it will be longer and dirtier." Aladar confirmed with his blue eyes, his Adam's apple moving as though he swallowed some of the words he wanted to say, and his voice was cloudy, "In my factory we have long switched to manufacture for the army. Maybe it's time to stock up on food." Ilona said, "Politics is very bad," and Kata did not mix in. Wars and politics are for the men and Ilona. She, Kata, thought about the successful deal signed that afternoon.

***

Next day, on the train back to Novi Sad, László said, "We need to think how to prepare." Kata put her hand on his knee and said, "It will be a little more difficult, but we'll manage like we did in the last war, no?" László replied, "No, this time it's going to be much harder."

"What should we do? What do you think?"

"Maybe sell the business and send the money somewhere, maybe to Palestine."

"Palestine? What do we have in Palestine?"

"I think the war will not get there."

"But it's all desert there, no? Think of another place."

When they got home they found Miki, their younger son, standing at the door, "I was waiting for you, I need to talk to you." The three sat down in the eating nook, drank tea and munched on cookies. Miki was nineteen years old then, a smiley youth, whose auburn curls fell on his forehead, and when he pushed the curls aside in a coquettish movement his bright brown eyes were revealed.

"There's going to be a war soon," he said to his parents and his cheeks reddened. "True," said László, "we talked about it, Mama and I." Miki looked at Kata, "Mama, I don't want to be drafted. I don't want to be killed like an idiot." She examined his face, "what do you want to do?"

"Go to America."

They sat silently and thought the same thought, each in their particular way. "It's a good idea," said Kata and looked at László, "Miki will go to America and we will move part of the business there, to save it." László gazed at her, then at Miki, smoothed his bald head with his hand and said, "it may be a good idea... you'll open a branch there, find tailors who will sew the coats," and while still looking at Miki with tender eyes he said to Kata, "but should we let him just go? All alone?" She looked at her son with tight lips, drummed with her fingernails on the table, and nodded her head in acquiescence. Miki smiled to his father like a boy permitted to go on a great adventure and László patted his arm, "Go. You will know how to manage there. It's good you took those English lessons, you see?" They sat back in their chairs and Kata said, "This is a good plan."

Suddenly the door opened and Sandor stood there, red-faced and panting, "I had a baby boy!"

***

Six months later Miki sailed to the United States with a large sum of money in his wallet. "They gave him everything they had," my friend Agi told me, "They sold most of the business and gave him the money and added more from their savings. He came to America a rich man. His brother Sandor was very angry. He always felt slighted."

On the ship Miki met Klari, who was born in Novi Sad like him, and like him escaped to the United States just before the war. But not like him, she was with her parents and her sisters. "A good family of Hungarian Jews," noted Agi. On board the ship, surrounded by water, Klari fell in love with the handsome and good natured young man, who diligently demonstrated his talent in kissing, and maybe his kisses were especially sweet because she knew he was rich. Her parents, who had heard of László and Kata Steins still in Novi Sad, were delighted with their daughter's friend and embraced him warmly, and he, being alone on his journey to America, understood that he was lucky, and gave himself to them.

They settled in New York. Miki began building his business, married Klari and sent his parents the bride-and-groom studio photo. A reply letter from Kata began with the sentence, "Dear Miki, mazel tov, but why the hurry to get married?" And since then Klari bore her a lifelong grudge, which over time she drained into it all the other grudges of her life.

During the war Miki escaped the draft. "He was right," said my friend Agi, "why did he run away from Novi Sad? To join the army in America?"

***

Back to Novi Sad, January 1938. Kata looked at Robert, her one week old grandson, who, small and wrinkled like a newborn chick, cried incessantly in his mother's arms, his sobs weak and screechy. He cried and cried until Kata lost her patience and said in a hard voice, "Give me, I'll soothe him."

She extricated him from the blanket, wrapped him in her arms and put her lips to his tiny forehead. The sobs ended, and suddenly she felt something crackling in her body. An almost painful tenderness spread all at once in her. She took a deep breath, held the baby to her chest and walked around the room whispering, "Shhhhh... sleep, Robi."

I did not imagine it would happen to Kata. She hardly hugged and hardly kissed her sons, and suddenly this tiny Robert woke in her a tumult of feelings and a sea of tenderness flowing toward him. She hugged and smelled him, kissed and caressed, washed and dressed, fed and put to sleep... "The child was her joy," Edit told me, "She was with him every day. He was with her more than with his mother. At night he slept in his own house, and in the morning they brought him to my aunt again. Sometimes he even spent the night with them."

***

The war broke out in September 1939, and after fourteen months Hungary joined the Axis powers along with Germany. Yugoslavia was occupied and Novi Sad was annexed to Hungary again. But wars and politics never interested Kata, and in the meantime, in the combustible hatred fumes and in spite of the spreading violence in the city, the routine of life continued. Ernő went out to the company's offices where he worked as he did every morning, and László still managed the little that was left of the business. Vera continued to go to the market and cook, and Kata dedicated here time to her little grandson.

"Come to me, Robi!" She would stretch her arms to him and he would leap to her from his father's or mother's arms in a babies' gleeful laughter. Kata would press him to her in a long hug, kiss his cheek and hum love murmurs to him. She sang to him and played with him, listened patiently when he began to speak, and laughed when he prattled his baby talk in a tiny voice. When he was three years old and already walked and talked "like a big boy", she would hold his little hand, and despite the tension in the streets, as long as it was possible to walk from the house to the Danube Park, she took him there. They would stand by the pond, which was surrounded by large stones, look at the water lilies and the goldfish, and throw breadcrumbs to the ducks and the swans. On the way back, she would carry him in her arms, and he would hug her neck and press his nose to her, "Oma, you smell good!"

***

Novi Sad, early January 1942. László let go the last of the agents he had left and locked the business's office. He sits in the small guest room and reads the newspaper. Ernő does not go to work any more and has shut himself in his room. Vera sends the Serb help to the market and he brings the necessary items. The house on Dunavska Street fills with cooking aromas.

Fifty-one years old Kata sits in her living room facing the portrait and four-year-old Robert sits on her knees. She hugs him and plants her face in his black curls. The child, all dark eyes and perfumed tenderness, eyes the portraits, eyes his grandmother and smiles, "two Oma Kata." His smile melts her. Her face beams and now she is more beautiful in my eyes than ever before.

Outside it is bitter cold and there is an unpleasant noise. I am so scared, that I barely type, but the plot continues on its own, whether I write it or not. Little Robert hugs Kata's neck and I have no way to prepare him for the things awaiting him in the depths of the story.

THE FROZEN DANUBE

The Hungarian gendarmes stationed in Novi Sad received directed encouragement to mistreat and harm the Jews, Serbs, and Gypsies; rob, beat, arrest, expel, and in January the order arrived to kill all at once. After the war, documents were found and testimonies taken, trials were held and sentences were carried out. All the details are known today – research was published, books were written and movies were made. But even if I hear hundreds of testimonies and read thousands of documents, I will never understand.

January 21, 1942. Novi Sad is covered with a cloak of snow, the cold stabs at anyone who stays outside. The temperature sank to twenty below zero and the Danube water turned into a thick layer of ice.

Early in the morning, the gendarmes are getting ready for the Razzia. The official target of the raid is to find and punish partisans for their attacks, but the off-the-record order is to kill Jews and Serbs, Gypsies and the Hungarian Fascist regime objectors. The gendarmes are assigned groups and tasks, prepare their guns and ammunition, get the vehicles ready, pack sandwiches, put on warm coats and hats, scarves and gloves.

Outside daylight rises. The gendarmes scatter in the streets, bang on doors with force and yell, "Police! Open up!" They check identity cards and take out families, among them children still in their pajamas, still warm from sleep under thick blankets. They gather them and lead them down city streets with shouts and shoves, half an hour, an hour, until they reach the Strand.

There, on the banks of the frozen Danube, next to the silent recreational facilities, they force everyone into a long line with armed gendarmes positioned around them. People stand with their families, hardly able to breathe the searing cold air. They look at each other, try to comfort the children, unable to understand what is happening. But there is no one to ask.

The gendarmes single out a group at the head of the line, lead it away a small distance, stop and shoot every person. The shots are heard by everyone, but there is nowhere to run away to; those who try to escape are shot immediately. They see and wait for their turn. The gendarmes return and take another group. The group moves away, shots are heard, then silence.

Saved as a Painting

The gendarmes are edgy. They shoot together at the thick ice on the Danube, create large holes and throw in the bodies. Other gendarmes guard around them.

Kata and László, Vera and Ernő sit in their house on Dunavska Street, hiding behind locked door and shuttered windows and do not dare venture out. Shots and shouts are heard from the distant streets. Kata looks at László, he rests his hand on her arm and gazes at her with concern. Vera covers her mouth and looks at Kata, and Ernő crosses his arms and stares at the floor. All four are tormented by anxiety for Sandor and his family. László says, "I'll walk over and see how they're doing." Kata shakes her head, "You can't leave, Laci, it's too dangerous." They look at each other helplessly, ignorant of what takes place outside.

Next day, January 22, grey light rises slowly. Familiar city noises enter the house on Dunavska Street, but the whole family stays behind their locked doors and shuttered windows. They do not know what happened at the Strand. They sit together, eyes burning with fatigue, eat a little, drink a little, hold in their sighs and wait for Sandor. The three Serb house employees have gone out and only one returns. He mumbles, "The city is such a mess..." and goes to sit in the kitchen.

Today too the gendarmes pull people out of their homes, march them to the Strand, line them up and shoot everyone. The edges of the holes in the ice turned black and the water beneath carried the bodies away. Where were they carried to? Did anyone find them?

Third day, January 23rd. The cold bites, and again a long line of death is stretched at the frozen Strand. Somewhere in the middle stand a husband, his wife and two children. The father carries the boy, about six years old, in his arms. The girl, about thirteen, presses herself to her mother. They shiver. Behind them stands an elderly couple, dressed in heavy coats. The old man leans on a cane, his wife holds his arm, supports him or leans on him, and sighs. She finds it hard to stand. Sandor and his wife stand behind the old couple. Four-year-old Robert stands between them on the snow that turned to ice. Why don't they pick him up? I don't get it.

Another group of people is separated from the line, taken away and shots are heard. People hold their breath. An hour passes slowly. It takes time to throw all the bodies through the ice. The old man who leans on his cane turns to the father with his child in his arms, "Please, let's change places. We will be in front of you. We are too tired to stand so long."

They exchange places. The gendarmes arrive galloping like hounds and take another group, push the people forward with their rifle butts and scream. The selected people try to hurry, slip, some of them fall down, get up and continue to stagger forward. The last people in that group are the elderly couple.

Shots are heard. Screams are choked back and moans rise from the waiting lines, but soon they die and silence takes over. A group of gendarmes gathers, they whisper, read from a paper that passes from hand to hand and suddenly they turn to the people standing in line and one of them yells, "Home! Go home! Nobody stays here!" frenzy in his voice and madness in his eyes. An order has come from Budapest to hold the fire.

One thousand two hundred and forty six people were murdered in those three days at the Strand, Jews and non-Jews.

These are numbers I can get, but when the numbers rise to hundreds of thousands and when these turn into millions, I don't get it anymore, I don't see faces and pictures, everything turns black, like the edges of the holes in the ice. The girl who pressed herself to her mother and heard with her own ears the old man's request to change places, later told her children about it, and eventually I heard about it too. I heard two testimonies about that day at the Strand, and when I asked my friend Agi what happened to Sandor and his family, she answered in a thick voice, "they returned home and went to sleep."

I don't know if they managed to fall asleep and I don't know how much this event affected Robert, Kata's and László's grandson. He was only four years old, and it is impossible to know the damage to his soul standing at the Strand with his parents in the freezing cold, but I am sure that some harm was done, and maybe that is the reason for the letter he sent to Jessica sixty years later, a letter that unsettled me.

***

That day, before the massacre at the Strand is stopped, the Hungarian gendarmes go wild in the streets of Novi Sad. They have Serb collaborators and lists of addresses. The pogrom is planned in detail.

Mid-day. Kata and László, Vera and Ernő sit in the living room. Faint daylight penetrates the shutters and brightens the colours of the portrait which hangs above the piano. László stares at it and listens to the screams and the gun shot sounds outside. He holds a documents file which he has prepared when the screaming began. "If they come in," he says to Kata, "I will put it like this, under the coat." She answers softly, "this is smart, Laci." Vera nods her head in consent. She is grey and worried. Ernő is silent.

Kata understands that the situation has become dangerous and in her mind she thinks of their prospects, either they are be taken to some place where they take the Jews, or... "I need to write to Ilona," she says in her metallic voice, "I need to leave her instructions."

How come you are not afraid, Kata? How come you are not covered with cold sweat and how come your mind does not freeze? How can you think about practical instructions at a time like this? Kata pulls her chair to the table, opens her bag and, with the self-control of a pilot whose plane is about to crash, she says, "I will leave them instructions for what to do with the property and the business." László looks at her and tears fog his vision. She takes a pad of writing paper out of her bag and a fountain pen with a silver cap, opens a new page and writes a letter to Ilona.

I stand outside, facing the house's entrance. The road is covered with white snow turned to ice. The cold burns my face and penetrates my body through the coat and through the scarf which is wound tight around my neck. I tremble. Behind me, not too far, I hear screams and shots. Six gendarmes come running, two stand next to me with their guns directed at the entrance, and four stand by the heavy wooden door. One of them bangs on it with his fist, "Police! Open up!" The door opens a fraction and I see the Serb employee's face. One of the gendarmes yells, "Show your documents!" and they burst in. Something in the entry hall falls to the floor and shatters noisily, maybe it is the blue vase that was standing on the carved cabinet.

Ernő is the first to be pulled out. He does not resist and walks with them as if they want to show him something. One gendarme yells at him, "Stand here!" The two next to me direct their guns at him and the other gendarmes go back into the house. Ernő stands three metres away from me.

Now they pull Vera out. She is seventy one. She wants to walk unhurriedly, but one of the gendarmes pushes her. She almost trips, directs an angry stare at his brazenness and straightens. The gendarmes guffaw and place her next to Ernő.

Immediately after her László is pushed out. He tightens his hold on the file with both hands and I can see in his face that he is surprised. He turns to one of the gendarmes to say something, but the gendarme thrusts the gun barrel into his ribs and pushes him toward Ernő and Vera. All three look confused. Their legs, as well as mine, tremble and we cannot control our trembling.

Kata leaves the house with two gendarmes behind her. She walks in her usual calm fashion because she knows no other way. A frozen expression is on her face and her lips are tightened. She thinks they are going to be marched somewhere, goes to stand next to László and puts her arm through his, but no one moves. Everyone stands in an odd silence. Kata looks about her. Three of the gendarmes move away and come back nervously, three already stand and direct their guns at Kata, László, Vera and Ernő. I hear the clock ticking in my living room. Ten seconds have passed since Kata left the house and then she grasps what is happening. She exchanges looks with László, who grasps it too. She looks at her mother, who grasps it a second after them, and at Ernő, who hasn't grasped it yet. Terror freezes time.

Kata looks sideways, like in the portrait, and remember the moment when, in his studio, Gábor Pahl turns to her slowly with blazing eyes. The blue velvet robe drops off her shoulders, her arms rise and circle his neck, she smells his tobacco scent. He hugs her with a sigh, sinks his face in the hollow between her neck and shoulder and his breath is warm. She becomes fluid, moves inside herself, moves with her artist, knows as she has never known, knows in her guts, in her lungs, in her heart... She smiles at him with lips wide open, breathes out purple syllables and he drinks them from her mouth, his hands sketch her on her body, something gathers in her and flows over, and Ernő breaks into the street with a wild dash. Kata hears the shots and stops three breaths away.

***

No, just a minute, I don't get it.
What just happened?

SEVEN MINUTES

Agi said that in her opinion, only seven minutes passed from the moment the gendarmes broke into the house until they shot and killed. "Kata didn't get to finish the letter to Ilona," she said, "They came in and pulled them out. The neighbours saw and related the events, and also there was the employee who hid in the kitchen, he told what happened, but it could be that he was the one who informed the Hungarians, there were rumours about him."

Saved as a Painting

An hour later some gendarmes came with a truck, loaded the bodies and took them to the Strand, where they were tossed into the Danube through the holes.

***

Kata, László, Vera, Ernő. Suddenly they are not in the story anymore. Turned into corpses. Disappeared under the ice. I was so scared that I did not have time to say farewell. Late in the day Sandor arrived, entered the house and found the unfinished letter. The pen rested on it without the silver cover.

***

A month later, in the United States, the artist Gábor Pahl died of an illness.

Part Two

Fingerprints

{ 17 }

Agi

Northampton, December 2007. One cold and snowy night I went out to a concert in the small music hall at Smith College. A few of my students who took voice lessons were going to perform and my position required me to show up. I had a part-time teaching position at the Ancient Near Eastern Studies department, where I taught elective courses. Every year I had three or four little groups, whom I taught history of the Ancient Near East, Biblical Hebrew and a little Biblical Studies. I enjoyed every minute of it.

I arrived just as the doors were closing, entered and shook the snow off me. The hall was full. Two of my teacher friends, nice Americans, waved at me from one of the front rows, and motioned to me that they were sorry but there was no room next to them. I waved back to them and was happy I did not have to sit with them. I found an empty seat at the back row and sat next to a woman who looked to be my age. Her dark hair was braided into a short Chinese plait and pearl earrings were fastened in her earlobes. She smiled to me politely, as people do in Northampton when a stranger sits next to them, and I smiled back.

The audience began to hush, and the woman with the Chinese plait took her phone out of her pocket and muted a ring. She listened, put her hand to her mouth and answered in Hebrew, "So give them chocolate milk and turn on the tv, and they'll fall asleep."

"You are Israeli?!" I almost yelled with joy.

The woman gave a little smile, "Yes, and I see that you are too. Pleased to meet you, I am Agi." And before she even told me her name, I noticed that her black-grey eyes are veiled with purple hue. I had never seen eyes like that.

I introduced myself, and she raised her dark eyebrows, "So, we're going to listen to a concert tonight," as if to hint that if she had her way, she would not have gone out of the house on such a snowy night. I answered that I came to hear a few of my students, because my position required it, and she said, "Oh, you teach here. I came to hear my son's girlfriend. She is a piano teacher, not an Israeli, maybe you know her," and mentioned a name I did not recognize. The lights came down, the audience clapped for the conductor who came on the stage, and under the cover of noise, I asked Agi, "Have you been here many years?" She directed an examining gaze at me, "Fifteen years is quite a lot of time, isn't it?" I answered, "I have been here nine years, how come we never met until today? I thought I knew all the Israelis in Northampton."

Maybe it was our body language which communicated before the words came out, or maybe my foreigner's loneliness which always looked for Hebrew-speaking corners to rest my head, either way, I immediately wanted us to be friends.

***

A week later we met in a small coffee shop which faced a church built with grey stones. Heaps of snow piled up in the street, the cold air was clear, and the coffee shop was warm and comfortable. Agi wore a light-brown corduroy hat, which looked to me like a "tembel" hat, and it turned out she had bought it in a prestigious New York hat shop. "I don't know any hat shops," I said and noticed that Agi was not surprised. Her light-brown hat suited her bright face and aubergine hair, which was gathered on her nape in a Chinese plait and made her look eternally young. Her pearl earrings looked like round and guileless drops and echoed her white shirt.

We stood facing each other, both of us of the same height and the same plump size, but Agi seemed to me narrower and taller, maybe thanks to the brown pants clinging to her body, fitting it in a sophisticated elegance, and her high-heeled boots. Something meticulous and festive arose from her, completely ignoring the fact that it was a mid-weekday in Northampton. Next to her I felt a little rumpled in my wide jeans, wide shirt and flat heeled boots.

We sat down, looked at each other and Agi lowered her eye-lids for a moment. The shadows of her lashes appeared beneath her eyes like another line of eyelashes. I became emotional. I asked, "Where are you from in Israel?" she waited a moment and suddenly we said in unison, "I am from Haifa."

We were delighted, and we exchanged childhood pictures from our city, but very quickly we realized that these images were completely different. She grew up in an immigrant family which made Aliyah in the fifties, and I grew up in a family of early settlers. They lived in Hadar, and I on the Carmel. For a moment, the remoteness of long ago buzzed between us, but we moved on to other subjects and it disappeared.

Agi did not ask me direct questions, rather went around, like a cat on soft paws, and I understood that she was interested in hearing why I was in Northampton. My personal stories poured out of me, and she listened with interest, nodded, focused her eyes on me and pulled me with invisible threads to tell her more and more, although maybe I wanted to be pulled more than she wanted to pull. When I asked her about herself, she dodged my questions with light pronouncements and proffered general details. Her husband was a U-Mass professor, History and Political Science, maybe I heard about him, she mentioned his name. I apologized, "I know only my colleagues at Smith College." We chatted for a long time, an introductory conversation, in which I situated Agi on my inner map, and she probably situated me on her map.

Our time together was good, and I did not want it to end, but Agi prepared to get up. I said to her, "Let's get together again next week!" Agi answered in an emphasized practicality that she was busy with her work and her husband and her children and grandchildren. They had three grandchildren, and she, like all grandmothers, volunteered to help, and there were many social obligations, too many, dinners and obligatory social gatherings, you know... a small quick smile, a glance at the watch, a short touch of the Chinese plait on the nape.

I instigated another meeting two weeks later, and ten days later she did. We started to talk on the phone every few days, and our meetings became more frequent. I did not know what attached us to each other. Agi – an economist in an organic food marketing company and a volunteer for an international nonprofit for third world's poor -- and I, a college teacher, she reserved and protective, I not, she suspicious, I not, she meticulous and I not. But despite our differences, we found common interests and our bond grew stronger.

In our conversations she spoke enthusiastically about social and political phenomena the world over, and displayed an impressive knowledge of literature and art, but when we approached the personal sphere, she became reserved. I told her my whole life story, and she only told me that she made Aliyah with her parents from Hungary when she was a child, and that she had a brother who was born in Haifa. I waited patiently for her to open up to me, was happy when she invited me for dinner in her home and introduced me to their friends, and I became excited when she exhibited a family-like closeness and introduced me to her children. She was always serious and seldom smiled but at the same time she did not seem to me to be unhappy and I did not feel that she hid some dreadful secret. My impression was that she was simply a reticent person who kept her personal stories to herself, and I assumed that she was prepared to expose them only in settings of affection.

Our bond was woven slowly in the Northampton rhythm. Here it would not have happened that way. Tel Aviv is a turbo-city which does not afford any sluggishness, a city which constantly pushes forward as if something bad is about to happen and it is important to hurry and do what we need to before that thing befalls us. In Northampton everything is peaceful, to the last squirrel on the trees, and here every accelerating motorcycle sounds to me like a real siren. Tel Aviv is a nervous city, being driven by tempestuous creativity and anxious expectancy, which quickens the cadence of breathing and heartbeats, which spurs its inhabitants to live fully, to live much, to live with all their might.

Northampton is a tranquil city in the Eastern United States. Life flows slowly, especially in winter, and that pace suited Agi, who managed our bonding carefully and with slight suspicion. But when spring arrived, with its green lawns and new leaves on the poplars and the maples, Agi relaxed. Once I even caught her laughing out loud, a Gypsy laughter, full of uncontrolled urges.

***

One day we met for lunch at the "Tea Pot," our usual sushi restaurant. Agi wore a light grey angora sweater and a dark gray silk scarf with purple lines was wrapped around her neck. "This sweater is gorgeous", I said to her, "Is it new? Wear it well!" She looked at her sleeves, at one then the other, as though looking for stains that evaded her eyes, "Yes, it was a successful buy, I've had it for ten years."

"It looks totally new; how do you manage to keep it like that?"

"I learned it from my mother. She has always kept her clothes like new, even now, being old. Taking care of our clothes is a family thing."

"And your mother learned it from her mother?"

Agi put her hand on her nape, straightened her Chinese plait and said, "No, she learned it from her aunt. For her mother, my grandmother, clothes were less important."

The waiter came, we ordered our favourite sushi and Agi sighed like someone who gave in to a harmful temptation. "We eat too much sushi. Had my grandmother known, she would have probably said we were going to look like tuna wrapped in seaweed."

"You had a poetic grandmother."

"Her name was Ilona, everyone loved her," said Agi in a tone of longing I was not familiar with.

"I am sure you loved her very much," I said, "What kind of a woman was she?" Agi hesitated for a moment, a cloud of suspicion hovered over her face and disappeared. She said, "She had a sense of humour, and she told me many stories about our family."

"I love hearing family stories..."

"For example, she told me that we had one woman in the family named Julia, who looked really good, tall with a good body and black eyes. She used to dress cheaply, with too much jewelry, and always wanted to go out to expensive places where there were rich people. She wasn't liked much by our family. She came from a poor family in Novi Sad. Maybe you heard of Novi Sad, it's a city in Serbia."

"Yes, I know."

"So two years before the war, that is, World War Two, Julia looked for a rich husband in Novi Sad, which was then still in Yugoslavia, and she was introduced to my mother's cousin. He was a reserved man and not very nice. He probably felt good that someone who looked like Julia was after him and he married her. His name was Sandor, a Hungarian name, and they had a boy, Robert, but my grandmother told me that Julia didn't take care of him and all the time was only busy with her clothes and her jewelry. She had lots of earrings and rings. My grandmother said about her, 'Julia had big and beautiful hands, each hand the size of a toilet seat cover.'"

Agi smiled as if she told me a dream, and something in me began to gallop into the mist. Maybe that was the moment the story took hold of me even before I heard it. A great wild urge took over me and suddenly I talked too loudly, "Your grandmother probably told you about the war time," but all of a sudden I halted inside myself, what is it with me and wars?

Agi blinked and her shadow-throwing eyelashes were like a screen between the world and the purple hue in her eyes.

"Did you know you have purple eyes?"

"Purple?"

"I mean, they have a purple shade in them..."

The waitress placed a wooden tray laden with sushi rolls before us. Agi held the chopsticks lightly, took one roll and dipped it in the soya sauce, put it in her mouth and chewed with her mouth closed. She looked pleased and I celebrated, finally she is talking! Albeit not like a bursting dam, but the gate has opened.

"Do you remember any other stories your grandmother Ilona told you?"

Agi finished chewing, swallowed, waited a moment and answered, "Yes."

I restrained myself from prodding her.

"There is a story about a painting," she said as if diving into herself. "Before we came to Israel, when we still lived in Budapest, there was a large oil portrait hanging in my grandparents' house, over the piano, of a woman called Kata. Every time my grandmother looked at it, she cried."

"Why?"

"Kata was her sister. She was murdered in the massacre in Novi Sad."

That word, murdered, fell like a stone among the seaweed-wrapped rolls. I could not take another roll and Agi was silent too, like a disabled person who mentioned her deformity.

In the end I asked almost in a whisper, "Tell me more about the painting."

"It was a large portrait," she spoke slowly, "I used to stand and gaze at it for a long time," she paused a moment, "my grandmother told me that Kata didn't want to be painted, but in the end, she relented."

"Why didn't she?"

"My grandmother didn't say. I have a photo of the portrait at home, I will show you."

***

On the following days Agi told me the story chapter by chapter, in their order and according to the time. She did smile her short quick smiles and glanced at her watch often – she had a difficulty exposing even an old family story – but finally her reservations evaporated, maybe not because of me but because of the story. I felt that she was discovering it anew.

She told and I wrote in my notebook. Every so often I stopped her and asked questions. She talked in disjointed sentences, and more than once confused the events or the people, or remembered something and went back in time, but I did not get thrown off and the story became full and clear. And then, one day, when white clouds slowly traversed the sky over Northampton and reveled in the peace, we sat in the breakfast nook in the wooden house Agi and her husband had bought in an old neighbourhood, drank coffee, and Agi reached the chapter on the massacre in Novi Sad.

"So, then," she said remotely, "on the third day of the massacre the gendarmes went wild. They entered the house on Dunavska Street, pulled them out and shot them right there, next to the entrance."

I knew from the beginning of the story that Kata and her family were murdered in that massacre, but it was the first time I heard all four were shot by the entrance to their home. I could not endure the moment of their death and I sealed myself on the inside against it. A silence fell between us. Agi sat before me and her face was frozen.

We sat that way for a long time, she looking to one corner in the room and I to another. I wanted to get up and hug her, but I was silent and did not move. If I could have wept at that moment, if I could have approached her and been with her... we became partners to the story like two sisters, but something stopped me, I did not know what, and Agi was probably stopped by the reticence that closed her within herself.

In the end, she got up with an expression of that's-how-it-is and went to the bookcase in the living room. Her husband, a handsome man, had a large collection of books. From the bottom shelf she pulled a tall and thick book and removed from its pages a brown envelope of documents, "Here, have a look." The purple hue in her eyes was damp and her stretched hand shook some. I grasped the envelope, peeked in and saw a stationery paper, thin and yellowing with blue writing on it. I pulled it out with the tips of my fingers and let it fall and Kata's last letter dropped slowly on the table.

"Read it to me," I whispered, "and translate for me."

Agi read in a steady voice, a sentence in Hungarian and a sentence in Hebrew.

"Novi Sad 23.1.1942

Dear Ilona,

> We have not been able to leave the house for three days. I don't know what will happen to us. If they take us away, I ask that you try to talk to the store manager. Maybe he can help us or maybe only the good God, if he wants to help us. Here are my instructions if something bad happens to us: I leave you half of the house on Klauzál Street number 17"

In my imagination I see Kata holding the pen in her right hand and in her left she presses the writing pad to the table. Her fingerprints are stamped on the paper with the dampness on her skin. The blue letters are drawn with a thin nib, in uniform letters, flowing and attached in a meticulous penmanship, curl in a restrained coquetry, stand clear, assembled in words on straight lines of equal length, one deletion in a decisive line and back to the determined writing, without trembling, without missing any letters. A level-headed race against the imminent pogrom.

I did not hear any noises, the same as in scary movies, when I lower the sound to nothing sometimes out of fright. I saw one gendarme approach Kata. She has no time to finish the letter, puts down the pen and gets up. He grabs her arm roughly and leads her to the door. She goes out and stands next to László, holds his arm, is shot and falls. It happened so fast that I had to replay the picture in slow motion so that I could comprehend it, but I did not.

My fingers hovered over the letters and I felt as if I touched a damp cloth. I pulled back, but immediately I moved them over it to feel it. Kata, it is me, my name is Noa and now I add my fingerprints to yours. For a moment, a strange darkness enveloped me, not real darkness but a kind of no-time, and then the light returned. I looked at the letter and suddenly I was seized by a strong feeling of tragedy in the room, as if Kata's fingers captured the moment of her death and kept it alive all the years since then.

Agi stood next to me with her Chinese plait and her innocent pearl earrings and smiled gently as if telling me that she understood, it does not matter what, but she understood. I was grateful to her and said, "This letter should be put in the Shrine of the Book next to the Dead Sea Scrolls, under the same conditions of preservation."

Suddenly I felt cold, "Just a minute, Agi, what happened to the portrait?"

"Yes, it's a problem... at some point it disappeared."

"What?"

"It's a long story, I'll tell you sometime."

"And Robert? Did he live? How old is he? Where is he now?"

"Yes, he lives in New York. He must be seventy. Would you like to meet him?"

"Maybe, but before that I need to meet your mother."

18

Protected Houses

I met Old Edit, Agi's mother, when I came to Israel for a visit, before I ultimately moved back. The story had not been written yet, and the notebook in which I wrote it as I heard it from Agi was full of notes I had made for myself, "ask Edit," or "check with Edit."

The door was opened by a woman with thick white hair cut in a flattering feminine line, befitting Kata's niece. She beamed a wide smile to me and said in a thick Hungarian accent, "Agi called that you are coming!" Despite being bent and leaning on a cane, she had a young air, maybe thanks to her meticulous attire, or maybe thanks to Aladar's clear light blue eyes, which peeked under her droopy lids with Ilona's spark of mischievousness.

The bedroom door was open and right away I saw a framed photo of the portrait hanging above the bed. Framed photos of her parents, Ilona and Aladar, as a young couple, and photos of Agi and her family and her brother and his family stood on the cabinet in the living room. An embroidered tablecloth covered the coffee table.

We seated ourselves, I in the armchair and Edit on the sofa. She was excited like all the residents in Seniors' Homes, who rejoice like children when they have visitors, and I also saw some sadness in her, like the sadness I knew in my parents before they passed away. I put my open notebook in my lap and said, "Don't pay attention to me writing." Edit smiled warmly and with open face, like the girl from Budapest who capers in the pinkish muslin dress, "Agi said you like writing." My cheeks burned, "I like writing, but I don't always succeed." Edit grew serious, "Ask anything you want."

I said, "I see that the photo of the portrait is hanging in the bedroom."

She sighed, "Yes, sorry..." and little tears began to trickle down her cheeks and slide in the wrinkles' ruts. She wiped them in an embroidered handkerchief and raised her gaze at me, "My mother never stopped crying about my aunt."

"How old were you when it happened?"

"I was eighteen."

"You already lived in the house on Klauzál Street at that time?"

"Yes, when my aunt bought half the building she gave us one apartment."

"Agi told me that Sandor came to you in Budapest two days after what happened in Novi Sad. What did he bring with him?"

"My aunt's letter and the portrait and a few more things, like a fur coat, jewelry."

"Do you remember what happened when he entered? You had no idea..."

"Do I remember? You can't forget such a thing!" Edit pulled her nose, "We knew that there were problems in Novi Sad, that they deported people, took their assets, and killed. We were worried, but we didn't know what went on that day. My mother and me, we saw my cousin Sandor's face when he walked in with the portrait, and we also saw his shirt with the tear, like that, and right away we knew something terrible happened."

"What did your mother do?"

"She hugged him and cried."

"Why was his shirt torn?"

"After the terrible tragedy, they gathered all the families of those there who got killed, to be like a funeral, they did like a funeral... Sandor went, and there they made that tear."

"And then he went to the house and found the letter?"

"No, the letter he took right away when he came in the evening, and the day after, after the gathering, he went in again, to take the portrait and a few more of my aunt's things, to bring to my mother."

"And what happened after that?"

"It was like this..." she sighed, "After three weeks Sandor came from Novi Sad with Julia and Robert. The boy was only four, little, like, and they moved into the apartment next door, that my aunt put in their name."

***

Budapest, February 1942. Outside it is frosty and on European soil the war devours humans. Ilona and Aladar's apartment in the building on Klauzál Street is neat and quiet, and the portrait is hanging over the piano in the living room. Ilona stands in front of it and her face is different. The massacre in Novi Sad did to her what a rapist does to an innocent girl. Her mother, sister, brother and brother-in-law were lost in one moment. Her insides are clenched, and her eyes are filled with tears. Edit goes to her and hugs her shoulders and the two of them stare at the portrait. In the painting Kata sits erect, her lips pressed together, and her gaze is turned to the side. The blue velvet robe is open over the alabaster silk negligee, her left hand rests in her lap, and her right hand, as usual, is dropped to the side. The grey-green background colours behind her, impenetrable like a safe's door. Ilona muses, Gábor Pahl cannot imagine what happened, he is in America, maybe we should let him know. She does not know that he is sick, and his days are numbered. The dying light of the end of day seeps into the room, and Sandor and Julia's voices can be heard from the next apartment they had just moved into.

At night Robert's crying reaches over the wall and wakes Ilona up. She lies and listens and her heart aches. How long does it take for them to wake up and go to him? In the morning, when she is alone in the apartment, she says loudly to her sister on the wall, "He is a lonely child, Kata, poor little Robert, he probably misses you very much."

At mid-day she hears a knock on the door. Ilona opens and finds Julia standing at the door holding little Robert's hand. His curly head barely reaches the middle of her thigh, and his dark eyes examine Ilona. She smiles at him and he lowers his gaze. Julia says in a sweet tone, "We just got up, auntie..." Her thick black curls quiver over her forehead in a short bob, and her black eyes glance through the heavy makeup. Her lips are painted red, a gold necklace on her neck and big gold earrings are attached to her lobes. The blue silk sleeves of her blue blouse with black polka dots and the tight black skirt can be seen through the fur coat. On her legs she wears silk stockings and on her feet she has high-heeled black shoes. Like there is no war, thinks Ilona, like they didn't stand in the Strand a month earlier and like nothing happened to the family... What's wrong with her? What party is she going to in the middle of the day?

Julia drops Robert's hand and tightens her fur coat around her body, "Can you look after the boy? I have to go out." Ilona lifts him in her arms, "can you smell the good smell coming from the kitchen, Robi? Let's go see what's waiting for you." His mother turns and clicks with her heels on the long deck, which encircles their floor like a gallery, and Robert looks after her. Ilona senses that he listens to the clicking as it moves away, she presses him to her and thinks of Kata, this Julia, when she was a baby, so much hair grew on her head that it ate all the good sense that was in there and left nothing. Now she has an empty head and tough hair.

The family did not like Julia, but I feel for her, as if she were a small starling fluttering with her small wings and screeches with her twits, I want to live! I want to live! I do not have enough information about her. I know that her hands were, each of them, the size of a toilet-seat cover, and she was a reckless young woman who was drawn to the pleasures of wealth. Maybe I should have gone deeper into her character, she is Robert's mother, after all.

"Any minute you will drown in a sea of details, Noa," Editor-Rafi calls to me, "Where are you going with all this?" I forgot that my five Deceased Loves are sitting in the living room. I forgot to miss Avry. I am not here. "I sew with a basting thread, Rafi, and you will do the final sewing."

***

Budapest, spring, 1944. The war is heavy and continuous, the Nazis had invaded Hungary already and reality turned black. Now they transfer Jews to special residential areas in what they call "relocation." When I asked Edit, "Did you know what was happening? I mean... to the Jews in Europe?" her face looked solemn, "My parents and I didn't know. Maybe others did. Later we heard that people knew. Our friends went by trains, we didn't know where. And they sent postcards saying they were fine, you know, those postcards. But rumours started that all the people who went by trains died. It sounded unreal to us. Died? How died?"

"Were you scared?"

"We weren't scared, but we were worried."

Edit obtains fake identity papers of a Christian woman and travels to hide in a small resort far from Budapest. She does not put on a yellow star; hence she can go on any tram and thus she travels to visit her parents occasionally. Her heart is heavy, her boyfriend is sent to a labour camp and she finds out that he got sick there. She does not have any detalils and she fears for him.

Ilona and Aladar have no idea where the trains go. Their main worry is their relocation, because for them nothing can be worse than leaving their apartment and moving to a new place.

And then Aladar manages to get for Ilona, himself, Sandor, Julia and Robert the Swedish Wallenberg's immunity certificates. With those certificates they will move into the protected houses with the Swedish flags flying over them and avoid the relocation. "Later we'll return to our apartments," Aladar says to them and puts his hand over Robert's curly head distractedly.

They are only worried and hope for the best, but I am very frightened because of the violence in the city, the killings and the robbing, the detentions and the deportations by train. I know where the trains go, and I see what is happening in Poland and what happens all over Europe below the black war cloud, things they will hear about only a year later. And I am extremely anxious, concerned that something will go wrong in my retrospective story, that I will have a writing accident and somehow, they will be put on the train. I write very carefully.

Old Edit told me that their immunity certificates were forged, "but nobody could see like, they were like original! And there was this Swiss, Lutz, who helped a lot," she added, "but my parents had Wallenberg's certificates."

***

Ilona and Aladar stand on chairs on either side of the portrait and together take if off the wall, careful not to damage the heavy wooden frame, with the leaves and engravings painted in gold. Ilona enfolds it in a sheet, wraps it in a heavy blanket, and coils a rope around it. No choice, Kata, she thinks to her sister, all of us must leave the house, you as well. They carry the portrait together and go down to the cellar. A silent dimness welcomes them with a strong smell of coal. In the good days of yore, the cellar was full to the brim with coal, and the inhabitants used it for cooking and heating. Now only the smell and the black stains on the walls are left. Faint light penetrates through the arched openings near the ceiling. Ilona and Aladar go to a far corner, where there is scarcely any light, and lean the portrait against the wall.

Aladar returns to the apartment and Ilona stays a moment longer, because only when alone can she speak to Kata aloud. "You understand, if they hear me, they may think that I am out of my mind and speak to the walls." She looks about her and touches the wrapped painting leaning against the wall, "if only you were with me now, Kata... the world has gone topsy-turvy." Then she goes back up to their apartment. Aladar has already closed the two overflowing suitcases, shut the shutters and locked the windows. "Everything is shut, Ilonka," he says, "There will be no air circulation," and looks at her with his ever clear blue eyes. His Adam's apple moves as if he swallows tears and Ilona shoves the grey curl that fell on her forehead, lays a hand on his chest and smiles sadly, "Lately my tears flow the other way too."

She is fifty-one. Her graying hair is gathered on her nape, her shoulders lean forward, and the skin of her face begins to age, but Aladar does not see that. Neither does he see her wrinkled neck nor her thickened waist. He always sees the young woman whom he met at the beginning of the century in the metal casting factory, and he always hears the clear voice wishing him a good morning. Now worry eats at his heart and he tries to conceal it from her. Worry eats at Ilona too, and they hear each other at night, ticking inside themselves like termites inside a wooden closet door.

They put on their coats with the yellow star sewn on their fronts, take the suitcases and leave. Aladar locks the door behind him, they walk on the corridor deck and Ilona's dress catches in a curlicue in the wrought iron. She releases it and whispers, "No need to hold on to me, I will return." Downstairs on the street, next to the green wooden door, Sandor, Julia and Robert stand waiting already, each of them with a yellow star sewn on their coat. Robert stands between his father who carries a suitcase, and his mother who carries a suitcase, with a pack on his back, too large for his small frame.

They prefer not to take the tram, because they are permitted to climb the last car only, which is always crammed to capacity and so they turn to walk on side streets. They walk on the pavement in a line, close to the sidewalk – only there are Jews allowed to walk – the suitcases are heavy, Wallenberg's protected building is still far, and Robert's legs hurt. He slows and Aladar picks him up and continues walking with the boy in his arms.

Nobody discovered the portrait. But the three young Jews who hid in an alcove next to it were discovered, taken out and put on the train. I am aware that the portrait is only a canvas daubed with oil paints, but a voice in me says that Gábor Pahl, with his brushes and paints, left Kata here, on this side, in a kind of existence. And this voice insists that Kata, from the corner in which she was hidden and through the blanket and the sheet she was wrapped in, saw and heard what went on next to her in the basement, when those three young men were discovered.

***

Budapest, spring, 1945. Aladar turns the key and opens the door to the apartment. Everything is in its place, exactly as it was when they left it, but they themselves are a little different, bitter stiffness clinging to them. Aladar throws open the windows and the shutters, light of day enters together with a wave of fresh air, and Ilona says, "Now Kata can come back home." They bring the portrait from the basement, remove the blanket and the sheet and hang it in its place above the piano. "If they hadn't been taken out that day, they would have gone to Auschwitz, like everyone else in Novi Sad. But maybe they would have been able to avoid it..." And Aladar sighs. Sandor, Julia and Robert return to their apartment as well.

A week later, Edit returns to her parents' home, and anxiously awaits her boyfriend to return from the labour camp. A friend of his, who has returned, brings her a letter and says, "he doesn't feel well yet." She bursts out, "What's wrong with him?" and the friend swallows hard, "He was punished by beatings."

Seven-year-old Robert, gentle and silent, clings to Ilona, "You smell like Oma Kata." She embraces him, "you remember her smell? That's excellent." He passes his hand on her sleeve, "her dress was always smooth, like yours." Ilona kisses his forehead, looks at the portrait and thinks, what do you think about your grandson, Kata? The boy was only four years old. It has been three years and he remembers everything, nothing is erased, he has a strange mind.

The war is over.

19

Budapest, Haifa, New York

A heavy curtain of iron fell on Eastern and Central Europe, shutting it tightly, and a heavy curtain fell on me too. I wrote for hours, I did not know when I slept and when I got up. I did not go out for refreshing walks, only sank deeper and deeper in the quicksand of the story and gave myself to it in a zeal of writing. My Deceased fell asleep, except for Editor-Rafi who only dosed off and opened his eyes every so often. The crows couple disappeared, and Avry flickered in me, came into my thoughts and disappeared.

***

Budapest, 1946. Sandor travels to Novi Sad, which has become Yugoslav again, sold at a loss whatever was left of the family business and found that his parents' house on Dunavska Street was turned into City Hall. He returned to Budapest and looked for a way to buy exit visas to the West. His brother,

Miki, sent a family reunification request documents, and the official process was long and nerve-racking, but after a year the visas finally arrived. Sandor took his wife and his son and sailed to America. Agi smiled contemptuously, "My grandmother said that in New York Sandor stood in front of Miki like a dummy, with his pockets turned out."

Sandor does deserve a moment of my time. He was the one who arrived at his parents' house immediately after the massacre, he is the one who found the unfinished letter and was the first to be struck by the emptiness. But I hurry to his son. One day I may write another story with the dedication, "To Robert's father".

***

New York, 1947. On 81st Street West, next to the blooming park, at the entrance to their house stood Klari and Miki with their three-years-old twins, Jessica in Klari's arms, and Jonathan in Miki's. A taxi stopped in the street in front of them and Sandor, Julia and Robert stepped out. They took out the five suitcases and stood close together next to them in heavy clothes, buttoned to their necks, and heavy winter shoes. For a moment everyone was silent facing each other, and in the next moment Miki regained his composure. He put Jonathan down next to Klari, stretched his arms and advanced to his guests. "Finally, you are here." The familial meeting excited everyone, and a festive atmosphere permeated the house, although Miki tried to sit alone with Sandor and failed. "He wanted to talk to him alone after nine years of separation," said Agi in dismay, "After all, two brothers, after nine years of not seeing each other, but Julia wouldn't let them. She pushed herself in all the time."

When Miki went with them for a stroll in the park, he put his hand on nine-year-old Robert and walked with him on the path among the bushes and the flowers. Sandor and Julia walked a few paces behind them and looked about them in wonderment, their new reality not sunk in yet. They did not ask Robert what he and his uncle Miki talked about and did not notice the happy expression on the boy's face. "Miki loved Robert from that first day," said Agi, "there was chemistry between them."

Klari was small and round, light skinned and with a narrow face. She rarely smiled, even though Miki used to say to her, "smile more often! You are beautiful when you smile!" But she exuded sourness. She did try to host her brother-in-law, sister-in-law and their son Robert, who seemed strange to her, with a generous spirit, but after a week, hosting them began to weigh on her. She was busy with the twins and found it hard to take care of an additional family, and Julia did not lift a finger to help. "That one, only wants to be served!" protested Klari in Miki's ear. "I know where she grew up in Novi Sad. I wouldn't set foot in that neighbourhood." Klari's nerves slowly became frayed. After ten days the festive atmosphere vanished, and a bitter dispute over inheritance erupted between Sandor and Miki. Frankly, if the sisters-in-law had not poisoned their husbands with their suspicion and anger, they would have settled things in peace, but tension mounted. In the end, the brothers arrived at some agreement and each went his own way.

Sandor, Julia and Robert settled in Boro Park, Brooklyn. Sandor opened a small fabric store in a dilapidated shopping mall, close to the train station, and bought a small apartment in a three story walk-up not far from there. "Why did you choose this place?" asked Julia and looked about her in revulsion. Sandor explained to her that several Hungarian speaking families lived in the neighbourhood, even though they were ultra-orthodox and there was little chance of having any contact with them. "Anyway," he thought out loud and Robert raised his dark eyes to him, "when you live in a foreign place, it's good to have a few people around us who speak our language, you never know when you might need them." Julia twisted her face, "Everything is so ugly here. Is this America?"

Sandor's few customers were ultra-orthodox Jews, who felt sorry for him because in their eyes he was a refugee from That Hell, and among themselves they said that he was half goy. "Anyway, he wasn't like his parents," said Agi decisively, "He had no head for business. Everything he invested was lost. In the end he sold the store and had no money."

A STRONG BLESSING

Budapest, spring, 1949. Ilona stood in front of the portrait, enfolding in her arms her two-week- old granddaughter, Agi, who was born to Edit and her husband four years after his return from the labour camp, sick from the beatings. Both families lived together in the apartment on Klauzál Street. Most of the other apartments were nationalized. That morning the men went to work and, for the first time since giving birth, Edit went out to get some fresh air. She said she would walk to the Danube and be back in time for nursing, and finally Ilona was able to talk out loud to her sister in the portrait.

She raised her eyes to her, "Kata, here is Agnes, my grand-daughter. Look how much she resembles you, like two drops of wine!" A reflexive smile lit the sleeping baby, and Ilona kissed her on her forehead, "may you grow healthy, my Agi, and may you be independent and strong like your great grandmother, her name was Vera." Tears flooded Ilona's eyes, she sat down in the armchair in front of the portrait and rocked the baby in her arms. "Kata, let's bless Agi with a strong blessing, things Mama would have said, if she were here."

"Rafi, are you awake? I need your help... I know exactly what blessing Ilona wants to extend to Agi."

"So what's the question?"

"Don't play dumb, you heard my thought."

"Yes, and I don't like your idea."

"Why?"

"Because if you start quoting here all kinds of other authors, you will end up with something ridiculous."

"But the passage I think about has been coming back to me for years, in different contexts. It is written perfectly, and it says exactly what I want to write here... It is by David Gross-man, you know, he formulated and wrote it, but as soon as he published his book, it is as if he gifted it to me. Anyone who reads his book is gifted it , you understand?"

"Noa, why do you need me if you do whatever you want?"

"Forget it, Rafi, go back to sleep."

This is what the author David Grossman wrote regarding the boy who was just born, in the paragraph which ends his book *See Under: Love* "---All of us prayed for one thing: that he might end his life knowing nothing of war --- We asked so little; for a man to live in this world from birth to death and know nothing of war" (Translated by Betsy. Rosenberg, [New York: Farrar Straus Giroux, 1989], 452).

***

Budapest, 1952. The family sat around the table in the apartment on Klauzál Street after dinner. Agi was asleep already. Ilona said, "We got a letter from Miki in New York, he wrote that Robert came to live with them. Maybe because Sandor is not working. Miki will take care of him." Edit said, "Miki with his money can afford it." And Ilona said, "Poor little Robert."

***

Budapest, 1957. Agi and her parents left the house at night, wearing dark clothes and carrying heavy bags. They climbed onto a car which waited for them in a dark corner and drove to the Hungarian-Austrian border. There they met a border smuggler who took most of their money and led them in the darkness into Austria on a difficult and barely navigable path. A car waited for them on the other side of the border which took them to Vienna, and from there, after several weeks, they arrived in Israel. Agi was eight years old then. I asked her where they lived and what they experienced when they got there, but she made a face and answered unwillingly, "It wasn't easy, but we managed."

***

Budapest, 1961. Hungary's exit gate opened officially for a short time, and Ilona and Aladar made plans to sneak through it before it got shut again. They stood, each on a chair, on two sides of the portrait, lowered it from the wall and brought it to a framer. Ilona asked him to remove the gilded and carved frame and take the canvas off the stretcher. The framer looked at the painting for a moment and his breath caught. Ilona whispered, "She was my sister," and he said nothing. After the war people did not ask questions. Ilona took in air, "Separate it carefully, not to tear it," and hoped that he would not identify the artist's signature. "I hope he does not even think to steal the painting," she said to Aladar, "Kata is going with us to Israel."

***

Haifa, 1961. Agi and her parents lived in a comfortable apartment in Hadar. Their apartment building was surrounded by tall pine trees, with pink cyclamens growing among them in the winter. From the apartment's balcony it was possible to see the Mediterranean glittering all day in changing blues, the white trim of the beach going up north to the Rosh Hanikra cliffs, and the bay and the industrial area with its two "upside down espresso cups". "You see, Grandpa? These are the refineries where Daddy works," explained Agi and called into the apartment, "Grandma! Come to the balcony, you must see the view!" Ilona came out and stood next to Aladar. From the back they looked like one entity: both with their elbows tight next to their waist, leaning on the railing at the same angle and with their heads leaning to the right at the same way. They looked to the sea all the way to the horizon, and together inhaled lungsful of air.

Edit helped her parents unpack and found the portrait rolled and wrapped in a piece of material torn from an old beige curtain. She opened it, looked, and was startled, feeling as though Kata was breathing on her. Immediately she rolled it back, wrapped it in the beige material and laid it aside.

***

Haifa, 1963. "Mama, I remind you that I am taking the painting with me," said Edit as she was packing a suitcase for her flight to New York where she was going to meet her cousin Miki. Ilona answered feebly, "Yes, yes..." and had difficulty hiding her gloomy thoughts. Contrary to her opinion, Edit entertained thoughts of immigrating to America and hoped that Miki would help. "Help with money," Agi explained to me, "Miki left the family in Novi Sad when he was only nineteen, and my mother didn't know what kind of a person he became, maybe he became miserly? She thought that seeing his mother's portrait would have an influence on him..."

***

New York, 1963. Miki had invested the money he received from his parents in a housewares store, which over the years grew and spread all along the East Coast. The logo was designed according to his request as a ladle, with the name "Steins" written on it. Now Miki is a rich forty-four-year old man, who cannot control his growing belly because of his appetite for high-fat foods and white flour pastries. His brown eyes shine, and his eyebrows are carefully trimmed. His large mustache looks like a thick brush and his ears and nostrils are cleared of hairs. His nails are manicured monthly, and his greying auburn hair is combed back like a small mane. He flirts with his eyes with the young women passing before him and smiles to himself, her too if I only wanted, but he prefers not to want, because even if he hid it from Klari, she would know.

He stands at the entrance of the Waldorf-Astoria hotel, dressed in a tailored suit, holding a bag that looks like a small suitcase, and peers around him with pleasure, as if New York with all its treasures was created just for him. He glances at his watch and wonders if Edit is already there. She preferred not to stay at his house and took a room in a small hotel but responded with pleasure when he invited her for lunch at the magnificent Waldorf-Astoria. Miki enters the lobby and sees her standing by the window, gazing at the street. For a moment it seems to him that her blue suit is one of his mother Kata's suits, and his heart quickens.

On one shoulder Edit carries a black leather bag, and on the other a whitish canvass bag, long and narrow, which resembles a sleeve but is twice as long. She turns her face, sees Miki and he spreads his arms. They walk toward each other with a look of amazement, and he clasps her in a strong embrace and mumbles something in Hungarian. Edit bursts into tears, "so many things happened to us, Miki!" He too tears up for a moment and passes his fingers on his mustache, "Many years, Edit'ka!"

Before they sit down Edit removes the long canvass bag, pulls out the portrait which is rolled in the beige material of an old curtain, and lays it on the table. Her cheeks are crimson and her blue eyes flutter, "this is the portrait..." the surprise on Miki's face confuses her and she raises her voice, "Put it in a frame and hang it at home over the piano!" It is obvious to her that they have a piano. Miki holds the cylinder and suddenly it seems to him that he touches his mother's arm. He pulls back his hand. "I didn't remember that the portrait is so big," he mutters, "I will open it at home." Edit feels a faint taste of disappointment.

But during the meal the ambience is warm and familial. They update each other on the details of their lives and Miki smiles, "True, many things happened to us." After dessert he showers Edit with gifts, for her and for the rest of her family, "Take this bag," he says, "Everything in it is for you." She is surprised by his generosity and her eyes fill with tears. "Sorry, I am emotional," she says. "In the end he paid for her flight and the small hotel," Agi smiled with gratification.

Edit and Miki speak Hungarian in an old jargon, and she remembers how in her childhood he waited for her with Sandor on the railway platform, their faces hidden by bouquets of flowers. "How is Sandor?" she asks. Miki shrugs, "We hardly see each other. Robert has been living with us for a few years. Now he is in Med School. But tell me, how are you in Israel?" She describes their apartment in Haifa, paints with dark colours their difficulties in adjusting to the language and the culture, but suddenly she smiles like a projector, "Agi is the best student in her class!" Miki puts on an expression of not-surprised, "it was to be expected, no?" She takes a deep breath and tells him about her immigration wishes. He gets excited and wants to help.

But in the end Edit changed her mind about immigrating. "My mother was already forty," said Agi, "she came back from New York and became pregnant right away. I was fifteen when my brother was born."

"Why did she give up immigrating to the United States?"

"Because it was difficult," Agi responded angrily, as if I asked only to nitpick, "When we emigrated from Hungary to Israel it was difficult. My parents and my grandparents were too exhausted to begin all over again."

"In the end you are the one who immigrated to the United States and they stayed in Israel."

Agi grabbed her Chinese plait as if I stepped on the most sensitive landmark on her map.

YOU HAVE NO PLACE IN AMERICA

During Edit's visit Miki kept the portrait in his office without opening it. If I show it to Klari she will tell me right away to return it to Edit, and this is out of the question. But opening it in the office is out of the question too, because Klari will sense it immediately and will ask. Yes, each thing needs to be given its own time. First let Edit go away.

At the airport he parted from Edit with a warm hug, and later, in his office, he put the whitish sleeve bag on his desk and walked around it as if there was a live creature in it. In the end, he slung it on his shoulder without opening it, and drove home. Klari received him at the door, looked at the canvass bag and asked in Hungarian, "So, she left? Everything OK?" He answered "yes," and dodged the report. During dinner, when Jonathan and Jessica sat with them, he told them that Edit returned to Israel. "What did she want, Daddy? Money?" asked Jonathan in an American English, and Jessica chuckled in the same English, "In Israel everyone wants money." They were nineteen then. Jonathan was tall, skinny and wide shouldered. His face was thin like his mother's, but unlike her, he smiled often, and his auburn hair like his father's was coiffed in President Kennedy's style. Jessica was tall and wide as well, with green eyes and clear cheeks. Her thick auburn hair came to her shoulders, always combed and held at the back with a clip, and she smiled with pressed lips. Miki looked at her and restrained himself from saying aloud how much she resembled his mother, because every time he said that, Klari was sick with a headache for two weeks.

He said in Hungarian, "Edit gave me a gift from my aunt Ilona. It is a portrait of my mother, which was hanging in our house over the piano."

As usual, when the family members who were murdered in Novi Sad were mentioned, the necessary quarter-of-minute-of-silence fell around the table, and after that Klari asked in a heavily accented English, "What do you want to do with this painting?" Miki answered her in Hungarian, "I think to frame it with a frame similar to the one we had in Novi Sad and hang it over the piano."

"Come, show it to me," she said to him in angry Hungarian.

Miki unrolled the painting and shuddered, "Look..." he whispered to Klari, "I remember when it was brought home." Klari studied the portrait and made a face, "too bad Edit left. I would have told you to give it back. Sorry, Miki, but I cannot handle having your mother on the wall in front of my eyes."

Jessica peered at the painting over her father's shoulder and for a moment had no words. Maybe the magic that exists in art, which makes the observer sink into his soul for a moment, worked on her. Or maybe I only imagine that she had no words, because she immediately twisted her mouth, "It looks to me like a tattered antique, Daddy, forget it." Jonathan looked at the painting with curiosity and chuckled, "give it to Robert, he likes such things." Jessica let slip a laugh, "yes, he will hang it in his room and all the girls will run away because Grandma is staring from the wall."

Miki sighed and rolled the painting, wrapped it in the Budapest framer's beige cloth, inserted it into the canvass sleeve and descended to the basement where he laid it on a remote shelf next to some old carpets.

A week later he called Sandor by phone. Julia answered and he said, "it's Miki, Julia, how are you?" "Fine", she answered dryly. They had not seen each other for five or six years and Miki said, embarrassed, "I thought to come over." Julia answered, "We are home."

***

Miki went to Brooklyn and parked on a side street in Boro Park, got out of his car and slung the sleeve-bag on his shoulder. He passed large garbage containers, full to bursting with scattering trash, walked down a street with grey three-storied wooden buildings on both sides, with uniform fronts, their slanted roofs covered with black tiles, and with a multitude of chimneys, tall and short. The buildings were stuck to each other like an angry urban wall and all their windows were shut. In the small yards next to the entrances there were no bushes or ornamental trees, no planters and no flowers, and papers were strewn on the ground. Men and women went on the sidewalk in a hasty stride, and a few children in black skullcaps and small sidecurls stood in a group and followed him with their eyes.

Train noises were close, with the rattling of the tracks, the chattering of the locomotives and the creak of the brakes.

Miki recognized the building's number. The door was not locked, and urine smell filled the dark stairwell. He went up the stairs to the second floor, knocked on the door and noticed that the peephole opened. His brother opened the door and for a moment the two leaned to each other in a primal impulse to hug, but Sandor recoiled and crossed his arms. His resemblance to their father warmed Miki's heart, he wanted to say something pleasant, but the words got stuck in his throat. Sandor's bald head and his facial featured were those of László, but Sandor was leaner and taller than their father. László always stood straight, and in contrast, Sandor's stance was limp and bent. He wore a wrinkled striped pajamas, with a heavy body odour rising from it, and Miki wondered if he was sick.

"Hi, Miklos, come in."

They spoke Hungarian, of course. Sandor never learned English and did not understand what people said to him on his rare sojourns out of the house. He closed the door and sat at the corner of the double bed which stood at the centre of the room, facing the entrance.

The air in the apartment was thick. Two reading lights, brown paper pyramids, stood lit on the night stands next to the bed's sides, and cast a weak light. An armoire stood by the inner wall, and the television was placed under the window. On the left of the entrance door, by the wall, stood a small dining table with three chairs around it. Julia sat on one of them and watched television. She was made-up, bejeweled, and her large curls, dyed charcoal black, encircled her face in a youthful haircut. She had returned home an hour earlier from the shoe store where she worked and where she also made friends.

She stood and shook Miki's hand flaccidly, "What happened, you remembered us?" returned to her seat and pointed at another chair, "Sit." Miki sat, focused his eyes somewhere on the wall between his brother and his sister-in-law and said, "Robert is studying nicely, he gets good marks." Julia stretched her long fingers, gazed at the rings on them and said dryly, "We don't hear from him, he doesn't come."

Miki removed the sleeve bag off his shoulder and rose. "Edit was in New York and brought you this." Julia tensed and Sandor looked at him as if he told a bad joke, "Edit brought us a gift?" Miki's voice shook, "Look, Sandor..." He pulled out the portrait, removed the beige cloth and opened it. Sandor stood on his right, and Julia on his left. Miki held the portrait at the top and the bottom and his hands struggled with the canvass which fought to roll back into itself. The portrait shook a bit in his hands and for a minute it seemed to all three of them that Kata herself was moving there. Sandor held his breath, Miki smiled and Julia wore a mocking expression.

Kata sat facing them in her eternal erectness, her white hands resting motionless, her gaze shifted sideways and the light from the side illuminating her face and is caught in her white gold earrings. "Here is Mama, Sandor," whispered Miki, and Julia went back to her seat which faced the television. Sandor contemplated the portrait and blinked. Maybe he shed for a moment the anger that stuck to him since he was born and maybe he succumbed to the soft warmth that the word "Mama" promised him. I do not know what Sandor felt, and anyway, in an instance the ancient expression of bitterness returned to his face. He sat at the tip of the bed and asked in a flattened voice, "Why did Edit bring it?"

Miki felt offended for their mother's sake and looked at her face as if asking for advice. "Maybe you want to frame it... I will pay, of course, you can hang it here in the apartment!" Julia turned her head to him and said furiously, "you probably brought it because Klari doesn't agree to hang it at your place. Listen, Miki, I don't want your mother in front of my eyes either."

Miki passed his fingers on his moustache and rolled the portrait, wrapped it in the beige cloth, inserted it into the sleeve bag and hung it on his shoulder. "OK," he smiled, "let's go out, I invite you to dinner. Julia, is there a restaurant in the area you like?" Sandor said, "You go, I don't want to go out." Julia raised her head and I saw on her face an expression of a girl who was robbed of a dream, but Miki noticed on her face an expression of settling a score, "Never mind, forget it."

He returned home and descended to the basement to the old carpets shelf, lay the sleeve bag next to them and rested his hand on it, as if to quiet a lament. "Mama, you have no place in America... But know that I think about you and Papa a lot." He moved his fingers on the cloth sleeve and the rolled painting returned his touch from inside. Miki sighed, "I miss you with your strength, Mama, everyone around me is wretched."

***

About two months following Miki's visit to Boro Park, Julia got up one day, packed a suitcase and moved in with a young Hispanic man, but six months later something happened, and she died. "It is possible that she committed suicide or became ill suddenly," Agi said to me, "nobody knew anything. Sandor told Miki there were all kinds of rumours." I asked Agi if Robert went to see his father and she answered, "I don't know, maybe he went to see his dad and maybe not."

***

In his solitude, Sandor closed himself up in his small apartment, but hunger forced him to get dressed and go to the Jewish soup kitchen, where he met several Hungarian men he had met in the days of his fabric store. They spoke Hungarian to him, drew him in and under their influence he learned to pray and became religious. He began to frequent the orthodox synagogue in his neighbourhood, but when he was matched with a new wife, he refused. Ten years later, at the age of sixty-six, he dropped suddenly and died of cardiac arrest in the middle of prayers. His Hungarian friends arranged a funeral and informed Miki.

Robert did not come to the funeral.

{ 20 }

The Frozen Lake

When Robert moved from his parents' apartment in Boro Park to his uncle Miki's house, he was fourteen years old, and the twins, Jessica and Jonathan, were eight, ordinary children and a little spoiled. They were not thrilled with the older brother who was foisted on them, and under the influence of Klari's acerbic attitude, they saw him as a poor and strange parasite. But Miki held determined against his wife's headaches and insisted on caring for his nephew.

The twins, like many children of immigrants, understood Hungarian, but refused to speak it. However, Robert, whose English was American and devoid of any foreign accent, preferred to speak only Hungarian with Miki. Jessica and Jonathan ridiculed him, maybe the same way my friends and I in the elementary school in Haifa ridiculed the immigrant children who spoke with their parents in other languages, not Hebrew. "Igen migen hapt a fligen!" we used to tease a Hungarian boy in our grade... We were such a cruel group of children, that I shut my eyes not to see Agi there.

Jessica and Jonathan amassed many hours of television watching, did not read much and studied well for exams. Agi smiled, "After my brother was born, I flew to the United States with my mother and we stayed with them. They were in college and Jessica told me, "I don't need to read novels to tell me what to think. I can think for myself.""

Robert was short with wide shoulders, thin and pale. His head was full of black curls, big and thick, his eyes were grey-black veiled in a purple hue, his lashes short and dense and his cheekbones high. His nose was straight, his lips full and his teeth big and white. A light smile was always on his face, like a remnant from a dream. He spoke little, and his silence was distant, like a long contemplation. Among his classmates he was the one standing to the side. He listened to their conversations, every so often uttered something, but most of the time he was silent, and maybe his long silences were what drew girls' attention.

He always had a book in his hand, in English or Hungarian, and if not a book – a newspaper or a magazine, which he read not skipping a word. A perpetual cigarette was between his lips or his fingers, and always, since his youth, there was a woman with him, mature or young, short or tall. Agi lowered her lashes, "He was a women's man, as they say... women loved loving him."

Poor Robert... the hungry yearning to get close to women never deserted him, to touch, to cuddle with them at the together-time which was soft and warm and gave him a momentary victory over his loneliness, but then left him lonelier, sad, and freezing.

I hear movements behind me in the living room and I turn. Rafi my editor is completely awake. He straightens for a moment and moves his body in his checkered shirt. Childhood-Love-Moosh releases his crossed legs and stretches his arms. His egg face is pinkish, and the oily straw strands are glued to his forehead. I would have made coffee for them; too bad they are dead. My other three Loves are still asleep. Itamar in his fatigues sleeps sitting on the carpet, his head between his arms. Husband-Yossi sleeps erect as if he is awake. And Old-Prince-Shaul's head leans down and he snores lightly. No problem, they can continue to sleep.

"Noa, you are losing control! You are getting too close to Robert!"

"What do you want, Rafi? I thought you'd encourage me to get into his head."

"To get into his head is good. To get too close to him is not good. When you get too close to him your writing becomes flat!"

"Moosh, what is that nonsense coming out of his mouth?"

"He-is-right, Noa."

"Where did I get too close?"

Rafi gets up and stands next to me, "Here," he shows on the screen, "Poor Robert with the three dots. Throw it out!"

***

Sandor and Julia never spoke with Robert about the war, never mentioned the massacre in Novi Sad, and, in fact, never spoke to him about anything. His early childhood memories stayed with him clear and precise, a trait Ilona identified when he was young, but when he got to high school, these memories were closed in his soul in a bolted and forgotten corner.

Saved as a Painting

A year after he moved into his uncle Miki's house, Robert heard from him about the pogrom in Novi Sad, the murders on Dunavska Street, and finally about the massacre at the Strand. "You were there, Robi, with your parents, until you were sent home. I hope you don't remember," Miki said to him.

That day Robert began a journey of information-seeking about his personal holocaust. He read hungrily books and articles in English and in Hungarian, found newspapers from the war time and the days after it, rummaged through survivors' stories and memorial books, and browsed in coverages of trials which took place after the war. Research clutched him like an animal clutching its prey. He widened his study about the war, sat hunched over books hour upon hour with his black curls falling forward, like additional, sensor eyes. He did not write summaries, did not take notes and did not file articles, only committed to memory and traveled in his imagination in the regions of horror which were beyond imagination. Until suddenly he stopped reading and looked out the window, focused on a faraway spot and dove into the pictures of that day at the Strand.

The piercing cold, the people whose coat tails and shoe-clad feet he sees from below standing in the snow which froze into ice, the father who holds his son in his arms, the elderly man with his cane and his elderly wife, who are too tired to stand, his mother, who tightens her coat to her body and says far above his head, "What are they doing? Did they go mad? They're shooting at people!" and his father who does not answer her, and both not looking at him, and his legs already hurting.

He was all alone on this journey, with the paralyzing fear, with the questions which had no answers, with desperation and loathing, and he did not have a teacher or a guide, a psychologist or a friend to help carry the load. Robert did not mention his quest even to Miki. Agi said, "Miki did feel that Robert delves into those things too much, but he waited for everything to work out by itself," and a minute later she summed it up practically, "Miki was right. At the age of fifteen you don't get depressed by history books. In the end Robert stopped."

Jonathan and Jessica treated Robert condescendingly, and at times even spoke about him in malice and ignored his presence in the room. Once, when all three sat in the living room, Jessica said to her brother, "I wonder what the world looks like from low to the ground," and he answered nasally, "Any midget can tell you." But all in all, Jonathan was a nice person. In college he joined the football team, wore the blue uniform and the white sports shoes, and was busy chasing girls. Jessica dressed conservatively and used to conspicuously avoid what she termed "nonsense" – literature, art and music. She believed that the world was driven by market forces, studied diligently and prepared herself for the big race.

Robert conversed with Miki a great deal, but in the company of Klari and the twins he was silent and withdrawn. He hardly talked to them, but sometimes, during dinner, he would suddenly cover his mouth as if he tried to stop the words which threatened to escape, and his face wore the expression of black curled vagabond Charlie Chaplin. Only the little mustache was missing. "Listen to this!" he would say in his thick low voice. They would fall silent and Robert would tell them some story he read in newspaper. Every time Klari and the twins were surprised anew that this guy had a voice and his speech was as fluent as a television anchor's.

One winter weekend, when Robert was already at university, he said suddenly at dinner, "Listen to this! I read in the newspaper about a man who drilled a hole in the frozen lake and got into the water. He was pulled out blue and half dead."

Miki's gaze rested on Robert for a long moment, "Which lake was it?" Robert mentioned the lake's name and Jessica broke into their conversation, "What's so interesting about that?" Jonathan mumbled, "Just someone crazy," and Robert said in a gloomy smile, "but the man got into the hole of his free will." Jessica looked at him disparagingly and turned to Jonathan, "Did you get it? I didn't."

Next morning Robert disappeared. Miki got into his car hastily, drove down snow- cleared roads and among white fields stretching on both sides until he got to that lake. Robert stood there with his back to him and watched the winter fishermen, men in balaclavas and heavy coats sitting on folding chairs in the middle of the frozen lake. They turned hand-held drills energetically and drilled holes in the ice, dropped down fishing lines with bait and waited for the fish.

Miki advanced in heavy steps breathing quickly, and when he stopped Robert turned to him with a tortuous expression and said, "I wouldn't have gone in, but thank you for coming."

CARRIED AWAY

Robert was accepted to Columbia University Medical School in New York. "Miki wanted him to go to the most prestigious university," Agi told me, "that's how it was with Miki, he always wanted the best and was prepared to pay for it."

At the university Robert walked the corridors alone, brushing against the walls and his wide shoulders moved a little as if in a dance. He was the shortest young man among the guys, and even most of the girls were taller than him, but his presence was felt in his expression and his loaded silence. When some of the students tried to get to know him and befriend him, he looked at them in astonishment which they interpreted as reluctance, said nothing as was his habit which they understood as aloofness, and they left him be. And then, after they gave up on him and became indifferent, he emerged suddenly out of himself, and told them a wise-funny story, which at once drew them to him.

***

A class in forensic medicine in the Institute of Pathology in the city. A dead young man with an open chest is laid on the table, the students stand around him, some of them moving from side to side in embarrassment. It was explained to them that the police investigators need to indicate the cause of death in their report.

The pathologist who is to give the answer approaches from the corner of the room and stops at the table. He lifts a thin pointer and points at the internal organs. "What have we here," he asks dryly, omitting the question mark. The students do not react, and the pathologist continues, "No injury is visible. Maybe you see an injury." Silence. The pathologist says, "Poison is disproved," and sounds as if he talks to himself, "We opened to make sure. No foreign object was inhaled, no sharp object was swallowed, no organ was damaged. So, what have we here?" He aims the pointer from organ to organ, names them and sums without inflection, "Everything is intact." He leans over the heart and stares at it closely, as if he discovered something, straightens and looks at the students, "Any questions." No one speaks, and no one moves, everyone wants the class to be over. The pathologist looks at the dead and says, "In such a case we say that the cause of death is unknown." Suddenly Robert's low and thick voice is heard from the side, "Pardon me, Doctor, do we know what this man did when his breathing ceased?"

The students stare at Robert as if the floor they stand on trembled and move their eyes to the pathologist, who raises a thin smile, "You can read it in his file, but it does not concern us here. Why do you ask?" Robert does not smile and does not lower his eyes, he looks like a sad boy, "Maybe he died of fear."

The pathologist narrows his eyes and touches the tip of his nose with the pointer. The silence in the room is heavy, one of the students coughs and the pathologist says, "Fear is a subject for poets, their department is in your university, not here." The students master their smiles, the pathologist ends the lesson and in the university's corridors Robert begins to be called the doctor-poet.

Never in his life did he write a poem, but he loved poetry. He was drawn particularly to pacifist poems, and in his backpack he regularly carried the poetry books of Allen Ginsberg and Robert Bly, and read them again and again. He was sure that all wars erupt and spread like an epidemic because of a violent fear-virus carried by humans. In one of his conversations with

Miki he said, "The fear-virus takes over people's immune system and they become sick with violence. Then they spread this virus all over the world and they don't know that wars break out because of them."

"But mankind was always like that, Robi, there were always wars, it's nothing new."

"Maybe someone with no fear should be found, to save the world from this virus."

***

Robert was fifteen when he conducted his research into the massacre in Novi Sad, and since then, he matured and stayed away from the obsessive preoccupation with that war, but one of the dozens of leaders and generals he had read about did not leave him, and surfaced in his thoughts all through the years, including the time he studied at the School of Medicine – Josip Broz Tito, also known as Marshal Tito.

Robert faithfully read all the news published about the Yugoslav leader and discussed him with Miki, who was not pleased about it. "Why Tito?" he protested, "OK, he is a decorated soldier, a partisan who fought the Nazis and a strong and much accomplished president, but there are other leaders like him, not less fighters, not less heroes, but less communist. Why him of all people?" Miki was troubled. Vera, his grandmother, did admire Tito and before the war was a communist, or may have only supported their ideology, and his aunt Ilona and uncle Aladar supported her views to his mother Kata's chagrin, but communism here, in America? "Robi," cried Miki with indignation,

"Tito does a good job in Yugoslavia, but he is a tyrant and a communist!"

"And he has no fear," answered Robert.

***

New York, 1963. Robert is twenty-five, short, thin and broad, his thick black curls are mussed, and a soft smile is spread over his face. He stands on campus in worn-out jeans thrust into high shoes with brown laces, with no socks. He does not wear an undershirt under his checkered red blue and white shirt which is missing buttons, and his black and dense chest hair pokes out of it.

A young female student approaches him, and they converse. I stand there to the side and observe them. The student smiles, touches her hair and wets her lips. He leans his head to the side and says something, she giggles and turns to go, and he follows her with his eyes. She turns her head and he nods to her, lights a cigarette and smokes in a limp posture. I tremble. I will go to him now and talk to him, and in the evening come to his room...

"Are you OK...?" Rafi speaks to me from the balcony and his voice tenor is strange, "Noa... you are confused, please take a break." What is with him? Perhaps he dreamt something while sleeping? Maybe he woke up on the wrong side? When Rafi wrangles with me about my writing, he is rude and readily reprimands me, but now he speaks in a hesitant tone. What troubles him? My other four Loves too, all awake already, sit tense and look at me with worried eyes, even Itamar's fawn eyes are wide open.

"What's with you? What's the problem?"

"You-got-carried-away," says Moosh the writer gravely, 'it-happened-to-me-one-time. It's-hard-to-get-out-of-it."

"What are you talking about?"

"It's-dangerous, when-we lose-the-distinction-between-the-story-and-real-life."

"I don't lose any distinction, Moosh."

Husband-Yossi gets up and comes to me decisively, as he used to do in our life when he thought that I overdid it in eating or writing. Now he looks to me somewhat ridiculous in his determination to save me from myself as it were.

"What's the problem, Yossi?"

He stands near me and his face is different. Something troubles him. "I beg you, consider this direction," he says, "for your own good, Noa."

This "for your own good" makes me start with fury, as it was in his life. "What do you want from me? You don't understand what I go through when I write! You are simply jealous!" He retreats to his armchair, "You don't listen to anyone, only to yourself."

"And you do? You are locked in your rage! Tell me, what are you so angry about that you gnash your teeth? All our life together you were like this. How did I irritate you? What did I do to you that such enormous rage accumulated inside you?"

Never in his life did I ask him this question.

"You did not irritate me. I was not angry at anything."

He denies. He was angry, I am sure he was angry... And maybe not? The dead do not lie. Maybe it was not anger but fear and I did not notice the difference? How could I not understand him... And what is it that scares him now? What am I doing anyway? Just writing about Robert.

Rafi enters from the balcony and approaches me heavily, "Noa, you are going to an interesting place, but dangerous. You are carried away, enough, take a break."

IT IS ONLY A STORY

I fell asleep and suddenly I woke. My crows couple cawed loudly. What is this, do they never sleep? Why do they scream in the middle of the night?

Later light of mid-day woke me, and I heard a helicopter with its ticking as it came near, passing and flying away in a hum. Immediately the city hummed to me too, with the honks and the rattles and the screeches and people voices on the sidewalk.

I stood on the balcony and early summer heat washed over me. I put on light clothes which I found on the high shelf in my closet, and when I looked at the mirror, I was seized by a strong yearning for Avry. I told myself that we had not met for an awfully long time and I called him, but he did not answer. I sent him a text message asking him to call.

***

I took Robert with me as I had left him on campus, with his mussed curls and his red white and blue checkered shirt with the missing buttons, and with his worn-out jeans, and together we descended in the elevator. He was so real, even though I knew he was entirely imagined.

"Let's go out, I want to introduce you to a poet I love."

"Is he also a physician?"

"No, he is only a poet."

Mid-day. The air is hot, but the shade of the large ficus trees cools it a little. Robert walks next to me, a bit shorter than me, he is the tourist and I am the local. I hope he notices the abundance of greenery around. The ornamental trees in the small yards are laden with yellow, pink and purple bloom, which falls on the sidewalk and pads it into a colourful carpet. The dense hedge hands us its hibiscus flowers.

We reach the wide Ibn Gabirol street, and the fact that Robert walks here for the first time excites me. The clear light of early summer rests on the big apartment buildings lining both sides of the street with their four-five balconied floors, and heavy heat begins to weigh down, but the tall palm trees with their thick trunks are indifferent to it. They rise in local pride from the long narrow concrete structure that divides the road into three lanes going north and three lanes going south, and all the lanes full of clattering crowded vehicles – cars, taxis and busses, accelerate and slow down. An ambulance weaves through them with its siren whining, approaches us, increases its hooting, and finally manages to pass and drives off. The air stands still, but the street flows back and forth, by car and by foot, and I say to Robert, "Don't let the noise bother you, if you listen carefully, you can hear that it's like a melody with a special beat." He smiles and looks around him. The heat rises.

The sidewalk is wide, people walk to and fro, and we walk slowly on the shaded side, under buildings' patios which are supported by columns, teaming cardo of stores, offices, cafés and snack bars. On our left, on the sun-struck part of the sidewalk, is the cycling path but many prefer to travel in the shaded part and ring insistently for us to move to the side. "They ride on this side even when it rains, not to get wet. You have to watch out," I say to Robert, "that's how it is in Tel Aviv."

Pails with bouquets of flowers, doormats and brooms, metal stands laden with newspapers, flat containers full of nuts and seeds, bicycles waiting to be repaired, small tables and chairs with people who wipe hummus with pita, shawarma smells, coffee, and bakery pastries spill out of shop entrances, sounds of laughter and voices, ringing of bicycle bells and cellphones fill the air. People lead dogs, stand at bus stops, young and old in summer clothes, slow elderly men and women, a young father carrying a child on his shoulders, a woman-girl pushes a pram, stops in front of a shop window, peeks in and continues.

Two labourers in stained work clothes cross our path. They walk behind each other, keep a certain distance between them and halt, block our way. Exactly between them, in front of us, a woman nears and stops. She seems to me a typical Tel Avivian, in her pink tulle shirt and wide pants of light cotton in grey and black toe sandal. Her abdomen protrudes a little through her shirt, her neck thick and her hair reaches her shoulders. She removes a clip from her bag, gathers her hair and looks about her like a bird preparing to fly. The labourers continue to walk behind each other holding a sizable mirror.

Robert and I cross the street at the foot of Century Tower.

Here, too, the sidewalk is half-lit, half-shaded. We stand in the lit part close to the road. Behind us cars move and in front of us people pass by. The building's façade is all display windows and glass doors, as in every mall, except that here, elongated glass panes are placed on the stretches of wall separating the stores' entrances, and on each of them a black and blue inscription is printed - a human silhouette with clean lines and sharp angles. Each pane displays a part of the body, here shoulders, there legs, here chest and there head. Twelve panes are affixed to the façade of the building and on them fragments of Shlomo Ibn Gabirol's silhouette, silent hints to the suffering youth who lived in Spain a thousand years ago and wrote poems in Hebrew. Segments of his poems are printed on the silhouettes in clean and quiet letters.

I hold Robert's hand which is very cold despite the heat.

"Come," I whisper to him, "meet the man for whom this street was named." We move to the shade zone and approach one of the poetry panes. "Here... look at this poem!" I raise my whisper in rapid breathing, "Amnon I am sick..." Robert looks at the pane then looks at me. "Do you get it?" I sweat, "One thousand years have passed, and it is as if Ibn Gabirol wrote it now, like a chat from one keyboard to another! As if he corresponds with the guy with dreadlocks, the one who sits all day with the computer at the café on the corner of Arlozorov and Ibn Gabirol."

We stand in the shade, but the hot air envelops me in sticky condensation. Robert is attentive, I pull him by his cold hand and go from one pane to the next, read the poems to him and almost choke, "here, 'See the sun...' You see? He cried when he wrote this poem, and he was so young at the time!" Robert asks, "Who did he write about?" I reply, "About the man who always cared for him..." He smiles, "his Miki."

Saved as a Painting

Light and shade blend. Heat tightens around me; Robert's cool hand is still in mine. Passersby do not pay attention to Ibn Gabirol's poetry panes, perhaps they think that these are advertisement billboards. Agi too, when she came for a visit from Northampton and I brought her here, said to me, "I passed by so many times and I never saw this." A wave of people on the sidewalk grows and it becomes crowded... ugh, Rafi my editor is coming. What do you want? Do not bother me now. You think I did not notice that you followed us?

"No-a, wait, you must be careful!"

I did not want to hear Rafi and he disappeared. My eyelids were heavy and Ibn Gabirol's poems became blurred. Robert drew his head to me, and I was aware of his cigarette smoke. His grey-black eyes were covered with that purple hue and he looked into my eyes. I shivered, "Robert, you are close to me, but I don't know who you are, I don't understand why I became attracted to your character and why I write about you..."

Suddenly I became dizzy and everything about me blacked out. I startled, leaned against Ibn Gabirol's glass pane, and when light returned Robert wasn't with me any longer. I said to myself, I better sit down before someone calls an ambulance and I will be taken to Ichilov Hospital. I entered the mall and sat at a small table in the café. People who were sitting there may have thought that I was an odd person who talked to herself, but Tel Aviv is full of them.

I was lost.

"It's only a story, Noa," Highschool-Sweetheart-Itamar's asthmatic voice sounded, "You better get out of it and back to reality." He talked to me from my living room, where he sat on the carpet. I had no energy to reply to him, I may have even fainted for a moment, and it is rather peculiar because I never faint. I ordered black coffee, sweetened it with lots of sugar and drank. Slowly I regained my spirit.

*　*　*

I walked out and suddenly my phone rang with Avry's name on the display. Surprise and excitement confounded me and I did not know how to speak to him except with that enhanced merriment which is necessary for me so as to ford the first moments of conversation with him. "Hello! Avry!!!" I called, so cheery that Century Tower shuddered above me.

"How are you?"

When he begins with that how-are-you, in such a reserved tone, it is an indication that he has an issue with me.

"I am fine, and you?"

"As usual."

Perhaps it was his live and real voice or maybe my yearning for him and maybe, really, as a couple, it was time to meet. It is true, we have an unusual together-arrangement, but we are still a couple. And if not a couple – what is he to me? And what am I to him?

I saw him in my mind's eye, with his honey eyes bounded by sad lashes, with his crooked eyebrows, pale cheeks painted with dark stubble, and three scars on his chest.

"I want you to come."

"When?"

"In an hour."

"The day after tomorrow is okay?"

"Okay," I confirmed, although I wanted him to come directly. I understood that he called me only because I sent him a message with a request to call, and it was clear to me that he had other relationships which may be better suited than me in this respect. Something in me clenched, but I shook it off quickly, it is only a story, in two days Avry will come to be with me, and that is the crux of it.

Next day I received an email from him, without mentioning my name and without a softening opening sentence. "The time doesn't work for me. Let's stay in touch."

{ 21 }

Nomadism

New York, 1963, A year before Robert's graduation from medical school. A weekend in Miki Steins' family home on 81st Street West, next to the park.

"Robi, come with me, I want to show you something," said Miki at the end of dinner and ran his fingers over his brush moustache. Robert tensed. Miki opened the door to the basement, turned on the light and descended the stairs. Robert followed him, and his tension intensified. The neon light flickered. "I should change it," Miki whispered as if someone was sleeping there. The basement chill clung to Robert and crawled up his back. When they reached the bottom, they stood under the flickering light and Miki said, "wait here." He moved away, was swallowed by the shadows, and a minute later returned holding an off-white bag which looked to Robert like a long sleeve.

"Edit brought this for me from Israel."

Robert remembered Edit and her parents, Ilona and Aladar. From the day he and his parents moved from Novi Sad to Budapest, his uncle and aunt were warm and welcoming to him.

He saw them in his mind's eye sitting with him at the dining table in their apartment on Klauzál Street. Aunt Ilona always made tasty dishes for him and was the only one to explain that his Oma Kata would not come back.

Miki pulled out of the bag a long cylinder and when he took off the beige cover Robert's breath caught for a moment, that is the portrait! Miki stood next to him, a head and a half taller, spread the cylinder, and held it at the top and the bottom, "Here she is," he whispered, "Look, Robi."

Robert's eyes lingered on his grandmother's face. In the flickering neon light, it seemed to him as if she blinked, and the memory of her warm embrace stirred him. Oma Kata, you are here. The bewilderment of her sudden disappearance hit him again, real and paralyzing as on that cold day, when he asked his father to take him to her house and he answered, "She is no longer there." Has she gone away? And when will she come back? Here she is and now she will embrace him, he will encircle her neck with his little arms and will thrust his nose to it, "Oma, you smell good!"

Robert inhaled, looked long at his grandmother sitting erect, and knew that she had the strength to sit like that for ever and ever, she would never fatigue. Here she is in the open blue velvet robe revealing the alabaster negligee with its lace in front. Her left hand rests on her lower abdomen and the right falling to the side, her wedding band on her middle finger. Her nails are clean. Morning light in its eternal flow is absorbed in her auburn hair. Her lips are applied with purple-pink and pressed together and her small smile dances at their edges. Her eyes are grey-black and the purple hue veils them. She looks to the side, but perchance will she turn her head to him and smile?

The dark-grey background colours transformed to green before his eye, and like in the past, looked like the door of a safe. He knew their every detail, since he stood every day in Aunt Ilona's house and stared at the portrait, until he went to America. He knew the safe's code since his childhood in Novi Sad, and he also knew that the entry was behind the chair his grandmother was seated on.

For a moment it seemed to him that she turns her head to him and smiles, and the next moment the safe door behind her opened. He entered a well-lit large room, like a gallery hall, and began to move among the images hanging crowded on its walls. Here is Vera standing in the snow, dressed in the grey coat which no longer closes over her big abdomen, and her Ferenc fondling it like a Gypsy lover. Here are Kata and Ilona striding with their mother on Dohány Street in Budapest and standing to look at her rich parents' house. Here they are in the National Salon gallery, and Vera holds the girls' arms, one on each side, and here is Kata standing at the counter in the tobacconist shop, arranging the violets in a vase, and László Steins gazing at her. The big house on Dunavska Street and the portrait which hangs over the piano. Kata writes a final letter to Ilona. Robert moves on from image to image and sees his own life as well, here he stands in the Strand between his mother and his father, and here he is by the frozen lake, I would not have gone in, Miki, but thank you for coming.

"I remember this portrait hanging in the house in Novi Sad," said Robert, and Miki stared at him in amazement, "You were four years old, Robi, how can you remember? Maybe you remember it hanging at Ilona's in Budapest."

"There and in Oma Kata's house too. In both houses above the piano."

Miki smiled to him as if he were his son, and returned to look at the portrait, "Oma Kata was a beautiful woman."

Purple pearls slid down Robert's cheeks.

"Yes, that's how it is..." sighed Miki, left the bottom of the painted canvas and enfolded Robert's shoulder. The portrait rolled into itself, and Miki covered it with the beige cloth and slid it into the sleeve bag. Later, when he laid it in the darkness on the shelf next to the old carpets, he heard Kata unspeaking to him from the strangled canvass. Miki felt a heaviness in his heart and ignored her silence, because what can he do with the silence of a dead mother? Mold stains had already stalked her, and Gábor Pahl's oil paints had already begun to crack.

At night, in his room in the students' dormitories, Robert dreamt that he is sitting on Kata's knees in the living room in her big house on Dunavska Street. She cuddles him, her embrace warm and her whisper caressing. The portrait on the wall is illuminated through the sheer curtains and Robert sees his grandmother twice, sitting in the painting and sitting with him. She puts her lips to his forehead and her embrace is so pleasant that he hummed in his sleep.

Suddenly he woke up, turned on the light and saw that his pillow was wet. I must get out of here, he said to himself. I need to travel.

A week later he quit Medical School.

Miki was not surprised. He was quiet for a moment and said practically, "Maybe you will return and finish your studies later. And what will you do now?"

"I am going to Novi Sad."

Agi said, "He could enter Yugoslavia with his American passport. Exactly then Marshal Tito opened the borders a fraction for trade with the west." I nodded to her, eager to return to Robert, but she added knowingly, "at that time everyone in Yugoslavia was poor, but everyone had a job, and everyone had a place to live, even if the apartment was tiny. There were no differences like today, everyone got education and social insurance and health insurance.

"Yes, Tito took care of them, he was everybody's Great Father."

Agi gave me a reproachful look and for a minute it seemed to me she was her great-grandmother Vera, "He took care of his people!"

"Oh, Agi, really... it is well known that it was very sad there, even if everyone had social insurance."

"If you knew the poverty of the third world up close, you would not have said that it was sad in Yugoslavia in the sixties. It was OK there." I said nothing and Agi added, "Noa, some poverty is worse than death!"

***

In mid-summer of 1963 Robert sailed from New York to Europe. Agi said that he was afraid of flying, and he always went by ships, trains and buses.

"What is the reason for your visit in Yugoslavia?" the border police asked him with suspicion as he leafed through his passport back and forth. "I was born here," replied Robert in his soft smile. The police saw a strange man before him and let him go. In fact, they sent someone to "keep an eye on the American", but it was a matter of routine.

*** *

In Novi Sad, Marshal Tito's image dominated everything, in statues, reliefs, on stamps and on signs, with his pictures displayed at the entrance of every public building, and his photos in the first section of the newspapers, which sang the undisputed leader's praises. Robert looked longingly at the image of his fearless leader and hoped to be able to see him even if only once.

He walked in the city centre, alien to himself in his early childhood regions, and indifferent to the architectural grandeur of the opulent buildings of the eighteenth and nineteenth centuries. He did not experience any excitement, no clenching in his gut. When he passed by his grandmother's house on Dunavska street, he glanced at it, did not slow down and did not stop. When he drifted by the pond in the Danube Park with large stones surrounding it, he did not pause to gaze at the water lilies and the goldfish. And at the Strand he walked among the bathers who sunbathed on the sand, stood at the water edge to look at the white swans floating on the water, and after a few minutes moved his backpack from one shoulder to the other and walked away.

Most of the people around him spoke Serbo-Croatian, a language he understood and even spoke a little. His family spoke

Hungarian, but quite often they spoke Serbian too, particularly his mother, when she was angry at his father and scolded him.

Robert climbed the tram and travelled from the centre to the distant workers' districts, which were erected at the edges after the war. He walked down the long streets, among long lines of apartment buildings, each with ten or fifteen floors, narrow entrances, small windows with roller shutters, small verandas with faded railings and heavily loaded laundry lines, small yards full of weeds, sad aridity. No cornices, no reliefs, no corners decorated with statues of figures from the past, only downtrodden and silent dullness. This too is "Serb Athens."

He rented a room in a cheap small hotel, and on the following day took a bus to his mother Julia's childhood neighbourhood. Miki mentioned to him once the neighbourhood in which his other grandparents lived. Robert did not remember meeting them, and Miki told him they had perished in Auschwitz. Old small dwellings stood on both sides of the street, sunken in the ground, patched with improvised add-ons, with plaster peeling from the walls and crooked asbestos roofs. Small vegetable gardens peered between them and large fruit trees leaned their branches over the rooftops. The pavement was cracked, and the threshold stones were broken. Children in summer clothes played with a ball in the street and laughed. Robert smiled at them.

A seven-year-old boy ran toward him, tried to catch the ball, slid and fell on the broken sidewalk pavement. He injured his knee and he sat down and moaned, holding his legs with both hands, looking at the wound which began to bleed. Robert knelt next to him, put his hand on his arm and said, "It hurts..."

The boy looked at him in surprise. Robert said, "Let me look, OK?" He pulled a first-aid kit out of his backpack, cleaned the wound gently, put an ointment on it and dressed it.

A woman of about fifty years, possibly the boy's grandmother, approached in quick steps, and stood over Robert, her hands on her hips and her face scowling, "What do you want with the child?" Robert stood and backed away, "Sorry, Madam, he fell and was hurt." The woman looked at the boy's dressed knee, looked back at Robert and her face softened, "Is sir a doctor?" He raised his shoulders, "Half a doctor. Remove the dressing in the evening." She smiled and invited him to eat potato soup.

"Thank you, Madam, it was good."

"It is too hot for soup today, but the boy likes it when I make potato soup for him in the summer too."

"On hot days do you go to swim in the Danube?"

"No. There is a swimming pool here, we go to the pool."

"You don't swim in the Danube?"

"You see... ever since what happened in the Strand, neither I nor my husband and none of our friends, we don't go into the water and we don't eat the fish. It's a bad river."

***

Robert hung around the workers' district in Novi Sad for ten days. At night he slept in his cheap and dirty hotel, which housed mostly prostitutes, and in the morning, he drank black coffee in the small kiosk next to the hotel. The kiosk owner never looked directly at him but saved him the Hungarian daily newspaper. Robert paid for it, sat on a narrow cement barrier and read it for a long time. When he was done, he folded it, returned it to the kiosk owner and left. His expenses were few. He bought cigarettes and some food, and at times he settled for fruits only. His dress was unkempt, his shoes scuffed, and his growing hair gathered under a grey cloth cap with a small warped visor. The locals sensed that he was a foreigner, maybe because of his American jeans, or in the acuity they developed to identify foreigners. No one spoke to him and no one bothered him, as if he were transparent.

One day he walked in a large shopping mall, a grey and indignant concrete mass in the workers' district and sat on a faded bench next to a man of about sixty. Despite the heat the man wore a thick shirt and a winter jacket buttoned to his chin. He sat leaning forward and stared ahead, his cheeks were covered with stubble and his breathing was rapid. Robert asked, "How are you, sir?" The man looked at him with a wet gaze, 'today not so good. I went to work this morning, but I didn't stay."

"Where do you work?"

"Here, in the grocery store, in the meat refrigerator."

"May I put my hand on your forehead?"

"Go ahead... what, are you a doctor? I am going to die anyway."

"Everyone dies in the end, but until then one can feel a little better. You have high fever."

"So I have a fever. What difference does it make?"

Robert pulled out of his backpack pills for lowering fever and said, "Will you give me your hand for a moment?" The man stretched his open hand. Robert put in it one pill and said to him, "Swallow it now." The man stared at him, "What, are you a doctor?" He ambled to a rusty fountain nearby, found a tap with a trickle of water and drank from his hand. When he returned to his seat Robert told him, "here are another two, for tomorrow and the following day. Now go to sleep. Sleep a lot and tomorrow you will feel better." The man opened his mouth to ask, but Robert was already on his feet and left with his shoulders swaying a little, like in a dance.

Thus, wherever he got to in the workers' quarter, he found sick or injured people, people who became dizzy suddenly and collapsed and people who sprawled on street benches. His eyes found them, especially the children, and he approached them, put his hand on their forehead, checked their pulse and calmed them with his low dense voice. He gave them American medications for lowering fever and reducing pain, sugar cubes or chocolate cubes, and departed before they were able to ask who he was.

One night he was awakened in his small bedchamber by a woman's moans and cries over the wall. He could not get back to sleep and went out to the darkened corridor, stood next to the adjacent door and listened. When the moans increased, he opened it a fraction, peeked in and entered. By the light of a small bulb dangling dejectedly from the ceiling he saw a young women lying in bed giving birth.

He approached her, "Don't worry, it will be fine," caressed her forehead and delivered the baby. "You have a beautiful daughter," he said, and rested the crying little creature wrapped in a towel in her arms, "Now drink, your strength will return soon." He supported her neck with his hand, lifted her head a little and let her drink from a plastic cup. Later he brought from his room a cup of tea and several chocolate cubes, "for the morning." The exhausted young woman whispered with her eyes shut, "Are you a physician? Who called you? Do I have to pay?" But Robert was out of the room already.

***

On the following day he travelled by train to Belgrade. Here too he wandered among the workers' districts, but several days later returned to the fancy city centre and followed from afar a group of photographers waiting for President Tito. Robert glimpsed him several times, leaving his car, stopping to talk to someone before entering a building, waving to his admirers, and at times waving again at the photographers' behest. Robert's heart was beating fast, it's him! It's really him!

From Belgrade, Robert travelled to Zagreb, but did not explore the sights of that beautiful city either. Instead, he went directly to the international fair which opened there, because the newspaper informed him that the president would arrive to give a speech. Robert walked amid the river of people which flowed into the fair, stood among the crowded throng far from the stage, and neither saw nor heard any of the speeches. He was disappointed and wondered if ever he was going to see and hear his hero in close proximity and turned away to walk slowly on the path winding among the fair's pavilions. Billboards invited the visitors to enter, but he walked distractedly, smoking and inwardly-absorbed, until he heard some English speakers and halted, as if finding old acquaintances from his campus.

They were American businessmen of Croat origins. They exhibited sophisticated agricultural equipment in the American pavilion and walked about in their suits like roosters who brought the Gospel. Their English was American in every respect when speaking to each other except for remnants of a foreign accent, but with the locals they spoke fluent Serbo-Croatian. Robert stood next to a brochure stand, leaned on the pavilion wall which carried the United States flag and shoved his hands into his pockets. Nobody said anything to him. The Americans did not pay attention to him or perhaps ignored him on purpose, and maybe like the locals they thought he was an American, one of them.

Several minutes later a large group of men came down the path, among them a few muscular men who looked every which way. At the centre of the group walked in a vigorous stride a short and bespectacled man, shoved into a brown suit, his grey hair combed back stylishly, like a Tito doll in a museum display.

He looked about him in satisfaction, stopped for the photographers, who immediately kneeled on the ground and snapped him, and continued walking. He stopped next to the Americans' pavilion, and the entourage quickly arranged itself around and behind him. He examined the brochure stand and turned in a heavily accented English to the American young man who stood next to Robert, "Where are you from?" The American jumped to attention and answered in Serbo-Croatian, "I am from New York, sir." The marshal raised a wry smile, "Good, good," and turned to look at Robert. His nomadic attire raised the bodyguards' suspicion, the President noticed it but ignored them and turned to Robert in English, "And where are you from?"

Tito was half a head taller than him and his sharp gaze through the glasses focused between his brows with a compelling firmness. All the thoughts Robert had had about him over the years, and all his ideas about the fearless man drained into his soul at that moment. His hero stood before him: high forehead, large and fair, that controls the whole face, glasses in a thick and dark frame, big cheeks, full lips and a decisive chin. Deep, measured breathing, erect stance with hands clenched behind, a domineering belly, passionate command and exploding crispness despite his seventy-one years. Yes, he is a slab of iron that nothing can break, not freezing cold and not hunger, not bullets whistling by, not explosions of shells and not cries of the wounded, not imprisonment and not beatings, not threats and not insults. He does not carry the fear-virus. He would have found a way to gain control over the gendarmes at the Strand.

"New York, sir," answered Robert in the same language, smiled and held out his hand. Tito shook it in a long and powerful handshake, and made a small bow, as if Robert was the United States Ambassador.

The Yugoslav leader's hand was sweaty. Robert was surprised and looked in his eyes. A broken smile painted itself for a moment on the President's lips and he turned to continue with his entourage. Robert looked after him and lit a cigarette.

From Zagreb he went to Budapest, walked about for several days and passed in front of the apartment building on Klauzál Street. The green wooden door decorated with carving of winding branches was closed. Robert glanced at it for a moment but did not stop. Then he traveled to Vienna and from there sent Miki a scenic postcard in which he asked for money, detailed the names of cities he visited and ended with a note, "It is over with Tito, Uncle."

***

Miki sent him cash in a warm letter of fatherly concern, with advice and family updates, and at the end a question, "When are you coming back?" Robert shoved the bills into his pocket, entered a pharmacy and refilled the medications and first aid supply in his backpack, bought several cigarette packages, a salami sandwich and a bottle of orange juice, and sat to eat on a bench in a clean and blooming park, in which the good smell of careful watering hovered in the air. If I were able, I would have told him, look how pretty! That is how it is with the Austrians; everything is tidy and cared for to the last leaf. But Robert was never impressed with such things.

On the grass before him a young woman lay with closed eyes, her head on a large bag, and exposed her legs to the sun. Robert finished eating, smoked and peered at her, and when she sat up, she met his gaze. He smiled at her and she got up and seated herself next to him.

They spoke in English. He told her a little about his tour and explained it as the grand-tour of a bourgeois student from New York. She told him that she studied music, held out her hand and gave her name. He told her his name and did not let go of her hand. She invited him to her student's room, and they did not leave it for three days. Robert was sure that his journey brought him to seventh heaven. "I love you," he said feelingly and looked into her face. "Stay with me, Robert," she said to him with wet eyes, but he felt the need to move on, took leave and immediately forgot her name.

Everywhere he stopped he found women who were drawn to him in spite of his strange and neglected air. Women fell in love with him and asked him to stay with them and he, too, fell in love with them and stayed for three days in seventh heaven's stops, but on the fourth day he always went on his way. Never did he ask any of them to stay with him and always forgot their names.

He hitch-hiked all over Western Europe, made his way to big cities like Paris and Rome and to medieval small towns that only ardent tourists, students and historians get to, those who later tell with pride about their travels, show videos and presentations and write academic reports about the architecture and the art they saw. Robert did not search for either Renaissance or modern art in Europe. Cathedrals and castles did not interest him, neither did museums, galleries or concert halls. In every place he went to the underprivileged neighbourhoods and looked for injured street children on broken pavements, prostitutes giving birth alone in filthy hotels, disabled people whose crutches broke and all the other wretched creatures. He relieved their misery for an hour with medications to reduce their fever and pain or with chocolate cubes, disinfected their wounds and dressed them. The afflicted never ended, only changed.

I have no idea if he was harassed by any lowlifes or if they tried to harm him in any way on his travels, I assume that he did meet with violence in the slums, but his neglected look and his preoccupied expression probably did not draw fire. He was not part of a group and did not have friends, he was alone. People noticed him only when he appeared suddenly like an angel of mercy. And when he disappeared, they did not search for him.

Miki sent him money, a little every time, Robert did not ask for much. At times he stayed in one place for several months, worked in restaurants, washed dishes and cleared garbage, saved some money and continued drifting. Sometimes he went into public libraries, found books in English, sometimes in Hungarian as well, medical journals, American newspapers. He sat and read day after day until he was sated. For weeks, months and years he traveled in circles and wandered in regions of squalor and the stench of dead-end. I would not have been able to tolerate the ugliness, but he tolerated it and yearned for it.

After three or four years he went to Africa, a leper continent, devouring its inhabitants. He did not need any certificates to volunteer in the makeshift hospitals. He was an American who studied medicine in Columbia University, and even if he did not complete his studies, he was good enough for them. Sometimes he joined the Red Cross, donned the white coat, but always claimed he was a nurse.

Hungry and diseased war refugees found him. Hundreds of thousands needed treatment but only a few hundreds were lucky to receive it. His frustration was intense. What to do? They die here in masses! He ate little and smoked much, washed when he could find a shower, shaved when he could find a razor, and did not get a haircut only tied his black curls at the back. At the makeshift dental clinic in the hospital where he volunteers, a dentist pulled two wisdom teeth that rotted. Agi said that as far as she knew, since then he never needed to see a dentist.

When Robert found English newspapers, he read them without skipping any item or any article. He did not have any special interest in Israel, but when he read that a war was raging in that part of the world, something inside him moved, like a spark of concern. He knew that Ilona and Aladar lived there as well as Edit, her husband and their children, a distant family, blood relations, and followed the news. After six days he read about Israel's grand victory but did not feel relief.

***

What kind of a grand tour did you plan for yourself? What the hell were you looking for?

He wandered outside the United States for seven years. Every two or three months, he sent a postcard to Miki to update him on his location and to ask for his financial support. Miki kept his cards in a small wooden box, sent him money and was the source of information about his adventures, although even Miki did not always know where Robert ended up in his wanderings. Agi said that there were stories in the family that he reached India and the wars on the border of Kashmir in his travels. "Some thought that he joined the fighters," Agi said to me, "but fighting didn't suit him. He probably only treated the wounded."

Robert never fought and never held a gun, but in one of the clinics where he volunteered someone gave him a khaki fatigue coat. He put it on, and since then the nickname "the fighting physician" stuck.

Saved as a Painting

***

In 1970, when Robert was thirty-two, he came for a visit in Israel. I saw him in a coloured photograph from that visit, standing with Caesarea's antiquities behind him, on his head a "tembel" hat with the word "shalom" written on it, and his black curls reaching his shoulders. His lips full, cheekbones high, and his expression sad.

Agi said, "My grandparents were extremely excited when he came. They raised him as their grandson for four years in Budapest, you know. But he was strange."

"What was strange about him?"

"He had an odd smile, but especially something in the eyes. His gaze."

"And how did he smell?"

"Noa! I don't know how... mmm... his clothes were like rags, my grandmother bought him new clothes. And he constantly scratched his head."

"How did he look in general?"

"Nice, harmless. He had a sense of humour and knew how to tell stories well, even though he was silent for long stretches. Suddenly he would open his mouth and tell an interesting story."

"Did you like him?"

"I don't know, I think that more than that I felt sorry for him, but my grandmother really loved him."

***

Two years after Robert's visit Aladar woke up one day and found that Ilona died in her sleep. "Maybe from cardiac arrest...

she was almost eighty," Agi said distantly, jealously guarding the privacy of her feelings, "and it broke my grandfather. He got sick and a year later died. We buried him next to her."

***

Robert sailed from Israel back to the United States, where he began to travel from place to place and from state to state. In Chicago he made a lengthy pause and took a paramedics course. After that, at any place he came to he presented himself in ambulance and firefighters' stations and volunteered, ate in small kitchens and slept with the people on duty. Each day he went out with the teams to treat the suddenly ill, car accidents injured and victims of murder attacks, brawls victims, rape victims, fire and avalanche survivors, drowning survivors, freezing survivors and women giving birth. When unintentionally he diagnosed and decided like a physician, the paramedics began to call him "Doctor", and so he left and traveled to another place.

"At times he came to New York to meet Miki," Agi told me, "He used to go to his office, not the house, and after he left, he sent postcards from different places, mostly when he was stuck penniless. And Miki, of course, sent him money."

Robert's hair faded and thinned, a bald spot became wider on top and his teeth yellowed, but his smile remained as it was and drew to him the women whose names he never remembered.

"Robert did not settle down anywhere; he did not get married and had no family."

"I think I want to meet him, Agi."

{ 22 }

Last Will

New York, 1988. Sixty-nine year old Miki Steins lies in his home on his deathbed. Klari, Jessica and Jonathan are at his bedside. Jonathan came from his office downtown, where he manages the family business of a chain of houseware stores, and Jessica arrived from the capital, Washington, where she lives with her husband and two children and works in a bank as an Investment Consultant. The family lawyer stands to the side.

Klari leans into Miki and whispers in Hungarian, "Shall we begin?" He nods weakly. At Miki's request, the family lawyer reads the will aloud, so that they hear it together while he is still alive. "We didn't forget anything?" he asks in a cracked voice. "Everything is in there, Dad," says Jonathan dispassionately and looks at his sister. Jessica gets up, "Everything is fine, Dad, everything is allocated as we decided." Miki looks at her and she seems to him tall and blurry. She resembles my mother, he thinks, but she doesn't want to know it. Never mind... He tries to lift himself on his elbows but gives up. Klari caresses his forehead and stifles her sobs into a handkerchief, "Did you remember something else, Miki?"

The man, wrinkled from sickness, without any trace of the handsome youth he was, closes his eyes and sees himself at eighteen, standing in his parents' living room in Novi Sad. It is afternoon and bright light floods the room through the sheer curtains. Miki remembers that light and the silence. His father, László, stands next to him wearing a black housecoat fastened with golden buttons. One hand grasps the chair's backrest tightly and the other is shoved into the housecoat's pocket. Miki moves his gaze to his mother Kata, who stands behind the chair, her elbows tight by her waist and her hands balled into each other. His brother Sandor stands away from her, thin and furious and with his folded arms pressed to his chest. They stare at the messenger from Budapest who pulls the framed portrait from the cloth wraps and leans it on the wall. Then his father László sees the messenger to the door and returns to grasp the chair's backrest tightly.

Silence in the room. The four of them stare at the portrait, as if it were a live creature that entered their house unexpectedly. Suddenly Miki hears his father breathe heavily and give a peculiar moan. He looks at him and sees clear tears trickle rapidly from his eyes, chasing each other on his cheeks and slide to his chin, hang there and fall on the black housecoat.

Miki opens his eyes, sees Klari, Jessica and Jonathan and says to himself, they will throw the portrait to the garbage. With an effort he raises his voice, "Give my mother's portrait to Robert, you hear, but don't give him lots of money, he has holes in his hands... give him a little every time, for food. Jessica,

I left money for him with you, make sure he does not starve to death... promise me."

***

After the funeral Jessica found in her father's little wooden box a colourful postcard sent by Robert from Los Angeles and said to Jonathan, "There's a phone number here, call him and inform him about Dad." Jonathan, obedient and efficient, called and was answered by a man from a mobile home park, who spoke in a Hungarian or Romanian accent, "yes, sir, Robert I know. No every day here."

Robert was fifty when Miki died, the only man in the world close to his heart. After he received the message, he sat on a torn armchair next to one of the mobile homes and looked at the sunset which coloured the horizon red. He sat awake all night, and in the morning went out to the highway. He hitch-hiked in eighteen-wheelers from west to east, crossed the continent and arrived in New York. He stood at the entrance of the Steins family home on the 81st street West, next to the park, after many years of absence, and rang the bell. Klari opened and did not recognize him. He smiled and said in Hungarian, "I am old already and bald, but it is still me, Robert."

***

"And then, Agi? Did she hand him the portrait?"
"Yes, she handed it to him, but later there was a problem."
"What happened?"
"After several years he sent a letter to Jessica."
"What did he write?"

"That if she doesn't send him one hundred dollars, he will burn it."

"Really?"

"Yes..."

"And what did she do?"

"She and Jonathan sent him an envelope with matches."

"Really?"

"Yes."

"And did Robert burn the portrait?"

"I don't know. End of story."

***

What is she telling me? End of Story? But the story cannot end like this. She is killing him. How come it is not important for her to know what happened next?! "Agi, are you getting it?" I almost yelled, "Robert threatened to burn Kata and you do not know if he burnt her or not!?" I breathed fast. Agi looked at me curiously. I did not comprehend her expression. I did not know how to speak to her. What is she thinking? This is horrible! The twins collaborated with Robert's criminal threat! And she too, she collaborated when she did not bother to learn what happened to the portrait. She has known the story for years, and it never occurred to her to check. What a family! Only money interests them, real estate, clothes, social standing. What happened to Vera and Ferenc's love gene? And what the hell made Robert send such a threat? And Agi does not care.

We sat facing each other at the dining nook in her house, avoiding each other's eyes. I breathed turbid air, a dirty screen unfolded before my eyes and Agi looked blurry. I went out onto the wooden deck, stood there with folded arms and burning cheeks, and I felt as though my world halted.

Some minutes passed, I did not know how many, and Agi came out. She put her hand on my arm and asked, "Shall we have coffee?" Her voice was pleasant and her touch – calming. I entered the kitchen with her, and she turned on the radio. Violin notes scattered around me and purified the air.

I stood and looked at her as she filled two cups with coffee and placed them in saucers on the table, took out milk and poured a drop into my cup, the right amount, returned the milk to the refrigerator and cast a look at me. Her grey black eyes, veiled in purple hue, gazed at me like Kata, and her full lips smiled at me like Ilona. "Let's sit down," she said.

I sat down and sipped my coffee.

What is going to happen? I wondered. How will I get to the end of the story? My fingerprints merged with those of Kata... What do I do next? Why did Robert send that letter to Jessica? I do not believe that he burnt... I must find the portrait, find Kata who survived in it, who was not pierced by bullets and was not thrown into the Danube, Kata who was left by Gábor Pahl here, with us.

"Agi," I said in an equanimity that surprised me, "we must complete the story. Let's arrange a meeting with Robert. Where does he live?"

"As far as I know, he lives in New York," she said. "After Miki died Robert stopped those travels all over the US and returned to live in his apartment in Boro Park."

"Can you find out his address for us?"

"Yes, I will send an e-mail to Jonathan... and I will try to find out what happened to the portrait, don't worry, Noa."

***

I tired of writing and got up from the computer. Summer assaulted Tel Aviv, and the air-conditioner wrestled with it with exhalations of cold air. I stood staring into space, and my five Deceased Loves looked at me. "Enough," I said to them, "stop pressuring me with those stares, I am too tired to write."

I opened the balcony window, and the city hummed to me from the heat wave as if asking where I have disappeared to. On both sides of the street stood apartment blocks, balcony after balcony, and to their south and west, more and more buildings crowded together with their yellow-white walls, lighted and shaded, hiding one another and appearing between one and another, with flat roofs laden with sun-heated water tanks, and with the green treetops between them. The rectangular, the triangular and the cylindrical structures of the Azrieli Towers glittered in the distance in silver-blue. From among them rose the skyscraper of the Diamond Exchange complex and stood in the solitude of one of a kind, a king from a future world. Next to it stood his neighbours, shorter but still towering, architectural backdrops of an urban play. If I were a crow I would have taken off and flown there, but who can go out in such heat. I closed the window.

Enough, I need a break. Maybe go away for a while, to breathe a different air which does not carry the smell my story, or search for a normal partner and quit the chronic aloneness... And maybe find a nice job here in the city, get up every morning and dress like Agi, button up like Agi, and like her, braid a

Chinese plait and wear hats from exclusive stores. If I were Agi, I would not have been attracted to Robert. Yes, he is her second cousin and they carry common genes, but she does not feel anything for him. If I were Agi, I would have distanced myself from Robert, and then it would have been easier for me to write him and get to the end of the story.

"It-is-not-accurate..." says to me Moosh the writer, my childhood love, and his voice is squished. His back is bent in a cross-legged position on the carpet, and his oval face sinks to his chest. "Moosh, what's with you? Can dead people get sick too?" He shakes his head, "I-simply-begin-to-fade-away."

"No, Moosh, you can't leave before I write the last chapters about Robert!"

Editor-Rafi gets up from the couch, stretches his full body, his glasses shiny on his nose. He paces the room, stops and watches me, "Perhaps you should give up the last chapters."

"No way."

"Understand No-a," he says in a forced affability, and a bad tone is blended in his voice, "the last chapters about Robert are superfluous. You don't have to deal with that material. Simply skip to the end, write about the trip you took with Agi to New York and finish the story."

"But I cannot skip such important material!"

"Listen, in order to work on these chapters you need cojones. You need guts to tell, but you haven't got it..."

How dare he say such a thing to me?!

Rafi smiles his on-off smile and gestures with his hand a movement of what-did-I-possibly-say.

"Don't get started, Rafi! Once you sent me to learn from a well-known writer how to shape a character and you must remember the fight we had! I don't want to write like him, do you hear me? I don't want to write like anyone, and I don't care if I have it or not!"

***

I opened my eyes and saw that it was daylight outside. Did I sit at my desk all night? I prepared coffee and opened the windows. I was beyond tired. The bad taste of my argument with Rafi was almost completely gone, only a few bitter traces were left in my mouth. Not so terrible. We had arguments in the past too, that is how he is with me and I with him.

My crow stood silent on the cypress branch. Where is your mate? She turned her little head to me, turned it right and left in her black collar, and looked at me in some bird knowledge, as though she understood something I did not.

Part Three

Purple Pearls

{ 23 }

Thick Darkness

Boro Park, Brooklyn, 1995, winter. White snowflakes whorl before the grey buildings standing in the background, fall slowly and pile up on the sidewalks and fences, naked tree-branches and roofs. Robert is fifty-seven. After Miki's death he returned to live in the apartment he had inherited from his parents and joined the rescue forces of ambulances and firefighters in Boro Park, but it has been over a year since he last went there. He sits in his apartment in the dark, drinks beer and smokes. A hush around him and a hush inside him. His face is tormented. His large bald spot is surrounded by a thin long grey band of hair, gathered at the back and braided into a plait as thin as a shoelace. He wears heavy jeans that were not washed in years, an old woolen shirt buttoned to his chin with a zipped fleece over it. His feet which are in two pairs of socks bore into an old woolen blanket on the floor.

The room has not changed since his parents, Sandor and Julia, lived in it. A double bed, an old mattress with a dip and on it a crumpled sheet, a bare blanket piled in a heap and two big pillows, crushed, full of yellow-brown stains. Next to a sizable armoire across the room, under the window, a small turned-off television stands on the floor. Next to it rests an old telephone, unplugged, and next to the wall four tiers of books in English and Hungarian lay on each other in a row.

Near the entrance against the wall stands a small dining table and three chairs around it covered with piles of clothes. Several newspapers are strewn on the table, four books next to them, a spiral notebook on which stood an empty soup bowl with a spoon, and a glass with hardened coffee grains next to it. Murky daylight slides in through the window and merges with the darkness. The room is cold.

Had Robert not had this apartment, he would have been homeless perhaps, and would have slept in the grime of subway stations. In my eyes his apartment is his castle, a safe corner from which he cannot be banished, but he sees in it a mere stop. He has no bank account, no credit cards and no cheque book. Every month Jessica sends him an envelope with some cash from Washington, DC. The envelopes arrive by mail with the money, without a letter, without a note, without half a note.

I am shocked by the loneliness, the cold and the darkness in which he sits. Why did he get to such a state? If I were to ask Agi how it happened, she would most likely evade the answer in order not to be drawn into this burrow with me. She would have likely said that it happens to some people, and that he has always been a "poor thing".

How did you sink so low, Robert? How come all the ills of the world devoured you? You were trapped in a cold and dark reality, why did you not flee? Why did you not raise a family?

Why did you not complete medical school? You could have been a successful physician and lived comfortably!

But comfort did not interest him, I know. He is so lonely... Women are still attracted to him, but those relationships always end. Several years earlier, when he first moved back to Boro Park, he had an orthodox friend, an older woman, willowy, married with no children. The first time she saw him naked, she stared at his member and said in surprise, "But they say that you are a Goy!" Robert observed himself and smiled at her, "You will never be able to set them right."

Under her brown wig she had short light curls, and under her many layers of clothes she wore sheer lace underwear. According to her, she never laughed, neither at home nor anywhere else, and as for her husband, she sighed, "him, he does not have much desire, even though he is younger than me." Every time before she arrived Robert prepared a stock of amusing stories from the paper, and in bed he attempted to innovate and surprise her, although it became not as simple over time. One day she arrived, stood at the door and told him in a tearful voice, "I shan't return, please do not look for me..."

Time passed in silence. A day, then another.

One evening he went out for a drink and strode down long streets with apartment blocks closing in on them from both sides like walls, crowded together with small windows, dark entrances and shut balconies. Garbage containers fermented odours of rot and rats scurried among them. Streetlights stood along the pavement, some of them dark, cars drove by and traffic lights changed their colours. Robert kept walking until he reached a pub and entered.

A woman sat by the bar drinking beer. A colourful woolen wrap covered her shoulders, and on it rested a thick braid, long and white. Robert lowered himself on an empty seat next to her, drank and peered at her. She peered at him and he told himself that he had never seen such blue eyes. A sad lonesomeness rose from her and touched him. He stood and without introducing himself simply said to her, "Come."

They went all the way to his apartment in a quick pace, panting and not a word passing between them. Every so often she stole a glance at him, and he stole a glance at her and when their eyes met, they smiled.

Being with her felt good. She was amiable and fragrant and for a long time later they still lay in an embrace, until she sat in bed and considered him in the weak light emanating from a pyramid lamp on the nightstand. Her braid unraveled, and Robert gathered a lock of white hair in his hand, swung it like a horse's tail and asked the woman her name. She replied and at the same moment Robert forgot it. "It was good," he said to her, turned and fell asleep.

He did not know that the woman slept with him, and in the morning, when he awoke to the smell of coffee, she stood over him dressed and her hair gathered. Her colourful scarf was wrapped around her neck and her black coat rested on her shoulders. She looked at him as though examining if he were awake, and her eyes were so blue that Robert thought he was dreaming. Her face was full of small lines and he could not guess her age. "I made coffee," she smiled, "let's drink it together."

"Together?"

"Yes."

"What's together?"

"What happened here in bed last night is together."

"If you want another together, we can."

Three days they sailed from together to together. Among the woman's tiny wrinkles Robert found treasures of ivory skin, he saw her forehead which peeked at him through her white hair when she licked his body like a cat who found cream, heard her pleasure moans and was drawn into her smile. He was in seventh heaven, surprised and thrilled, and said to her, "I love you!" But when he saw her blue eyes widen and her forgiving smile, he mocked himself, this is the only song I know how to sing, and I am always off-key.

In the morning of the fourth day they drank coffee and chewed on some crackers the woman found in a cupboard. Robert said, "Now I want to read." She was still for a moment then said, "Fine, I will clear the mess here."

He sat next to the small dining table and slowly drank the black coffee, lit a cigarette and delved into the free newspaper he had brought from the grocery store four days earlier. The woman behind him buzzed to herself like a working-bee, entered the kitchen, and he heard the water running in the sink, the glasses and spoons rinsed and set aside, heard the rustle of compressed paper bags.

The woman hummed to herself and entered the room, opened the windows, changed the beddings on the bed with clean ones she found in the closet. "What a lovely embroidery," she said in a melodic voice, "where are the beddings from?" Robert answered without lifting his head, "from the market in

Budapest." She piled the dirty clothes in a corner, added stained hand towels to them and proceeded to clean the shower and the toilet. She laboured there for a long time and then approached Robert in soft steps, put her hand on the back of his neck and her fingers toyed with his shoelace-plait.

"What?"

She kissed his bald head, "May I go into the second room?"

Robert pulled his shoulder, "Go ahead."

It was his childhood room, from the time his parents still hoped to create a home in America. The woman opened the door, entered the room and did not utter a word, not even a sigh, when the stench hit her. The small window was shut and the little light that penetrated through it was lost among the naked walls.

On the floor there were heaps of old newspapers and among them were scattered empty bottles and crushed beer cans, tattered travel bags, a comb with broken teeth, old shoes and inside-out socks which looked like they were made out of plaster, a grey cloth hat with a warped visor, crushed and filthy, and a stained "tembel" hat with the word "shalom" in Hebrew, which she could not read. Old books were piled amid torn shirts, men's underwear with holes in them, used condoms, a mesh bag with shrunken lemons covered with mold, empty sardine cans, dry orange peels and a rotten apple with little worms writhing in its crumbling flesh.

The stench was dreadful, but the woman with the blue eyes and the white braid opened the window and commenced cleaning. She went down and up the stairs back and forth and filled the garbage container in the street, emptied the room of the filth and washed the linoleum floor.

I would have done the same had I met Robert in a pub and slept with him till morning. She fell in love with him like many other women who were with him, and whose heart he broke. Ugh, like Avry, who is in fact neat, clean and well kempt, but they are both messed up, stuck in their connected-separated, chronic loners who are not capable of any together.

The woman finished cleaning, stood next to the armoire and mumbled, "Now it's a bit of a home." Perhaps she hoped that it would make Robert give her a smidgeon of a smile, but he was silent and did not look at her. "Shall I tidy the armoire too?" He pulled his shoulder again and heard her pull out clothes from the shelves, mumbling, "This for the wash, this to fold..." singing softly to herself. Suddenly there was a quiet moment followed by her astonished voice, "Who is this?"

Robert turned and saw that she held the open portrait with both hands. He stood and stared at her, and later did not remember if he answered. She had a strange expression. She trembled, put the portrait on the bed and left the apartment saying nothing. The portrait rolled back into itself from a habit of years, and Kata's silence flooded the room.

Robert dressed quickly and left the apartment, bought thumbtacks and returned as in a frenzy, as if the portrait were going to take flight. He attached it to the wooden wall next to his bed with many tacks, so that it did not roll back into itself, and then lay in the bed on his side and looked at his grandmother.

Saved as a Painting

***

Two years later, 1997. The light in the room is off and darkness is so dense that Robert can barely find his way to the bathroom. He feels his way, turns on the light and urinates. The urine smell is strong, and Robert turns his face away. His sensitivity to smell increases daily, but he does not sense his own body odour. He coughs and spits into the toilet bowl; turns off the light and reaches his bed, lays and says aloud, "I don't blame anyone, Oma, this is my life."

In the morning he glances at the mirror above the sink. I haven't shaved for that long? His cheeks are sunken, his lips cracked and his teeth yellow. A shiver of cold shakes his body, but he turns on the heat only on the coldest days. He enters the room, puts on his coat and pulls the zipper to his neck, looks at the table and thinks, I have two cigarettes left. He rummages in his jeans' pockets and finds a twenty-dollar bill and some coins. It is middle of the month and this is what he has left of his monthly allowance sent by mail by Jessica.

He hardly utilizes electricity and uses an old gas burner left from his past travels to boil water for his coffee. He stopped paying for cable as well, and his television has two free channels that he watches sometimes, only the news.

Most of the time he is engrosses in obsessive reading of the newspapers he salvages from the paper depots, and there he finds his knowledge-of-the-world which he is compelled to pour into himself each day. Wars and earthquakes, famine, tsunami waves and rapes, drought and terror attacks, avalanches and beaten children, war planes bombings, hurricanes and murders, car accidents, massacres, fires, executions, illnesses and degrading poverty. These are the images of life that he is compelled to browse through day after day. There is no other life, he knows, he went through it.

He thinks he hears Kata urging him to go work and he answers her aloud, "I will, but today I didn't go out. Everything bears down on me, Oma." She looks to the side, sitting as usual in the light in the portrait. If only she would have turned her head and smiled at him! "Perhaps you look when I don't see," he says to her out loud, "poor Oma, you were so afraid of poverty and now you are trapped in it with me."

Kata's lips, cheeks and neck are riddled with small cracks, the blue velvet on her shoulder is furrowed with lined fractures and her belly is cramped under the moldy silk negligee. Black mildew stains spread on her hands and her neck, and her auburn hair is broken in fragmented lines. Only her black-grey eyes are whole and undamaged, veiled in the purple hue and shine as if they were eyes of a live woman. Maybe Gábor Pahl mixed some special substance in the colour of the eyes to protect them from the ravages of time.

Days go by, nights go by, between darkness and light, between heat and cold. Robert sits at the table and reads, or lays in his bed eyes shut, every two or three days he goes out to collect newspapers from the papers bins, buys cigarettes and beer, something to eat, and returns home.

***

Mid-day. Steps are heard beyond the locked doors and a letter is shoved through the mail slot. Robert lifts it in amazement.

Saved as a Painting

It is middle of the month, how come a letter from Jessica? He sits at the table and puts on his reading glasses.

Dear Robert,

For your information, the money Daddy left for you will be gone by next month.

Jessica

He folds the letter, returns it to the envelope and puts it aside, lights a cigarette and sits gazing at a corner in the room for a long time. In the end he bestirs himself, takes a book from the table and smooths the cover once or twice. Avry does exactly the same when he takes a book off a shelf in his neat and dusted bookcase. How did I end up with two book strokers?

Robert opens the book and lays it before him. It is an anthology of novellas by the exiled Hungarian author who lives in the United States, Sándor Márai, stories that Robert reads again and again. He lights a cigarette, drinks the rest of the beer directly from the bottle – the tasteless beverage has lost its fizz – sits hunched over the book and reads. The grey shoelace-plait rests on his back and his bald head blanches under the weak daylight coming from the window. His breath is measured, and he reads for a whole hour without lifting his eyes off the pages.

***

Boro Park, 1998. Robert is sixty, lies in bed and regards the portrait. A strong cough full of phlegm shakes him, he coughs hard, breathes with difficulty, and when his breath returns, he pulls to himself an old plastic pail which stands on the floor, spits into it and wipes his mouth with his sleeve.

Electricity is disconnected. The bills sent by the city remain unopened, and when his hunger brings on a headache he shaves and goes down to the kosher restaurant across the street.

After receiving Jessica's letter he entered that restaurant and asked the proprietor if he could wash dishes and clear the garbage in return for a dinner. The well-shaven man wearing a black skullcap thrusted his hand deeply in his black jacket pocket and with his other hand touched for a moment his collar, "If you return shaven and dressed properly, you can eat here." He spoke English in a Hungarian accent and when he noticed Robert's surprise he smiled apologetically, "I came from Budapest." Robert answered in Hungarian, "I from Novi Sad." The restaurateur grabbed his arm excitedly, "My mother had a cousin in Novi Sad, her name was Julia!" Robert's face froze, go figure how many Julias there were.

Since then, once a week he shaves, inserts his shirt into his pants, laces his shoes and goes to his possible relative. "Szervusz", hello, he says in his low dense voice, stands at the door and waits. The proprietor invites him in and sits with him at the corner table. The waiter serves them goulash heavily seasoned with paprika and potato puree in a reddish sauce.

They are both sixty. The first time they sat together they told each other details of their childhood and even mentioned names of elementary schools which they had attended in Budapest. The proprietor hinted that he was put on a train with his parents but did not elaborate and since then they avoid mentioning the past. Every week they eat together, look at each other in a warm companionship and chat in Hungarian. At the conclusion of the meal, they drink black coffee and then Robert insists on washing all of that day's dishes and clearing the garbage. The proprietor relents to make Robert feel better, and before Robert leaves, hands him a bag with another meal to take home.

Once, in the fall, the Hungarian proprietor gave him an unusually heavy bag. Robert raised questioning eyes to him – Robert raised his eyes to most people, except for children – and the man whispered, "tomorrow is Rosh Hashanah. Shana tova to you." In the bag he found his usual meal with the addition of a bottle of red wine, coffee, candles and razors, an apple and a small jar of honey. Robert thanked him and left. "He is my cousin," the proprietor said to his employees who stole glances, and added, "He is a good man. He is not homeless and not a thief, I heard he is a doctor.

***

And there was the Italian restaurant, a larger one, located among a string of stores facing the railway station bridge. Robert approached its owner, a heavy and sweaty Italian, and asked if he could clean there twice a week. The man dressed in a striped suit examined him, "You look familiar!" and told his head waiter, "let him work." Robert would arrive twice a week, eat leftovers in the kitchen and wash the dishes, clean the toilets and clear the garbage. With the money he earned he bought beer and cigarettes.

One day, the heavy Italian sank to the floor clutching his chest. In a flash Robert was next to him, bending over and releasing his tie. The man's eyes rolled, and he fell unconscious. Robert turned to the anxious staff with equanimity, "He will be fine, call an ambulance!" and began to perform CPR on the man stretched in front of him. The paramedics arrived and accepted Robert's medical diagnosis unquestionably. They placed the Italian on the stretcher, and Robert joined them in the ambulance which left to the hospital, siren blaring. During the ride he sat at the Italian's head and when he asked for a stethoscope, he immediately received it. The paramedics were young, and Robert did not remember working with them in the past, but he thought to himself, maybe they know me. In the Intensive Care Unit he sat next to the Italian's bed, held his hand, wiped the sweat off his forehead, and when he opened his eyes occasionally, Robert smiled at him and told him to go back to sleep. Only when the Italian's wife, round, frightened and panting, arrived, did Robert slip away and leave.

He walked through several streets until he reached the Brooklyn-Manhattan bus stop, a private bus serving the Orthodox Jews. Its bearded driver with the skullcap would break only for people he recognized waiting at the stops or if one of the passengers yelled, mostly in Yiddish, "stop, he is one of us!" A bus braked and Robert climbed in, dropped a coin in the metal receptor next to the driver and looked for a seat.

Only men sat at the front of the bus. Some of them were like the Hungarian restaurant proprietor, shaven, wearing brown and grey hats and dressed in business suits. The rest of them had beards and sidecurls pushed behind their ears, wore long black coats and their heads were covered with black brim hats. Women sat at the back covered with wigs, hats or headdresses and attired in long sleeved dresses buttoned to their necks. Most of them sported bracelets and rings, necklaces and earrings, their nails manicured, and their bags adorned with straps and buckles, some chatted, some read Psalms, and others stared through the window.

Robert found a seat next to one of the men. He did not know who called the bus driver to stop, he did not recognize any of the passengers, but felt that they knew who he was.

***

When the Italian returned to the restaurant, less heavy but no less sweaty, he drew Robert in for a hug and pressed his head to his chest for a long moment. Finally he released him from his grasp, kissed him on both cheeks and said, "You saved my life, now you are my brother! Tell me what you want!" Robert raised his eyes and from his wrinkled face emerged a child's smile, "Thank you, nothing. I will come twice a week as usual." The Italian shut his eyes and bobbed his head, then embraced him again, "Whatever you say, sir!"

Since then, whenever Robert finished cleaning, the head waiter handed him his wages with a lowered head and a bow, as if he handed alms to the son of God. When Robert discovered that his wages were doubled, he did not protest. Now he had a little more money for beer and cigarettes.

The Power of
Antibiotics

Boro Park, winter 2002. Robert is sixty-four, his face grey and lined and his lips cracked. He wears a coat that used to be green, a knitted hat of indeterminable colour covers his ears, and a faded brown scarf is wrapped around his neck over the shoelace-plait. He looks like a homeless person, far different from Chaplin's cute vagabond, but there is still something in him that attracts me, maybe his child's expression.

Despite the intense cold he goes to the small park in his neighbourhood which is not a real garden because even in summer neither grass nor flowers grow there, only two reedy Maple trees which look dead in winter and between them a bench. In such an area this is considered a park. Robert seats himself on the frozen bench and immediately a dozen grey pigeons fly to him. They blow at him a strong smell of damp down, land at his feet and stroll about him with energetic nods of their little heads, back and forth. He follows them with his eyes and scatters dry breadcrumbs. They swoop down on the meal like an excited ball of feathers and peck swiftly.

Robert shivers with cold and rubs his coat sleeves, tightens his scarf around his neck and folds his arms, but the shiver grows and he rises to walk home. The pigeons hop aside, flutter their wings and promptly resume their search for crumbs.

His broad shoulders hunch forward in his coat, his steps are sluggish and his hands are shoved deeply into his pockets. At the entrance to his building he halts, looks around as if searching for something and enters the stairwell. The smell of urine hits him and he hides his nose in his scarf, climbs to the second floor and hurries to enter his apartment. He locks the door behind him, and without taking off his coat, hat and scarf sits in the gloomy dimness.

It is difficult for me to see him like that, neglected and sad, even though I know that occasionally he meets women in the Italian restaurant, in pubs or liquor stores. A leftover manly charm of old still bursts forth, and from time to time a woman invites him to her home. The relationship lasts one or two more meetings and ends. Robert does not invite them to his apartment and does not remember their names. He remembers that years before, a nice Orthodox woman whose face he had forgotten, used to come to him, and he remembers another woman who stayed in his apartment for four days and three nights, whose hair was long, thick and white and her eyes so blue that it took his breath away, but he does not remember her name either.

Always alone in this solitude which I cannot understand. I find it hard to imagine what it feels like not to have children, family or friends, save the Hungarian and Italian restaurant owners and the pigeons he feeds in the park.

✱✱✱

Evening. Robert has slept through most of the day and now he wakes up, stares into the darkness around him and very slowly reality adheres itself to his body. He sit up, still in his clothes, feels for his lighter and lights the candle on the night-stand next to him. The faint light illuminates the portrait and Robert gazes at it, takes out a cigarette and notices that it is his last one. He lights it, inhales, and crumples the empty pack.

"I returned from sleep, Oma," he utters and is seized by a coughing spell.

Kata turns her head, looks at him and the purple hue is moist in her eyes. She raises her right hand which is full of black mildew stains and says to him, "Get up! Come back to life. You can!" He smokes and keeps gazing at her, and when the cigarette is a short stub between his lips, he crushes it in the full ash-tray and whispers, "I can't."

"Why can't you?"

Robert clasps the empty cigarette pack, looks in vain in it for another cigarette, and sets it next to him. "Some people are weak, Oma," he says in a waning voice, "not everyone has an engine like yours, which is so strong that even after you are shot and thrown into the Danube it does not cease revving. My engine is weak, you see. It was always weak, and now it hardly works. Enough, I am done."

"This is rubbish, Robi!"

Robert shrinks and wonders if she ever really loved him. Kata hears his thought and it seems to me that I see discomfiture on her fractured face. Maybe she understands that she went too far in her inflexibility.

"Noa," Itamar calls to me in his screeching voice. He sits in his army fatigues as always, with his arms leaning on his gathered legs, and looks at me in his decent simplicity, "you forget that Kata is different from you. She does not get embarrassed by anything, rather she says to herself that Robert can think whatever he wishes. Now it is imperative to help him, and she understands that she has to push him to rage."

"Rage?"

"Robert has a problem because he is never given to rage over anything. His will to live weakened by pity for the world and himself. If he rages a life force will rise in him."

"But Itamar, rage is poisonous and destructive! It is not like you to suggest such a thing."

"A short and strong rage will have the healing effect of antibiotics. It is the chance Kata will take."

"No... I don't think she wants to help him. She is too tough."

Robert wants to smoke, remembers that he has run out of cigarettes, and rubs his thighs nervously. He has no beer either. He stands, takes the candle and goes slowly to the kitchen where he has left the paper bag with the tealight candles the Hungarian restaurateur gave him recently. The bag rustles between his hands. He takes out a tealight candle and lights it, returns to the room and places both lit candles on the dining table.

The table which is piled with various things in a jumbled heap is instantly lit, the linoleum floor is lit, the walls, the ceiling, the portrait. For a moment it seems to me that the room is well lit, but darkness grows, surrounds the two small flames and closes in on them. Robert looks at them with exhaustion – a little bit of wax poured into aluminum cups and in them short wicks which hold onto the fire. Such weak fire, he thinks, so dilapidated. He sits at the table, his back to the portrait. Again he searches for a cigarette and examines another crumpled pack lying there, leaves it and it falls onto the floor. He sighs and leans his forehead on the table. Kata's voice bursts into the silence of the room like steel nails, "Robi, you must go out of the house."

He raises his head and does not turn to her. I stand by the portrait, and it is clear to me now that Kata likes only strong people who can help themselves. Robert feels betrayed. Something burning rises from his throat to his mouth.

"I can't go out."

"Get up and go to the door! You can! Go out!"

He turns his head to the portrait and raises his voice, "You don't understand how it is to be at a dead end?! I have no money and I have no energy!" He is furious. "What do you want from me? Leave me alone!"

I am startled, it is not like him to explode like that.

Kata prods him, "what do you need?"

Tears of rage run down his cheeks, he raises his hands and his fingers straighten and stretch. His voice rises further, "but you know, why do you ask?! I need beer and cigarettes, that's what I need, damn it!" He ignites the lighter nervously, looks at the flame and extinguishes it, "I need cigarettes and beer!" His rage turns his voice hoarse, "Do you get it? I need one hundred dollars!"

Kata answers practically, "One hundred dollars? If that is what will get you out, write Jessica and she'll send you a hundred dollars."

"She? She'll send me?!"

He shakes with rage and I cannot stand by any longer. "Kata!" I explode, "How can you be so hard on him? Help him." She swivels her head and stares at me with all the tiny lines and slits on her face, and her horror indicates the fact that she is not comfortable with the way I think, speak and write. I see that she does not care to help him. "He brought this situation upon himself," she says to me and casts a worried look at him, "he needs to get out of it by himself."

Robert sits with his back to us and his quick breathing scares me. "No! Kata, we must help him!" I become dramatic, not sure how to convince her, "he suffers so!" She ignores me and looks at him, "well, take a piece of paper and write to Jessica!" Her metallic voice pierces my ears.

Robert leaps out of his chair, kicks it back and quickly approaches the portrait. His head leans forward, and his body is tense. He flicks the lighter and draws the flame near the canvas coated with fissured oil paint. Another fraction of an inch and the fire will touch it. Kata's face is fraught, and her cracked lips are parted in a pain I do not recognize in her. Now they talk but I cannot hear. She tells him something, and I see that Robert hurls words at her, spittle runs down his chin and his face is contorted. What did she say to him that he became so incensed?

Then I hear him yelling in a broken voice, "That's it? That's what you have to say to me?! Fine!"

He has gone mad, I tell myself.

Robert extinguishes the lighter, sits at the table wildly, opens the spiral notebook and searches for a pen. He has no pen. I have a pen in my bag, but I will not hand it to him. He finds a pen on the floor under the chair, looks at the page, exhales and the two tiny wax candle flames vibrate. All his body aches and I cannot endure his suffering. He coughs, searches his pockets and does not find a cigarette, puts on his reading glasses and writes.

Jessica,

> Take Oma Kata's portrait from me. I will send it to you for one hundred dollars. If I do not get the money in two weeks, I will burn it.

Robert Steins

***

Ten days later. Robert sits at his desk and hold an unopened envelope which has just arrived. At the top right there is a stamp and underneath it his address in Jessica's handwriting. At the top left two addresses are written, one is that of Jessica in her handwriting, and the other is of Jonathan's in his handwriting.

Robert opens the envelope and stares at a small book of matches. He leans with his elbow on the table, supports his cheek with the palm of his hand and shuts his eyes.

Several hours later, when darkness has descended, he gets up and leaves, walks slowly down the street, his hands in his coat pockets. In one pocket he has a few dollars he received at the Italian's restaurant, and in the other the envelope with the matchbook. His fingers toy with it and suddenly he stops and takes it out, holds it at the corner and lifts it a little. In his other hand he ignites the cigarette lighter and brings the flame to the bottom of the envelope.

The flame catches the paper and snakes on it in a burning line of orange and blue. It catches the matchbook inside the envelop and it bursts into flames in a blasting whisper, turns into a ball of fire, and immediately turns black and falls like a small lump, smoking and disintegrating. The envelope keeps burning, the fire nears Robert's fingers and when he feels its sting, he releases it. The remaining burning paper hovers to the ground and becomes a small mound of ash. Robert scatters it with his shoe, lights a cigarette and continues walking.

He ponders whether to go to the nearer liquor store or walk to the pub which is further away and chooses the liquor store. He turns left, takes a few steps and suddenly turns on his heels, walks back to the sidewalk where he was walking before, and continues straight. At the end of the street he turns right and continues along tall streetlights chasing his shadow forward and backward. People go by hunched into themselves, and old cars are parked next to the sidewalk, banged and dusty. Finally he arrives at the pub which looks as in the past, as though no time has elapsed since he was there last.

He enters. Low lights, amplified music and noises of chatter. His shoulders are slumped, his shoelace-plait hides under his coat and his face is calm. He sits on a high stool by the bar, orders beer and looks around, just looks, as anyone sitting in any pub does, and like them does not report to himself what he sees, it is I who talk all the time.

All at once he notices the woman. She sits alone at a side table, her back which is turned to him is wrapped in a colourful woolen shawl, and a thick white braid lays on it. A pleasant memory traverses through Robert and happiness sprays his heart. He does not remember her name. When was she with him? I want to remind him it was seven years earlier; I want him to approach her, but he sits on his high stool, slowly sips his beer and eyes her back. I try to nudge him with all my literary powers, but he thinks, she will not wish to speak to me.

The woman turns. Her eyes are bluer than he remembered, and her face is full of the wrinkles in which he found treasures of ivory skin. She smiles, comes over and touches his knee, "Robert, how are you?" He holds her hand and gazes into her eyes, "I remember every detail except for your name."

"Michelle."

***

In the morning, after they awoke, he made coffee, and they sat at the end of the bed and drank. Michelle said, "I moved to Florida. My daughter is a single mother, she has a baby and I help her. Yesterday I came to visit a sick friend and tomorrow I go back."

"Stay with me, Michelle."

"No, Robert. Come with me to Florida."

And so, at the age of sixty-four, after always pushing away women who invited him to share their life, Robert said in a trembling voice, "I was afraid you'd never say that" and shut his eyes. Then he opened them and dipped into the deep blue of her eyes, inhaled deeply into his shrieking lungs and looked at the portrait.

"Oma Kata," he said and did not know if Michelle who was seated next to him saw or heard, but it did not make a difference. Kata turned her head to him, her pressed lips, full of cracks, opened into a smile and the sea of her love flowed to him and flooded him.

WHY DON'T YOU STAY

Out of the blue, after a long silence, I received a short email from Avry, "how are you?"

I was angry. Why does he write instead of calling? Why does he go round-and-round with this non-committal how-are-you? I called him, and when he picked up, I heard happiness in his voice, but then I was disappointed, because he dragged the conversation into where-he-was-and-what-he-did, a kind of chatter of nonsense. I tried to be patient, I tried to sound cheerful, but I did not succeed. I cut the small-talk and said, "Avry, come over!" He replied coolly, "I am busy." I was offended, "Fine, don't come…" He was still for a moment and asked, "When?"

"Tonight."

"I'll be there."

Great, I made an appointment with him.

In the evening he arrived tired and absent-minded, we hugged lightly, and he did not look at my face. The smell of his perspiration was heavy and repulsive, his face was despondent. For a minute I resented him for allowing himself to come over like that, unwashed and listless, but I remembered that I pressed him to come, and suggested taking a bath together. "It will be good for both of us," I entreated him. He smiled in a tired lethargy, and a shadow of sorrow passed in his honey eyes, "will that make you feel better?" Suddenly my throat clenched and filled with tears. I shut my eyes tightly to block the tears and opened the bath faucets.

Avry undressed, left his clothes on the floor and leaned on the door jamb staring at the running water. Had I not said, "let's get in," he would not have noticed that the bathtub was full. I undressed, and we lowered ourselves into the water. He leaned his head back on a towel I had folded for him, shut his eyes and said, "I am tired." I said, "Soon you will feel refreshed," and we fell silent. After a few minutes I lost my patience to sit with him and be silent. I got out of the bathtub and he said, "That's it?" I replied, "I will sit here, next to you." He sank into the water, his hands limp on the bathtub's edge and his fingers still. The scars on his chest seemed more prominent than ever, and for a moment I wanted to trace them with my lips and write a love note between them with my finger-pencil, but these games were like a movie we had seen a long time ago.

His cheeks were pale, and the veil of dark stubble accentuated their pallour. I did not know where his soul wandered, I did not know how he occupied his nights and days and whom he met. He appeared tortured and distant, but there was a strong bond between us despite that. Or perhaps I was wrong, perhaps it was only an illusion of a bond, some story I told myself. Avry opened his eyes, stretched his water-dripping hand and placed it on my shoulder, "You were right to put me in a bathtub." I leaned into him, we kissed, and I returned into the water.

Later we sat in the living room, smelling of shampoo and melancholy. I said to him, "Say, Avry... why don't you ever stay with me till morning?" His face became distant and he fixed his eyes at the living room corner. I expected him to avoid a direct answer, but he looked at me and his face transformed. I saw in it a pained or maybe an offended expression, I did not know, I did not understand.

"Because I feel that you want me to leave."

"Really?"

"Yes, every time I leave your house, I don't understand why I need to wander the streets at that time of night and why you don't want me to stay with you."

"Avry, that's what you sensed in me?"

"I think you love only the protagonists of your story."

"We'll have to discuss it sometime," I said quickly.

He smiled a feeble smile, got up, got dressed and left. I locked the door behind him and was so sad that I was unsettled. I sank into the swivel chair, switched on the computer and told myself it is time to end this business with Avry.

{ 25 }

A Trip In The Rain

Robert sent the portrait to Jessica in Washington, DC on the day he moved in with Michelle in Florida. She placed it in the basement without opening the cylinder, which was rolled in a newspaper, but several years later retrieved it and sent it as is to her brother in New York. "Jonathan did open it," Agi told me in a telephone update from Northampton to Israel. In my mind's eye, I saw Jonathan peel the newspaper off the rolled portrait, hold it at the top and the bottom and look at his grandmother sitting in a pool of light, with her cracked colours and the mildew stains which covered her. Agi said, "He showed the portrait to his wife and she decided it needed restoration, so Jonathan did some market research and looked for the best restorer in town." I could hear Agi smiling over the line, "You know, the painting didn't interest him one bit, but that's how it is in our family, always the best. Finally he found an old restorer, a Guggenheim retiree, and that man, he took one look at the painting and immediately identified the artist."

Saved as a Painting

The mildew stains were removed, the paint was reapplied, and the portrait was stretched anew in a richly carved golden frame, but not like its predecessor, this frame was made of plastic, light and easy to carry. A messenger brought the package to Jonathan's house, who, while he was happy with the restoration, preferred to leave it in its cardboard packaging. He called Agi and told her, "This painting doesn't go with our house... You told me your mother misses it. She can have it as a gift from Jessica and me." When Edit heard it in the Seniors' Home in Tel Aviv she was as excited as if she were informed of the return of someone whom everyone considered dead.

All that happened about two months after I returned to live in Israel. "That's it," Agi told me on the telephone in a festive tone atypical to her. "Now we can finish the story, but we need to go to New York for that. Are you coming? We'll take my car and get the portrait." "Of course I am coming!" I replied, "and the timing is perfect because I haven't begun to write... But just a minute, Agi, did you ask about Robert? Is he still in Florida? I want to meet him."

"Jonathan said that Robert returned to New York and is living in his apartment in Brooklyn with that girlfriend, Michelle or whatever her name is. He also put the apartment in her name. Jonathan thinks that Robert is ill and that is the reason for the move to Brooklyn, because in Florida they lived in a mobile home."

"Robert is ill? Agi, perhaps we can visit him in Brooklyn when I come?"

"Well, we'll see."

Two days before flying to the United States, Agi called me again, "Noa, I have some sad news. I could have told you when you arrive here in two days, but I decided not to wait."

"What happened?"

"It's about Robert... he died."

"Robert died? And I wanted to meet him so badly before getting into my writing..."

"Yes, it worked out that way."

"Agi, would you go with me to Brooklyn? I would like to see his apartment at least. I must be there."

"Sure."

***

Northampton, January 2009. The day prior to our journey to New York, Agi and I walked to the town centre, and the stroll in the clear air was refreshing. Mounds of snow-mud were piled along the familiar streets, and every house and every tree, every store and every doorstep smiled at me as if I still lived there. "I love this charming place so much!" I rejoiced, and Agi answered, "yes, it is nice here."

We entered Northampton Brewery, a restaurant we both liked. It was teeming with people, and the air was full of the smell of nachos coming out of the oven with melted cheese, mixed with the smells of French Fries and beer, perfect for cold days and appetizing. We sat at a side table, and a wave of excitement rose in me. "Agi, can you believe it? We found the portrait! It is an amazing experience!" "Yes," she smiled a quick smile, "I see that you are a bit excited."

Saved as a Painting

***

A heavy downpour began next morning which melted all the snow piled up. I ran the short distance from Agi's front porch to her car, but I was drenched. We did not exchange a word until we were out of Northampton and on the highway. The rain increased and Agi turned on the wipers to their maximum speed. I said, "what a flood!" And she answered, "yes, the weatherman said it would be wet." At once I became angry, what is with her? She always clips my wings. Every "wonderful" of mine is her "OK." Every enthusiasm I intensify she diminishes, every sentence I elevate she lowers, she must be upset at me because I leech myself to her story. You would think I have nothing else to write about! In fact, I need to live seven lives in order to write everything that is waiting in me. So why this story? And what am I doing here, in this torrential rain, on this journey to New York, to get a portrait I have nothing to do with?

I waited for Agi to ask me what was wrong, but she did not ask. I peeked at her face and thought that she too was annoyed. I could not bear the discomfort and shrunk into my seat. Agi pulled a disc from the glove compartment, "Let's listen to music," and slid it into the CD player's slit, "This is road music." The music did make our journey pleasant, and Agi's smiles became longer. Rain kept pouring on us, the wipers ran back and forth on the windshield, and we began to chat. After three hours of rowing in the voluminous water we arrived in New York in a good mood and a sense of victory. Agi navigated directly to the family home on Eighty First Street West, next to the park. Before exiting the car, I told her, "You are an excellent driver!" She nodded slightly with her head, "Ah, it was not as hard as I had expected," put her hand back and arranged her plait.

***

At the Steins' house Agi introduced me as her friend from Israel, and I was received in a familial warmth. Jonathan looked very sporty and his wife was agelessly cute. They both smiled pleasantly their wide American smiles, but I was too impatient to look at them or listen to them. We had coffee with brownies, and the three of them talked. I pretended to be part of the conversation, although I did not know what it was about, and twice I got up with different excuses only to approach the cardboard package which stood waiting for us next to the front door. I remembered the portrait's dimensions, one metre twenty centimetres in height, eighty centimetres in width, and I even estimated its weight, because I knew that the new frame was made of plastic, not heavy wood as the previous one. But only now did I really understand how big the painting was. The package was about twenty centimetres in thickness, as if it contained some large furniture which required two porters to move it from place to place.

I was so taken hostage by the intense need to see the portrait, that I almost missed the crux of the conversation. Agi, in her minor tone and the delicate strings she pulls that make people tell her things, got Jonathan to talk, and he added meaningful details to the story. In the end he even gave Agi his father Miki's wooden box with the postcards sent by Robert from his travels. On top of them was the folded letter sent to Jessica, a torn sheet from a spiral notebook.

Saved as a Painting

Two hours later they finally rose, although not in haste. Jonathan and his wife saw us to the door and exchanged another sentence and another story with Agi. It was obvious that all three enjoyed the visit. I stood next to the cardboard package and said, "I'll take it to the car, it's light." I thanked them for their hospitality and forgave myself for not being able to hide my impatience. The package was heavier than I had thought and too big to be able to protect it with my umbrella. I held it with both arms in an embrace and rushed to the car in the rain.

Darkness began to descend, and when we reached the highway the rain intensified and discharged noisy torrents on the windshield. We were exhausted. We exchanged a few impressions about Jonathan and his wife, and quickly fell silent. Music played, and I took it upon myself to change CDs, which I did faithfully for three hours until we reached Northampton.

At the house I got out and carried the heavy cardboard package to the front porch, getting us wet. I stopped by the door, leaned it on me, and while Agi parked the car I said to myself, restrain yourself and do not press her! If she does not want to take out the portrait yet, wait until tomorrow. It will not run away! Remember that the story is firstly hers!

Agi arrived, wiped her shoes at the doormat and I bit my lip so as not to say something like, I'm dying already to see the portrait. But it came out. Agi smiled a quick smile and entered before me. I raised my load and entered. I stood in the living room with the portrait leaning on me and did not move until Agi came over, took it from me and propped it against the wall. Her husband entered the room, looked at us brightly and asked, "How was the journey?" as if we just returned from an excursion to the North Pole. Agi poured wine for the three of us and raised her goblet, "l'chaim!" we toasted with her and she said, "So, shall we open?"

{ 26 }

The Separating Border

July 2010. Summer days here oppress with their heat and humidity, and the exhausted city moves through them sun stroked. But when night arrives, she wakes up in buzzing sensual urges, her movements become alert and quivering, and the hot air fills with a sharp perfume, a mixture of honeysuckle and lavender scents. Only locals can identify this bouquet, as one identifies his own body odour... But what can I do all alone with these energies? Nothing...

Through the open window I heard my crow duo chatting noisily, if only I understood Crow... I was sick of looking at the screen, sick of sitting at home. I went out for a walk, strode for ten minutes and turned to go back. Maybe that is what you feel when you reach the finish line of a race, not the physical strength that wanes, but the will to be there.

On the way home I entered the convenience store at the corner of the lane. The owner, a young woman with an uncommonly beautiful face, received me with the tired smile of end of day. We exchanged pleasant sentences of no consequence, and it felt good to talk to her in her clean and neat shop, full of things meant to lift one's spirit when it has been alone far too long.

***

Morning. I sit within my four walls and stare at the screen. The text in front of me is frozen. I am stuck. Had I written yesterday instead of going out for that short walk, perhaps it would not have happened to me at this very moment when I am so close to the end! My five Deceased look at me in silence. Let them be silent, I do not care. But their stares bother me, and I raise my voice, "What can I do? It's not coming out and you are not helping." Their silence aggravates me. "Tell me," I raise my voice, "why did you come here? What good does it do that you are here? I can't go out with you, I can't eat or drink with you, not kiss, not make love, I can't do anything with you, only talk dead talk. Nothing. What do you think that it is so simple for me to be only with you all the time? I can easily be sucked into your side I'll have you know!"

What do I want from them? They are not to blame that I am stuck, especially not Itamar. My eyes seize on him. He sits on the carpet like a reservist on a break during military training, his legs gathered, and his hands lean on them, his head sunny and his face quiet. At once I realize that he is the only one in my life with whom I experienced a togetherness of two people who belong to each other in the most simple and complete sense. Ugh, Itamar... If only I could turn back the wheel. If only I could touch him! Kiss his lips! If only I could cross the boundary that separates us.

I go and kneel before him, and he raises his dark eyes which are like the earth of the valley after rain. "Embrace me, Itamar," I plead, "we'll be together, like on that night, this time to the end..."

He shakes his head.

I stand and stretch my hand to him, "Get up! Give me your hands and stand up!"

"Impossible, Noa."

"Why?"

"Because my legs were amputated."

"It can't be! Stand up!"

He smiles sadly and lowers his head between his arms which are leaning on the legs that all this time I thought he had.

I sit in front of the computer and do not quite get it. Itamar has no legs, how can it be? They were amputated in the war... Oh, no, Itamar, they killed you! I feel inside me that dreadful blow, darkness envelops me for a moment, and then I strike the floor with my feet and turn my chair with the momentum like a carousel. The living room gallops around me in a circle, my Dead are blurry, another faster turn, I spread my hands to the sides, turn more and more, and stop all at once, panting. I look at my Deceased Loves and a giggle escapes out of me, "come, let's change the rules of the game! Now each of you will cross to this side to be with me for an hour, only an hour! And I will come to you, Itamar, first of all to you."

A heavy stillness engulfs the room, as if it has not been here all this time, in this mausoleum.

I chuckle, "Why are you so startled?"

They do not move, do not even blink. I am sorry I worried them, "Fine, that's enough, don't worry. Here, I am going back to my writing. That's what you want, no? I am going to Robert, coming?"

They stare hard at me. What is with them? "Listen, Robert is indeed dead, and I did not get to meet him, but I went with Agi to his apartment, and when we walked in, I felt as if he were still there, as if he were lying dead waiting to be taken to his burial. Now I have to go back to him over there."

My Quintet sounds a medley of gasps and sighs.

"What happened to you? What's the problem?"

"Noa, don't-do-this," says Moosh in a squashed voice. He gets up slowly, swaying. The oily stalks tumbling down his forehead, and his blue pants gliding down. He holds them, and his oval face is pale, "don't-go-there."

"Why?"

He stands close to me, looking at me from above, almost-almost touching me and does not answer.

Editor-Rafi approaches and latches onto to Moosh's right, blocking the light with his big torso. "No-a..." he speaks in a soft soundtrack, "how about going back to the revisions in chapter one...?" His embarrassed speech confuses me, "Rafi?" His hands are by his sides, his left almost touches my shoulder, and he looks at me helplessly. I love his weakness and also his strength, and I am sorry again that we never realized the images we saw beyond the curtain of noise. He sighs, "Noa, we always loved each other, but that's beside the point, don't go there."

"Why?"

He does not answer either.

Old-Prince-Shaul elevates himself and clings to Moosh's left. His tall and thin body is bent, and his face is very grey, as if his death has intensified. A hoarse voice emerges from his mouth, "be wary, I beseech you."

He too?

Through a slit between Moosh and Rafi I see Itamar. He sits on the carpet leaning back on his arms.

"Itamar?"

He turns his face to me and I see a look of concern in it.

What is going on here?

Husband-Yossi rises and attaches himself to Old-Prince-Shaul. This is progress! Perhaps military secrecy links them. It seems to me that the old prince took under his wing Husband-Yossi who moves his big shoulders as if to release the tension in them. He says, "Noa, take a break from writing for a few days," and puts out his hand, almost-almost touches my cheek, "you need to rest."

"But I am not tired!"

They cling to each other and pant hard at me like ancient animals. I barely breathe. "What got into you?" I yell. They stand over me pressed to each other and their moldy smell fills the air between us, "don't go there!"

"But I must meet Robert!"

PURPLE PEARLS

Robert sits at the edge of the bed and smokes. He is naked and his thin body is shrunken in the cold air. His round bald spot is surrounded by grey, thin and long hair braided behind into his shoelace-plait. His neck is wrinkled, his chest hair snarled and his shoulders slack.

The room is dim. Heavy smells of old sweat and new sweat, a brimming ashtray and soggy clothes float in the compressed air. Two small candles flicker in round aluminum cups on the night table, and next to them rest two additional tealight candle cups, empty of wax. My clothes are draped over the chair in the corner.

Robert stretches his scrawny arms, drops ash into one of the empty wax cups, and looks at the quivering flames. I say to him, "it's awfully cold, get under the cover." He turns his black-grey eyes to me and out of his wrinkled face he smiles like one who has given up a long time ago, "yes, cold..." A shiver goes through his body, and he gives himself to the chill as though it is his intimate enemy. I cover myself with the blanket up to my neck and he asks, "Are you cold?" his voice thick and low. I answer, "No, I am covered".

Robert inhales the smoke and closes his eyes, opens them and gazes at the perfect rings he blows out. "Enough!" I say, "this city is totally frozen. Get under the cover." He stubs the cigarette in the ashtray Slowly and gets up, "This is winter in New York, Noa, this is not Tel Aviv... You want coffee?"

Noises of clinking dishes come from the kitchen and a slippery light-shadow moves in its doorway. A few minutes later the smell of coffee wafts in, and Robert, naked and shivering in the chilly air, comes with two cups full of the black liquid. He places one of them on the night table, sits on the edge of the bed and drinks in small sips. I sit next to him, wrapped in the blanket, drink the hot coffee and for a minute forget the cold air. "The candles will be done soon," I say. Robert looks around him. "I had more candles somewhere here; I don't know where they are." I lie down again and curl up in the blanket, "it doesn't matter, come to bed and get under the cover." His black-grey eyes are veiled in purple hue and he examines my face with a soft smile.

"Why did you come here?"

"I had to. I couldn't go on without you talking to me."

"What do you want to talk about?"

"About the letter you sent to Jessica."

"It's futile..."

"No, it's not futile. Come, lie down next to me and warm up."

He puts his cup on the night table, stands over me and gazes at me ponderingly. His limp member rests among faded fine curls and his stomach is concave, his broad shoulders lean forward and his arms are pressed to his sides in some steadfast, unexpected and maybe even protesting steadiness. I shiver and take off the blanket, "come". He reclines next to me and I say to him, "you are frozen." He presses himself to me and puts his cold head on my chest. A strong odour emanates from him, a sour stench of cigarette smoke and mildewy body odour. Slightly nauseated, I cover him completely and turn my head to the side.

Robert shivers, perhaps from the cold. I lift the blanket a bit and a wave of heavy odour rises to me. I breathe through my mouth only and whisper, "You will warm up quickly..." He replies, "I can't warm up..." I release my held breath for a moment and say to him, "Finally we are together." He nods with his head, "You are not scared?"

"No."

"You understand where you are?"

"With you."

He pushes himself up, presses himself to my side and encircles me with his cool arm. The odour is strong and hard, and I breathe through my mouth, tighten Robert to me and our legs intertwine. His body is cold, I am hot. My fingers glide over the small bumps on his wrinkled cheek, and with my pencil-finger I draw his profile from his forehead to his chin, return to his lips and draw them until a tremor of a smile skims them.

"How was it to live in Florida?"

"It was good."

"Did you tell Michelle about your life? About your journeys in the world?"

"Yes, I told her."

Something stirred in me, "Now tell me too."

"What?"

"Why you wrote that letter to Jessica."

Robert raises his head like a perplexed child, "Because I was angry at my grandmother."

"Why were you angry at her?"

He sits up and leans against the wall. I still breathe only through my mouth, seat myself next to him, thrust the pillow between my back and the wall, and cover both of us. He holds my shoulder and his fingers tighten on it, loosen and tighten. He feels under the blanket with his other hand, finds my hand and holds it firmly. Something in him is more determined than I imagined. He smiles as if he heard my thought, "Why did you come here?"

"I must finish my story."

He stays silent.

For a moment I breathe as usual and hover with my lips on his neck, "So, why were you angry at your grandmother?"

"I don't know," he sighs, "she made me mad as hell."

"What did she say to you that made you that mad?"

"Why are you asking?"

"Because I must know what caused you to explode!"

"Not everything is knowable."

"But how can I write if I don't know? I couldn't see when Kata made you blow up in anger and I couldn't hear what she said to you."

"It is most likely her secret," he says in his thick voice and he sounds as if he speaks love.

I shudder and nestle my head between his shoulder and neck. He hums, presses me to him and his cold right hand quashes my hand under the blanket. I want to continue with my questions, but he quashes my hand again, "shhhhh..." I wait a moment and resume talking, "I was so startled when you threatened to burn the portrait! I was afraid you lost your mind. What happened to you?"

"I think the anger kindled a fire in me."

I become dramatic, straighten and raise my voice, "one more millimetre, and you would have burnt it for real, but something inside prevented you and instead you only threatened to burn her. What prevented you?"

"Something did, I don't know what..."

"And why did you write to Jessica? You knew she would not forward you the money, and you knew she would tell Jonathan, and that they would ridicule you."

"Hmmm... I wrote, and I sent. The end."

"Robert, I must clear some things with you..."

He shuts his eyes and smiles softly. The cold air begins to gnaw at my shoulder, and I say to him, "I am cold." We lie down under the cover and embrace. "This is a good together," he says and his breathing rasps. I slide under the cover, barely breathing, and shower kisses down his chest. Salty-sweet dampness clings to my lips, the odour spreads inside my head and strikes my forehead from the inside, but strangely enough I get used to it and it becomes almost pleasant, like a swamp of sewage full of daffodils. Editor-Rafi is not with me, but no doubt he would have erupted here to say, shit, shit, Noa, really, call things by their names!

I pull my head out of the blanket and inhale, lie on my side and look at Robert. He turns his head to me, looks at me and suddenly I see his pain... I have no words with which to think of that pain, I only know it is terrible, too monstrous to look at. My eyes close for a moment. Maybe Rafi was right... maybe I cannot.

Robert's pain rises to me, putrid and full of perfume spray. His face is that of a grown-up, but something from his youth's good looks can be observed in his wide forehead, in his high cheekbones and in the shape of his nose. He is far away from me and at the same time so close, I cannot comprehend it. That smile, which reminds me of a remnant of a dream, appears on his face, "You think all the time, Noa, you are full of thoughts."

"Right, because I have questions. And I can't finish the story without the answers."

"Why can't you?"

"It has to do in the book's aesthetics. Without the answers it appears as if it has ugly holes in it."

"Life has these holes as well. Are they ugly?"

"Perhaps not ugly, perhaps frightening."

"Everyone has fears."

"Yes, everyone, even your Tito... Robert, what did you hold onto all your life?"

"Now we'll be together without talking, Okay?"

The odour is heavy and sharp but I withstand it. I am hot and sweaty. We cling to each other again, and his cold body cools my skin somewhat. He glides up my neck with his lips and I shiver again. I am aware that this meeting has to end immediately, but I embrace Robert fiercely and then let go a little. My fingers caress his nape and encounter his shoelace-plait.

"Why did you braid this silly plait?"

"Shhhhh..."

I sit up, "I have to go."

He sits facing me, sips the rest of the coffee from one of the cups resting on the night table, and eyes me the way men eye women in bed. All I wish now is to be with him, my body leans to him on its own, but I must go.

"Robert, my time is over."

He rests the cup next to the full ashtray, reaches out and grips my shoulders. His grip is strong. His lips move as though he speaks, and his eyes sink into mine. I hold his cheeks and bring his face to mine. Cigarettes stench rises from his breath, mixed with coffee, and his mouth opens to mine, our lips join, and he drinks me, I move to him involuntarily, pulled by a strong current and –

Boom! Something lands on me with a blow, like a huge chunk of stone. I recognize this terrible blow, but do not remember from whence and where. Everything darkens, I cannot move, I cannot breath, another moment and I choke. The black weight crushes and squeezes me. I try to push it off me, but I have no strength. Silence.

Fear freezes me.

All at once the pressure eases and ten strong hands hold my head, my shoulders and my arms, and pull me fast out of the darkness.

I open my eyes and move my head, breathe, straighten, and the light returns.

What happened to me?

We sit on the bed's edge and Robert looks at me as if I dodged him in some game. I glide my fingers over his lips, "I would have taken you with me if I could." "Wait," he says, opens the night table's drawer and picks up something, "Will you give me your hand for a moment?" I offer my hand like the man on the bench in Novi Sad, the one Robert handed pills for lowering his fever. He cups it softly, lays two purple pearls, and with the other secures my fingers over them.

Then he lays on his back with his head on the pillow. I get dressed and approach him, pull the blanket to his chin, and turn to leave the dim apartment. Too bad, he is really a women's man. Maybe another time. Robert smiles with closed eyes.

Strong light pours over me outside, warm air engulfs me, and in my hand, I hold tightly the purple pearls that I received from Robert. In a moment Rafi will pounce and scold me, get rid of this line! It reeks of perfume and is full of sugar! I do not need Rafi to tell me that. I know it, but right now I need some sugar.

Where am I? In my apartment on Jabotinsky Street, in my heat stricken city. My five Deceased sit in the living room, each in his place, like a welcome delegation. "My beloved, thank you for saving me."

Nude 37

The Hamsin intensified the next day, the air-conditioner froze me, and my throat was hurting. The previous night I was sure that the expression of gratitude to my five Deceased Loves was the final sentence, but this morning I realized that I was wrong, and I was left listless.

Why does the story not end?

I had no energy to get to it and I did not want to write, but late in the day I sat at my computer, uploaded the photo of the restored portrait and made it my screen saver. Here is Kata, I said to myself. Every time I turn on the computer, she will welcome me, and maybe she will help me reach the end of the story.

Her beauty was preserved in the refurbished portrait, the mildew ravages were undetected and there was no sign of the devastation of the paint which cracked. Kata sat in it erect as usual, but suddenly I noticed that her erectness was less stiff, and in the tilt of her head there was a mildness I was not familiar with. I was reminded of the tenderness I felt for her when I saw her in her house in Novi Sad sitting with four-year-old

Robert on her knee. The portrait shone to me with all its colours and Kata looked in it full of vitality as ever, forever. The Hungarian gendarmes did indeed shoot her, but they did not defeat her. Gábor Pahl triumphed over them and left her here. Later her grandson wanted to burn her, but she saved him. And what will happen to me? I do not know. I am spent. Kata, talk to me!

She turned her face to me and intertwined her fingers. The mildness I saw in her earlier disappeared and her gaze was severe, "What do you want me to tell you?" her metallic voice pricked me. She sounded practical and focused, as if she were looking at a proposal for a real-estate deal.

I weakened, "How shall I explain...?"

She wore a thin smile with pressed lips, "you don't know what you want!"

"Yes, I do!" I protested, "I want you to speak to me the same way you spoke to Robert."

Kata was silent and stared at me with a cool and detaching patience. Most likely that was the way she stared at the businesspeople who negotiated with her and fastened them to their seats when she did not agree to lower her prices. She refuses me. How shall I talk to her? What shall I say to her?

I became emotional, "I want you to believe in me, Kata!" and I raised my voice, "if you believe in me you will be able to speak to me!" And immediately I hated my tone. It does not matter, I thought, she will be able to see beyond it. But she sat in her baroque chair and stared at me with reservation, "you need to be clear and say precisely what you want."

Ugh, what a businesswoman! And her arrogance! She sees in me a woman who does not know her mind. In her eyes I am a foolish woman who chases men, a prattler who deals in words. She despises me.

"Kata, it's me, Noa"

"Yes, I know."

"I'm Agi's friend, I visited Edit, they told you about me."

"I know. So? What does it have to do with anything?"

"I am writing about you and your family. I held the letter you had written to Ilona... It does not matter to you in the least?"

"What do you want?"

"I want you to soften toward me... to give me the Kata that is inside. It is imperative for the story I am writing, you see. Otherwise I can't finish it."

Kata's eyes found mine.

"Madame Noa," she said matter-of-factly and cold, "tell me, what gives you permission to ask such a thing? You think you are Gábor Pahl? You think you are as talented as he was?"

At first, I did not get the meaning of her words, and then my heart sank. Tears choked me, but I managed to say to her, "Gábor Pahl in his genius painted you with colours, and I in my limitations paint you with words. That is all. And if you don't like it that I write about you, too bad."

Humiliation burnt in me, even though I had known from the start that she was destined not to answer me. We are too different. She is a fighter and I am soft, she has a capacity to live that I do not, Eros is with her after her death too, and he stuck me in the living room with five Deceased Loves.

"Did you hear that?" I sobbed to them with rage, "she can't stand me!"

Saved as a Painting

***

I strolled on the promenade along the Yarkon River, its dark water moved with the spreading darkness. The air began to cool off and touched me with a careful dampness, as if asking to become reconciled, but I was still possessed by humiliation. Suddenly four of my five Deceased Men appeared on the path next to me. Itamar, as usual, stayed home, he cannot walk.

Enough, leave me alone... You saw that Kata does not want me, it is over. There is no point in finishing the story, too bad I started writing it.

But they seemed determined like soldiers in an elite unit, including Moosh who overcame his weakness and raised his squashed voice a little, "You-only-got-a-bit-weaker, Noa, you-will-overcome-it. You-know-how-to-reach-her." Editor-Rafi protested in frustration, "Why do you cave in before her?!" Old-Prince-Shaul purred, "It is only her style, my beauty," and Husband-Yossi who marched next to me as if he were my bodyguard announced resolutely, "Listen, Noa, Kata is a strong woman, but you are not some weakling. Explain to her again what you want, that is all!"

And Itamar?

"You should get back to your computer," he sounded from my living room.

Fine, now leave me, please.

They disappeared, and I ambled by the tall eucalyptuses which were planted so long ago by dreamers. Cyclists pedaled slowly and many people strolled there like me, searching for a relief from the heat in the darkness, people with their dogs, couples, in groups and singly, and I alone but with them and they with me in an agreed upon reciprocity that we are here, in our city, at this time, and this is the life we traverse on the promenade along the Yarkon.

*****

At home I sat in front of the screen and browsed back in my text. I read Kata's passages and did not know what I was looking for. Rafi came and stood next to me, his belly almost leaning on my head. A rare expression of patience appeared on his face, the one that was hidden from me for so long and now finally returned. He said, "Noa, your answer is in the paintings, go to them."

"Rafi, you always say that."

His eyes lingered on me and he was with me as if we were gliding in a boat on the Yarkon, I in front and he behind me, rowing in my rhythm, breathing with me, getting excited with me, getting tired with me. "Let's look again at Gábor Pahl's paintings," he said.

I uploaded the research file onto the screen and swiftly skimmed over dozens of Gábor Pahl's paintings, those I had found on the internet and those I had found in other various ways, moved the cursor over them, enlarged them, went back, until finally, I found the painting with the caption Nude 37.

In it a naked woman stands in profile, her face turned away and cannot be seen. In accordance with the artist's will the painting was exhibited for the first time fifty years after his death and now it is in a private collection in the United States.

I am pleased that it is there, that way it will be properly preserved.

***

Here is Kata naked, and no one knows it is her. Gábor Pahl
promised, for László's sake and for the sake of her children and
her family, acquaintances, friends and customers. Promised and
kept his promise: the face is hidden, and the body is presented
in a strange and confusing pose, but it is Kata, I have no doubt,
and she is forty-six here, the same as in the portrait.

I recognized the studio right away. The sofa covered with
golden satin fabric and the glasses with coffee dregs at the bottom at its foot. The two small unframed portraits hung on the
wall behind the sofa and next to them the pleated heavy red
drape, like a curtain in the theatre. The floor padded with the
old wool carpets and the light, always the same morning light.
A mirror is positioned to the right of the sofa – I did not remember that there was a mirror there – in which the French
frilly screen is reflected with a blue velvet cloth dropped to the
floor and peeking from under it. It is clear to me that this is
Kata's robe. Gábor Pahl could not restrain himself, he had to
leave a hint.

The woman standing by the sofa looks as if she had just begun to turn right, maybe to stand with her back and buttocks
to the window and to the artist standing next to it but stopped
her turn with her body in profile and her face to the wall, hiding. Her auburn hair spread over her shoulders.

She is full-bodied, and her skin is ivory. A small fold of
flesh in her back above her waist can be barely seen. Her left

arm, which faces me, is lifted like a bird's wing, somewhat bent. Her underarm hair is sparse and dark. Her left breast is heavy and its nipple light in colour, her right breast is mostly hidden. Her small, round stomach descends to a mound with a hint of dark tufts of hair, her buttocks slightly sagging, and small, dense dimples can be seen on her broad thigh. Her right thigh is mostly hidden and a bit distant, as if her legs are separated to steady her turning movement. Her shin is long, muscular and narrows at the heel. She is barefoot, and her nails are white. Her right arm, the one away from me, is lifted as well, and the forearm is bent toward the unseen face, as if she put her hand to her mouth, but it is impossible to ascertain because her hand is hidden.

This posture is not common for a nude, with both arms lifted, as if the artist caught the woman in a stupid moment as before a sneeze.

"Kata?"

On the sofa next to her a light blue shawl is laid in a heap of folds and tassels, and a multitude of little violets in dark and light purple are drawn on it. Something is happening in the painting now. The woman straightens her far arm, the one that may have been laid on her mouth, extends it and lifts the shawl off the sofa. She spreads it with both arms, shakes it lightly and wraps her body in a quick movement.

"Kata, talk to me..."

The woman turns to me. It is a different Kata, who reminds me of Ilona, Kata with no make-up. Her black-grey eyes are full of light, her cheeks sweaty and her smile broad.

Saved as a Painting

Gábor Pahl stands behind me and Kata stands in front of me with her open smile, wrapped in the violets shawl like a towel after a shower. She sends a twinkling gaze which travels through me to her artist, and her brows lift in some kind of a hint. I do not know what gestures he makes or what he says to her, but suddenly she covers her mouth and tries to block a burst of laughter. "Enough!" her voice rings, " people will hear me. Phhhh..." And all at once a groan explodes from her, which turns into growing waves of a loud laughter.

Her hands are crossed, she leans a little forward and her hair falls in front of her face, her mouth is open and stretched to the sides, and her voice jumps in three bars of laughter forward and one back as she inhales, and then again, in increasing sounds, like a hundred silver bells all ringing together. Tears pool in her eyes, her shoulders quiver, and she laughs and laughs, the violets shawl slides off of her and her laughter grows, she clutches her stomach and crosses her legs, and waves of her laughter fill the studio, break out through the window and scatter in the streets of Budapest --- slowly she gains her composure and looks at her artist in a smile full of tenderness. "I will miss you so much," she says and extends her arms to him, "but we shall not think about your departure, now I want you to tickle me with your beard." She steps over the violets shawl which lays on the floor, passes by me with her stretched arms, and I do not turn to look.

Right Now she stands next to me here, in my living room, in the alabaster silk negligee and the blue velvet robe over it. Her eyes are made-up again, her hair gathered, and the white gold earrings gleam in her earlobes. She bends down a little to look at the computer screen. In spite of her receptiveness to technological innovations she is suspicious of it. I remember her fountain pen with the silver cap. Her gaze lingers over the nude on the screen, and a smile still lights her face. She straightens up and looks at me.

"Why did you laugh, Kata?"

"Because he made me laugh."

"I didn't know you could laugh, you seemed to me so serene and restrained, a kind of woman who has no laughter in her." She spreads her hands and leans her head to the side in a friendly expression, "So, you weren't totally wrong, but with Gábor Pahl I laughed a lot," and I notice that the metal shards disappeared from her voice.

"Ilona laughed a lot with her Aladar."

Kata smiles as if she remembered some joke and peeks at me mischievously, "to love your man," she imitates Ilona's alto and her speech, "is to laugh with him so much that tears run down your cheeks and you pee in your pants."

I rise and stand in front of her, close to her, "This is exciting, Kata..." She looks at me with unexpected fondness, "Yes, it's exciting. And you, Noa? You laugh with your man?" My throat constricts. She tightens her lips for a moment and like in the portrait looks to the side as if a thought went through her, but then she looks at me again with the same fondness as before. Now it seems to me that her face reveals understanding and compassion too. "You are sad with him," she says to me, "I am afraid that you don't laugh at all, ever..." I lower my eyes and she continues in a soft and intimate tone, 'but it's not only you, Noa, it's all of you here, where you live. Something is broken in all of you, like in Robert."

I inhale, and I have no need for words. Kata is close, the scent of her perfume is pleasant, and she possesses something strong which is transferred to me, some kind of energy, as if I stand in front of a burning fire in a cold night. The skin of her face is smooth and flushed. I want to touch her skin, hold her white fingers, but it is impossible.

She smooths her hand over her forehead, "Are you satisfied now?"

"Thank you, Kata."

I want much more from her, but she does not stay with me. That is it. She was in my living room and left, and no effort on the part of my imagination can bring her back.

The scent of her perfume still lingers in the air and her voice still echoes in me.

{ 28 }

Tel Avivian Firefly

Tel Aviv, August 2010.

That is it. "The End".

I turned off the computer, leaned back and felt as if I had a birthday.

I wanted to celebrate, I desperately wanted to celebrate! To eat a birthday cake or a birthday ice cream with someone, drink birthday wine with someone, sing with someone, dance, laugh, get out of my living room to some togetherness, any togetherness, so long as I am not alone in this celebration.

I opened the window and the Tel Avivian night energies floated into my balcony and filled my living room with summer perfumes. I called Avry and he responded in a cold politeness. For a moment I recoiled but I recovered and drew into a conversation of how-is-it-going, in the hope that he would warm up to me. He did sound more courteous and suddenly I lost control of my voice, "I finished writing, Avry, come celebrate with me!"

"You finished?" I heard excitement in his voice.

I knew it. I knew he understood the meaning, he would not leave me alone in this birthday celebration. "Wait," he said in a practical tone, "I'll call back right away." I understood that he had things to do, I accepted that too and disconnected. Fifteen minutes later he called, "What do you want to do?"

"Drive with you in the city and see it at night."

He answered that he would come get me and sounded eager as if I suggested some novelty in bed.

I wore a colourful light spaghetti-straps dress, long and flowing, and waited for him in the street. When I climbed into his car, he smiled at me, "Mazal tov! Congratulations!" and gathered me to him in a firm embrace. I was delighted, there, he opened to me! But as soon as we began driving, he withdrew into himself, his face shut down and the dark stubble enhanced his pale cheeks. I ignored it and held onto my celebration.

"I will tell you what is special about this city," I whinnied to him, and Avry smiled a forced smile. For a moment I was devastated, but I recovered directly, "it doesn't matter, what's important is that we are together." He turned his face to me as if he were pulled out of a faraway stream of thoughts, "What?" I put my hand on my mouth, enough, shut up already! We drove, and I was silent, even though waves of speaking kept surfacing. I stopped them, inhaled heavily and coughed. Avry may have sensed something in me, put his hand on my thigh and said, "You want Tel Aviv at night? Here, take it." I interpreted his touch as reaching to me and his generosity as love and my mood promptly improved.

We drove east, got on the Arlozorov Interchange and suddenly I saw the city from above, stretched around us in all directions. I could not restrain myself, "Go slowly, Avry, look, it's wonderful!"

The sky was like dark velvet and underneath it rose the glass towers, illuminated with white lights. More and more buildings crowded around them, tall and of medium height and low, a sea of buildings with legions of lit windows, sparkling with glinting strings and with brilliant jigsaw puzzles of light. Billboards turned on-and-off as if daydreaming, and the lines of cars under the bridge were long like blinking swarms of fireflies. I pressed into Avry's arm, "This is like a dream!" and a quick smile flickered on his face.

We descended the bridge and drove north. At the Rokach Interchange we went up the bridge and turned toward the sea. Tel Aviv was like its own hallucination, a night-city excited and insinuating, tempting with some kind of beauty which is hidden during the day and rises after sunset, smiling from its dark corners and small balconies, moving through its major arteries, ready to pounce from the side streets, a frenetic city which does not want to sleep, and I am in it and it is in me on this ride with my lover, his hand on my thigh, my hand on his thigh.

We drive and do not speak. Avry demonstrates his complete command of the streets and the maze of alleyways, and I already know these routes too, know when he turns and when he continues straight ahead. Dimness conceals the day's ugliness and reveals the night's secret treasures. The nocturnal treetops spread dark covers on the apartment buildings and on the small yards, parts of sidewalks are coloured in clumps of thick shadows, and darkness steals among the yellow streetlamps.

Saved as a Painting

We travel south along the coast, the water line wriggles in illuminated foam trains. People parade on the promenade, I know their expression and their walk, they are steeped in sea air and give in to it. Tel Aviv in a dark purple dress studded with sequins, secular queen thirsty for entertainment, and Yaffo flickering in the distance is her ancient palace.

We made a big tour and heaps of words accumulated in me. I said to Avry, "let's sit and drink something on Basel Square." He mumbled, "okay," and his expression did not alter. We drove there, circled the square three times and could not find parking. Avry became impatient, and my enthusiasm began to wane too. I was startled, lest my celebration run away from me! Finally we parked and left the car.

Basel Square hid its flaws and ignited its nocturnal beauty marks with decorative lamps of cafés and restaurants, and the orange-yellow flashes of light on the pavements. Many people were there, standing or sitting, as young as our children and as old as we were, dressed for a night on the town or dressed simply, and a lively bustle spread among them. At the entrance to the underground parking hung the epitaph "In Basel I founded the Jewish state," like an old song trying to infiltrate a party uninvited. The large stone plaza spread out like a white platform above the parking lot, drenched in night.

Smells of joints and beer mingled in the air, waiters moved like night cats among the tables, the conversations, the music and the phones ringing, people ate and drank, chatted, looked at each other, looked around them. Everyone belongs, the city does not choose by age or dress code, but by impulsive vitality, those who have it get in.

We found a table in a partly dim corner and I sat to Avry's left. We ordered white wine which was served in large goblets, we clinked them and I declared, "to our life and to the life of the newborn book!" I could not ask for a better celebration. Avry looked absent-minded, but I was already in take-off. I took a sip of wine and said, "I want you to know that had you not charged me with our love energy, my writing would not have flowed!" My heart pounded, and I raised my voice, "Can you believe it? In this story you were the charger!"

I waited for him to answer me with love words and I leaned over preparing for a kiss. He leaned back and put his hands on his thighs. His lips parted, then closed, and his honey eyes went far away. What is this? He is silent exactly at the most important moment?! And where is the kiss? I straightened and prepared to protest, say something, but suddenly a Tel Avivian firefly ignited in me and began to twinkle, tink-light, tink-darkness, and between the tinks she spoke in a nasal tone, "So, your charger doesn't feel like kissing! Never mind, go with the flow."

Suddenly his phone rang.

It was strange because whenever we met Avry used to turn off his phone. He read the display, got up and said, "Just a moment," walked to the corner of the street and talked. I saw him but could not hear his voice. He stood relaxed with his free hand shoved in his pants' pocket, talked and smiled, nodded and listened, talked and listened again. I said to myself, I stumbled onto a connecting-parting scene.

When he returned to the table, he sat down and did not look at me. I was dumbfounded, I did not know where to turn my thoughts to, and suddenly Editor-Rafi's voice sounded, "that's it, Noa. The story ends here."

Yes, it ends.

Bitter emptiness climbed in my throat and all I wanted to do was get away from there, get away from everything, but I was heavy like a boulder, I got stuck on the chair and could not lift myself. I closed my eyes and told myself I would never again open them, but they opened of their own volition and I saw Itamar in front of me, dressed in the army fatigues. He stood close to me in full height, in empty pants and without feet, stood for a long moment, looked at me with his brown fawn eyes and disappeared.

I rose and Avry gave me a surprised look. I leaned down and put my lips to his in a long kiss, straightened and said, "Our story is over. I will always love you, until I die and beyond, but we won't get together again."

***

The crows' calls woke me up in the morning. I looked around me and recognized my bed and the nightstand next to it. Then my heart shook violently and every breath I took ached in the emptiness in my chest. I did not want to get up, I did not want day light. That is it, everything has ended. I lay on my back with my eyes shut, my hands resting next to my body and my legs straight and close to each other. I breathed slowly... But I had no patience for this ritual, and I sat up.

The city hummed its morning sounds in rhythmic beats of a large heart. Sea breeze entered the room and raised my appetite for a breakfast of buttered fresh rolls, sunny-side-up eggs and strong coffee.

I got up and found Robert sitting on the floor next to the dresser. He was dressed in a wrinkled white shirt and old jeans and wore high top shoes with brown laces and no sox. His bald head shone, his face creases were soft, and his black-grey eyes were veiled with purple hue.

He said to me, "you hurt," and looked at me with a great deal of sadness.

What a man! He has no skin, everything penetrates him.

He smiled in embarrassment and got up, short, thin and wide, a seventy-one year old boy.

"Come, Robert," I said to him, "Join my friends in the living room. Your grandmother Kata sits there too, she arrived at night. Now we shall all sit together."

-The End -

Acknowledgments

My gratitude to the family of Magda Kantor for providing me with the core material and the theme of this book and their continuous support and advice from start to finish, during the creation of this work.

To my friends, Daniella Givon, and Judith Gurfinkel of Vancouver, Canada, thank you for their contribution of significant information related to the story and help with details and explanations I needed to complete my book.

To both, Judith and Daniella, thank you for the friendly spirit and heartening company on our trip to Budapest and Novi Sad to research and follow in the tracks of this story.

To Vesna and Mirko Stark, thank you for the generous hospitality in Novi Sad, for the guided tours navigating us through the city, and for the abundance of knowledge and information imparted to us.

Many thanks to all my friends in Israel and in Vancouver, Canada, who read the manuscript, commented, enlightened and added their personal knowledge and professional experience to my efforts: Tomer Golan, Ruti Dayan, Anat Kadishson, Sarah Barak, Prof. Nima Gefen, Dr. Sigal Ben Shmuel, Chanan Shamir, Dan Gelbart and Michael Halber.

In memory of Magda Kantor, born in Budapest, and passed away in Ramat Gan in the summer of 2015, whom I met for lengthy conversations about important details related to this book.

Tali Geva,
Tel Aviv, 2015

Tali Geva is an Israeli writer, resident of Kiryat Tivon, where she was born, grew up, married and gave birth to her two daughters. She has academic degrees in Literature and Biblical Studies and was an award-winning Hebrew Literature teacher at the local high school.

Tali decided to focus on her third Hebrew novel while relocating to Canada. Living for 10 years in Vancouver, she completed this book and was an active member of the Canadian Israeli community.

Saved as a Painting is Tali Geva's fourth novel, following *Lizard in King Palaces* (1987), *The Pistacia Tree* (1994) and *Love Suddenly* (2008). Now she lives in Israel, working on her fifth novel.

CPSIA information can be obtained
at www.ICGtesting.com
Printed in the USA
LVHW050604250621
691049LV00012B/1654